The Heart of the Guardian

E. PAIGE BURKS

© 2017

For information about this title or to order other books and/or electronic media, contact the publisher:
Infinity Flower Publishing, LLC
infinityflowerpublishing@gmail.com
www.infinityflowerpublishing.com

ISBN: 978-0-9984620-6-6 Softcover

Printed in the United States of America

Cover Design: Infinity Flower Publishing, LLC

Dedicated to Granny;
Without you, this book would have never existed.
I love you.

Chapter One

Snow fell lightly, coating the forest in a white calm. Joseph walked through the forest, his footsteps silent, the rubber soles of his boots muting them. His golden, wolf eyes scanned the trees, searching for any dangers. He had been traveling alone for some time now, and he knew he was far from his home. His keen, wolf senses allowed him to navigate the forest, but he didn't know where he was being led to. He felt a pang of hunger twinge inside him, and he fought the urge to wince. He couldn't remember how long it had been since he had eaten last.

A sudden noise made him jump, and he ducked quickly behind a group of trees. He watched as a pure white unicorn walked calmly, threading its way through the trees. A dove floated down from the trees and alighted softly on its back.

As he watched the unicorn, he noticed that it seemed to carry its own light. A soft, warm glow emanated from its purer-than-snow white coat. The dove was also the same ghostly white. He watched as it ruffled its feathers. The unicorn looked back at it, nickering softly. The dove cooed a quiet answer.

Joseph thought it an odd picture. He watched for another minute, then sat back in the snow. He felt his stomach rumble, and he grimaced, hoping that the strange unicorn moved on soon. He was starving, and he needed to hunt. He looked back at them from behind the tree, and was surprised to see a figure standing next to the unicorn. He stared at them, completely awestruck.

It was a young woman. She was clothed in a riding clothes and a cloak, which drug across the snow. She pulled back the hood of her cloak to uncover long, flowing hair so blonde it almost matched the snow. Her eyes, which were a cold, icy blue, seemed to jump out at Joseph, especially since her clothing was the same pure white as the unicorn. Her essence whispered the warmth and gentle grace of nobility. He watched as she placed a gentle hand on the unicorn's shoulder.

"We're almost home," she said softly.

The unicorn bobbed its head as if in response. It was then that Joseph noticed the vine of white rose buds that wound its way around the ivory horn.

"Yes, Snow Belle," she said, her voice a soft whisper. "I did notice that. I think whoever it was is nearby."

The unicorn bent its head to the snow, blowing tiny snow flurries as it searched for a scent. The unicorn took a breath, then looked in the direction of Joseph's hiding place. Joseph watched as it neared, realizing that he was about to be discovered. He looked around helplessly.

It was too late to run.

He watched as the girl also walked over. He was frozen in place as he ducked back behind the tree, hoping he hadn't been spotted. He felt his heart sink as their footsteps came to where he was hiding, and the girl's face suddenly appeared.

"Are you spying on me?" she asked, a dangerous look on her face. She held a bow in her hand, and she notched an arrow from the quiver on her back.

"No," he said quickly, his golden eyes narrowing as he eyed her weapon. "Or, at least not intentionally." He got to his feet. "My name is Joseph."

"Abigail," she said, eyeing him warily. Her response seemed automatic as she looked at him, taking in his broad shoulders, light brown hair and golden eyes. "May I inquire as to why you are here, trespassing in our land?"

"I'm hiding," he said brusquely, glancing over his shoulder. He hoped his distraction would work. "I can say no more." He looked at her unicorn. "I see you have an ice unicorn."

Abigail nodded. "This is Snow Belle," she said. She lowered her bow, putting her arrow away. She would let his diversion slide for now.

Snow Belle walked up to him and bowed her head.

Joseph reached out his hand. "May I?" he asked. Etiquette had to be followed when it came to magical creatures, and Snow Belle was no exception. Offending a unicorn was not at the top of his list of things to accomplish; they were known to place very harsh curses upon those they did not like.

Abigail paused, her ice blue eyes glancing at Snow Belle. Something passed between them, and then she nodded.

Joseph placed his hand on Snow Belle's shoulder. As soon he did, he felt like electricity was pulsing through him. Images flashed before his eyes, and he yanked his hand away. A voice like the chime of bells spoke softly in his mind. The beast inside him growled, protesting at the intrusion, but the magic was done.

'He can shape-shift,' it said.

He glanced at Abigail, seeing her nod. "I thought as much," she said thoughtfully.

Joseph frowned, the wolf twisting in his chest. "Do you know me?" he asked, extremely uncomfortable. Did they recognize him?

Snow Belle snorted softly. 'Certain things passed between us,' she said.

He crossed his arms. He was becoming more and more uncomfortable. Had they been sent by Bozal? What had Snow Belle seen?

"We need one like you to join us," Abigail said, looking at Snow Belle.

Again, Joseph felt as if they were speaking and he wasn't hearing their words. If he had been in his animal form, his hackles would have bristled. Secrets didn't make friends.

Joseph felt unsure of what to do as her eyes came back to him, seemingly piercing through him, waiting for his decision. He weighed his options. Was it worth it to join her? He supposed that if Bozal had sent them, they would have just accosted him and forced him to return.

The wolf inside him twisted, both distrustful and yearning for company. He had been alone for such a long time, and the beast inside him craved companionship. He needed a pack to join.

He sighed, relenting to the pressure from his other half. Anything was better than being alone and on the run.

"Okay," he said softly. "What must I do?"

"Come with us and work with us," Abigail said. She glanced away. "It is a lonely road that Snow Belle and I travel."

"Alright," Joseph said, looking at Snow Belle. "I'll go with you and your unicorn. Just tell me, where are you going?"

"We are on our way to Castle Corona," Abigail said. "Once there, we will retrieve Shalamar, the legendary bow. Have you heard the story of Shalamar?"

Joseph shook his head. He had heard only rumors.

"A long time ago," Abigail said, "back when unicorns ran the Gandorian Plains, a sorceress named Lady Charlotte was bonded with the woodland unicorn, Shalamar. Together they defended the Plains and Corona from demons. For nearly a hundred years this land was a peaceful place."

A quizzical look came to Joseph's face.

"You see, a bonded rider can live for many years more than the average human," she said, answering his unspoken question. "Then, Lady Charlotte's nephew, Bozal, attacked her and Shalamar. They were taken by surprise, and Shalamar was slain by Bozal."

"Saddened, but not disheartened, by the loss, Lady Charlotte took the pieces of Shalamar's horn and fashioned them into the shaft of a bow. She used hair from his tail for the string, and she used the bow to protect the land for the remainder of her life. But, shortly before she joined Shalamar, she fashioned her crystal ball, which contained all knowledge, known and forbidden, to the shaft of an arrow. She called it Precious, thus the Precious Arrow of Shalamar. She blessed it so that whoever wielded both could have the strength and the courage to be unstoppable."

She paused and saw that she had Joseph's full attention. He had relaxed, and he sat in the snow, his golden eyes fixated on her.

"So what does that have to do with you?" he asked.

"I am on my way to my home in Corona," she said. "Once there, I must retrieve Shalamar."

A surprised look crossed Joseph's face as he seemed to put the pieces together. "You're a Guardian?"

She nodded, a little smile on her face. "My father and brothers were Guardians before me," she said, the slightest hint of pride in her voice.

Joseph stared at the snow. Finding a Guardian was more than he could have hoped for, but it still left him to deal with other things. If he went with them, he would have to go back to the place he had fled from; the land of the Phoenix. Was that an option for him?

"So what's your answer?" Abigail asked, drawing his gaze.

Joseph arched a brow at her, wondering what she was thinking. What had her unicorn seen, and what had she told Abigail?

"You like to take risks," he commented dryly.

She smiled placidly. "I've seen many things, and a lot of it has been things that I feel no one should ever have to see. And the road can be a cold, lonely place." She glanced at Snow Belle. "And not everyone supports the cause of the Guardians. I can recall many nights sleeping in the cold because we couldn't find a place to stay."

Joseph knew what she meant. "I can relate," he said.

"Really?" she asked.

He nodded. "It's a hard life," he said, "being a wolf-child from Phoenix." He disengaged his eyes from hers. "If there's one thing I've learned, it's that people fear the unknown. They fear those who can shift, the land of Phoenix," he glanced at her, "and some even fear Corona and the Guardians."

Abigail nodded her head.

"But they don't understand," Joseph said, his voice becoming bitter. "The powers that you and I are blessed with are not evil. Only the bearer's heart can determine how the powers are used. Some people are too shallow to see that it truly is the person. That's why they're scared of us."

Abigail nodded. She looked into Joseph's face.

He was already so wise, especially for someone so young. She felt, strangely, a twinge of pity for him, but also a connection to him. She had been forced to learn early, too. She remembered the Great Divide and what it had meant for the mortals that lived in the north.

Magic and magic users were banished from the mortal kingdoms, except for the select few who keep the evil magics at bay. This was almost twenty years ago now, but already people had forgotten the shape-shifters and the way they had defended the mortal kingdoms against Bozal when he made his first grab at power.

"But I don't understand why they fear Phoenix," he said quietly.

"It is where the phoenix, the bearer of magic to our world, originated," she said. "And every so often they must return there. Only then can they die, by burning, and then be reborn from the ashes. Once they are reborn, they can bestow magic abilities to the people of the lands. The people fear the place because they feel its enchantments are of an evil sort. That is where the people who can shift gain their powers. The mortals try to forget, but there are still some who remember Bozal's campaign."

Joseph stared at the snow, silent. As Abigail looked at him, she saw he had his fists clenched. She also saw the look on his face.

"Bozal forced your parents to join his army, didn't he?" she said softly, reading his face.

He nodded. "My father," he said. "My mother and I fled at my father's orders. He said he'd come back for us later. So, we went. I was very young still, so we stayed with my aunt. After a while, my mother became sick. My aunt somehow managed to get the message to my father and he was able to come to us. He was there when my mother died. He stayed for a while, teaching me and telling me that I must never serve Bozal."

"I asked why he did, and he said it was because he had no choice. He was too old to run, and too weak to fight. But he said I was young and healthy, and that I could make a life for myself outside of Phoenix."

"My father always told me that our hearts, though pure wolf blood pulses through them, were kinder and purer that the snow. He would not let that end with him or me. Our family would continue to live by our ancestors' code of honor. We would continue to be pure."

He paused and looked at her. "So here I am," he said. "Homeless and on the run. I have nothing but the clothes on my back and my pride. Bozal may have forced me from my home and my family; he may have taken all my material possessions; but I have hope, and those are things he can't take from me."

Abigail nodded. "Yes," she said. "Our desires are the same." Her heart ached slightly for him. "Does this mean you accept?"

He contemplated it for a moment. Being with her was better than being alone. "I accept," he said, meeting her gaze. "But I must ask for payment."

She looked at him, her ice blue gaze piercing. "Name your price," she said.

"Well," he said, slowly. How much was too much to ask of her? "Ten gold pieces each day."

She grinned coyly. "Is that all you feel your life is worth?" He watched as she looked at Snow Belle.

"*Arrockneheshmen,*" she commanded. The sound was harsh and startling to Joseph's senses, and it made the innate being inside him snarl.

The wolf sensed danger.

Joseph suddenly leapt to his feet. He watched Snow Belle charge him, her horn, though soft pearl, a deadly point aimed at his heart.

He watched her come, then jumped at the last minute. He cleared her horn and touched momentarily on her back, before flipping off into the snow. He landed with a dull thud, his eyes watching Snow Belle.

Then he saw something flash out of the corner of his eye. He realized that Snow Belle was only the decoy. His ears pricked at the creak of wood on wood, and he turned in time to see an arrow flying at him. He hesitated, then snatched the arrow from the air. He twirled it through his fingers and threw it into the snow. He then drew his dagger from his boot.

Swifter than Abigail could bat her eyelashes, he had her pinned to the ground, his dagger at her throat. His breathing was quick, and it fogged the air. He noticed that his heart was pounding loudly in his chest. He met her gaze, which had softened.

"What are you playing at?" he demanded. The wolf inside him snarled angrily.

Pain flashed briefly across her face, and her hands came to rest on his. "I was testing you," she said easily, eyeing the dagger at her throat. "You don't think I'd hire someone without seeing them perform, do you?"

He searched her gaze a moment longer, then let her up. He slid his dagger back into his boot.

"I must say, your movements are unorthodox," she said as she sat up, her hand pressed to where the dagger had once been. "You move as a wild thing would. But your senses are keener than most." Her ice blue eyes shifted to him. "And I did rather enjoy seeing you make a fool of Snow Belle." She watched Snow Belle stand next to her.

Joseph still looked a little stunned. "What was that language you spoke?" he asked. He still remembered the way it had felt down to his core. It wasn't a normal word; it had been laced with powerful magic.

"It is the Unicorns' language put into words so that we may speak it," she said simply. "Truly gifted riders learn to speak as the Unicorn, with whinnies and such. But that is a very rare gift."

He nodded. His golden-eyed gaze shifted over Snow Belle, who stood with her head down near Abigail, her eyes trained on him.

"Where did you learn to move like that?" Abigail asked, drawing his gaze.

He shrugged. "I did a lot of hunting," he said, "when I lived in Phoenix. But I mostly just had to listen to the beast inside." He glanced up at her. "He protects me when my human senses prove too weak."

Abigail smiled, pulling a small bag out of her cloak. She tossed it to him.

He caught it. "What's this?" he asked. He turned it over in his hands, hearing soft *chinks* from inside.

"Enjoy your first paycheck," she said slyly. "Don't squander it."

Chapter Two

Joseph stared at the entrance hall to Corona. He had never seen a place so large before. Beneath his feet, a soft red carpet led its way to a staircase. He looked at the walls, which seemed to be coated in ice. The floor beneath the carpet was white marble, which sparkled in the light from the chandelier hanging from the ceiling. It too, appeared to be made of ice, and it had icicles hanging from its tiers.

"Abbie!" a voice yelled, echoing across the hall.

Joseph looked and saw a tall, young man at the top of the stairs.

"Harlie," Abigail said, a smile lighting her face at the sight of him.

He ran down the stairs, taking them two at a time. When he reached her, he flung his arms around her, lifting her from the floor to twirl her around. "I missed you," he said cheerfully. He seemed to be only in his teens, but he was much taller than his older sister.

"And I missed you too," she said, laughing as she hugged him tightly. "How did it go here?"

He nodded. "Fine," he said "I had no problems. You?"

"No," she said, holding him at arms' length. She glanced at Joseph. "But I picked up a guest while I was gone."

Harlie grinned slyly. "Yeah?" he said. He looked at Joseph, clearly giving him a once over. "I don't think you picked him because you needed protection." He looked at her. "I've mastered four kinds of karate, and you can still spin-kick me on my butt in two moves."

Abigail could not hide her smile.

"You're a fighter?" Joseph asked. He felt betrayed and lied to suddenly. What the hell had he agreed to do?

She nodded.

"Oh yeah," Harlie said. "She can beat anyone in hand to hand combat, but she's the best archer in the world."

Joseph arched a brow, suddenly on guard. What was her game? "Well, I suppose she must be to wield Shalamar," he said carefully. He felt very uncomfortable. What had he unknowingly stepped into? And how hard would it be to get out?

"Oh, how rude of me," Abigail said softly, breaking his thoughts. "Let me introduce you; Harlie, this is Joseph, Joseph this is my brother Harlie." She watched as they shook hands.

"Nice to meet you," Harlie said, grinning mischievously.

Joseph nodded. "Likewise." He noticed that Harlie very much resembled Abigail, save for their eyes; where hers were ice blue, his were a warm green.

"Harlie," Abigail said, drawing his gaze. "Joseph will be going with me when I go to retrieve Precious."

Harlie pressed his lips together. "Are you sure he's good enough?" he asked, his eyes raking over Joseph. It was clear he disapproved.

Abigail nodded. She did not doubt Joseph's abilities, but she also knew he could provide the one thing that she lacked; knowledge of Phoenix.

"I want to fight him and make sure," he said stubbornly, sliding into a relaxed fighting stance. He arched a brow at Joseph in a silent challenge.

Abigail shook her head, a small smile on her face. "Later, Brother," she said, eyeing Joseph's reaction. She noticed that he tensed and his back went rigid. He kept a wary eye on Harlie. "I'm sure he's just as tired as I am. I would like to rest before we begin anything."

Harlie sighed. "Yes, Sister," he said, bowing his head.

Abigail saw Joseph's shoulders relax. "Who's hungry?" she asked, walking toward the dining hall, which was to the left of the stairs.

"Oh, me!" Harlie said, jogging after her.

Joseph followed them silently.

They walked into the dining hall, which had a large table in the middle. On the wall opposite the door, a large fireplace had been lit. Joseph watched Abigail walk to the fire to warm her hands. He noticed that Harlie sat down and began to pile food onto a plate in front of him as servants finished putting down plates. He noticed that neither sibling sat at, or near, the head of the table. It seemed to him as if they were leaving seats vacant on purpose.

"Go ahead, Joseph," Abigail said, smiling, drawing his golden gaze. "You must be starving."

He paused for a moment, before selecting the seat beside hers. The scent of wonderful food wafted under his nose, and he felt his stomach rumbling. Once he started piling food onto his own plate, he ate until he felt like he would burst. Silence fell over the room; the only sounds were the clinking of utensils on china. It was at that point that Joseph realized that only he and Harlie were cramming their faces full of food. He looked over at Abigail, catching her ice blue gaze as she sipped at the red wine a servant had poured for her.

"Aren't you hungry?" he asked, pushing his empty plate away and smoothing his napkin on the table.

She gave a little smile and shook her head. "I'm not really hungry," she said softly.

"Not hungry?" Harlie demanded, staring at her. He took a bite of a biscuit, before pressing his hand against her face. "Are you feeling well?" Crumbs fell from his lips.

Abigail shook her head in disapproval, before she pushed his hand away and stood. "I'm fine." She moved to stand beside the fire again, her ice blue gaze distant as she gazed into the flames.

Joseph thought he saw a flicker of doubt on her face, but he was not sure. He got the impression that she was hiding something.

She turned to look at him, as if sensing his thoughts. "Are you finished?" she asked. He recognized her question for what it was, and followed along with her distraction.

He nodded.

"Then I shall show you to your room," she said, her voice tired suddenly.

He got to his feet, and so did Harlie, another biscuit in his hand.

"I'm going to check on the Dream Catcher," he said. He caught her in a side hug. "I'm glad you're back, Sister."

Abigail smiled up at him, returning his hug. "I'm glad to be home," she said softly. Joseph sensed sadness to her words and a bond that they shared that he felt excluded from. He almost felt as if the moment he had witnessed was private.

The siblings bid each other good night, then Abigail turned and led Joseph out of the dining hall. They walked up the stairs and down a hallway. Joseph stared at the paintings that lined the walls.

"So where are your father and brothers?" he asked. The castle felt strangely empty, despite the servants' activities.

Abigail lifted her hands slightly, motioning to the paintings. "Here," she said softly, "lining these walls." She looked over her shoulder at him, her gaze unreadable.

"Oh," he said, shifting his golden eyes away. "And your mother?"

Abigail sighed, but her voice tried to be nonchalant. "She has been sick for a time, so we sent her away for a while, to the north, where she can live with other mortals," she said quietly. "We would be with her, if not for the recent events." She brushed her pale hair over her shoulder, and somehow Joseph felt as if she was lying. Why would a woman who gave birth to a race of warriors whose destiny was to protect the sanctity of magic need to live among mortals?

Joseph watched her pensively as she stopped in front of a door.

"This is your room," she said. She pushed the door open. "I hope it is to your liking."

He walked inside and looked around. It was like the rest of the castle, except it had a bed, a bureau, a bathroom, and a balcony. He walked to the bed and sat on it.

"This is fine," he said, unable to imagine why it would not be. It was the lap of luxury, in his opinion, and it was a million times better than sleeping in the snow.

She nodded and gave a tired smile. "Then I suppose this is good night," she said.

He watched her for a second, noticing her weary gaze. "Good night," he said.

She walked to the door, catching it in her hand. "Tomorrow we will begin preparations," she said. She watched Joseph nod, his wolf eyes catching the faint candle light as she pulled the door shut behind her.

Joseph stared at the door for a second, then laid back on his pillow. He thought it odd how quickly her energy left her when Abigail walked into the palace. He knew there was something about her that she hadn't shared with him.

Abigail walked down the hall, toward her room. A dizzy feeling swept her, and she had to stop and lean on the wall. She thought back to her journey to the king's palace.

On the first night, she and Snow Belle had been attacked by some of Bozal's soldiers. One of them had struck her in the shoulder with an enchanted arrow, and she had not been the same since. She felt sick and weary, and she was afraid that the enchantment was slowly killing her. She and Snow Belle had been unsure as to what the enchantment was, but Snow Belle could sense that it was very dangerous.

They had traveled to see a sage about an antidote, but he had not been very helpful. He could only say that the enchantment would not kill her until Bozal wanted it to, and it would kill her the way he wanted it to. He then offered to tell her future so that they would be prepared, and that was when he told her that she would meet a Wandering Soul, one who would prove to be her greatest friend and worst enemy. She had wondered how someone could be your friend and enemy.

She stood up slowly, the dizzy feeling fading, leaving her feeling drained. She walked to her room and shed her clothing to climb into her bed. She was glad to be home, and the soft sheets felt good to her. She was asleep within minutes.

The next morning, Abigail woke to the sunlight streaming into her room through the window. Its soft rays landed on her face, and she sat up. She got to her feet and walked into the bathroom. She looked at her reflection in the mirror.

Her blond hair was greasy and dirty and it stuck out all over the place. Her eyes were tired, and she felt gross. She sighed as her stomach felt queasy, a sign that the enchantment was already taxing her body.

She walked to the bureau and pulled out a deep green, floor-length gown. She drew herself a hot bath and cleaned up, before slipping into the gown. After she changed, she brushed her long blond hair, shaking the water from the ends. She then left her room and made her way down the hallway to the winding stairs. She entered the dining hall to sounds of Harlie and Joseph gorging themselves.

"Good morning," she greeted. She watched as they both looked up.

"Hey Abbs," Harlie said around a mouthful of food. He leaned in as she walked to him and placed a kiss on his cheek.

"Morning," Joseph chimed as she turned her eyes on him. He noticed that she smiled brightly.

"Did you sleep well?" she asked as she sank into her seat at the table. Harlie nodded.

"Yes," Joseph said softly. He watched as she looked up at Harlie, lifting a glass full of juice to her lips.

"You want some breakfast?" Harlie asked, looking over at her.

Joseph saw her wrinkle her nose briefly, before she smiled and nodded. "Please," she said. He had a distinctly suspicious feeling as he watched Harlie place food on her plate. He kept his eyes trained on her for the duration of breakfast.

"I think after breakfast I'd like to see you two train together," she said, glancing between them. "It will be good practice." She saw them exchange looks, Harlie frowning markedly, while Joseph pressed his lips together.

"Sounds okay to me," Harlie said finally.

Joseph nodded. "Yes," he said finally in agreement.

"I need to tend to the unicorns before our session," Harlie said, finishing his juice and rising to his feet. Seeing to the horses had been what had allowed him to endure while his family was gone, and it was something he enjoyed immensely.

Both Abigail and Joseph watched him go, before their eyes met. Abigail looked as if she was about to speak, but Joseph beat her to it.

"You are ill," he said plainly, pinning her under his golden-eyed gaze.

Abigail's ice blue gaze widened, and she looked down at the table. "It's nothing," she said softly.

Joseph snorted softly in disagreement. He had realized what it was when she had sat next to him this morning, and he wondered why he hadn't picked up on it yesterday. "I can smell the dark magic on you," he said. "Something is killing you." He saw that her face had gone pale.

"Please keep this quiet," she whispered. Her blue eyes were desperate. "Harlie can't know."

Joseph arched a brow. "Why would you hide this from him?" he asked in disbelief.

Abigail swallowed thickly. Joseph realized suddenly that she was fighting down her emotions. "We have suffered so much," she breathed. "He can't know."

"And when you die?" Joseph demanded. "Then what?"

Abigail sat back in her chair, composing herself. "There is a cure," she said quietly. "I will not die and leave him." Her eyes were determined as she looked up at him. "You will help me find the cure."

Joseph narrowed his eyes at her. "Is this why you chose me?" he asked, an edge to his voice. "Because you think I can save you?"

Abigail turned her head, rising to her feet. "I chose you because I need you just as much as you need me," she said evenly. "If you'll excuse me, I must see to preparations for our travels."

Joseph frowned as he watched her leave, feeling uncomfortable again. What had he *really* gotten himself into?

A short time later, Abigail, Harlie and Joseph stood on the training field. The sun was starting to heat the air, and the early morning chill was beginning to abate. Abigail held her bow in her hand. A quiver of arrows was thrown across her shoulders.

"Okay," she said, turning to face Harlie and Joseph. "I want a fair fight. No weapons." She looked between them. "Understand?"

They both nodded, looking at each other.

"Shake hands," she ordered.

Joseph shook Harlie's hand, feeling the tension in his body. He was giving him a glare; one that said there would be no mercy. As they released hands, Joseph glanced over at Abigail, noticing that the spark had returned to her ice blue gaze. She raised her hand.

"On my mark," she said.

Joseph trained his eyes on Harlie. It was then that he realized for the first time, as rays of sun hit Harlie's face, how much alike they looked. The thing that set them apart was the fire in Harlie's eyes; the same one that Abigail contained but always hid behind her icy gaze.

"Ready."

Harlie's shoulders slumped slightly, a sign he was relaxing.

"Set."

Joseph felt his body tense and his fists clench, anticipation locking up his body.

"Go!"

Harlie tensed at the last second. That was the read Joseph needed to know that Harlie was starting on offense. He managed to block Harlie's kick, but it sent him backwards, throwing him off balance. As Harlie came at him again, he spun away, regaining his balance and dealing a blow to the back of Harlie's legs. He was surprised when Harlie barely seemed phased, using the force from the kick to flip and land on solid footing.

He watched as Harlie stood slowly from the crouch he had landed in. "I hope you're ready for this," he said, his green eyes sharp and piercing.

They exchanged more blows, evenly matched despite the differences in style. After matching one another for a long time, Abigail stepped between them.

"Let's make this more interesting," she said. She smiled as she tossed each of them a broad sword.

Harlie grinned, twirling the weapon with skill. "Watch out," he said, rushing Joseph.

He swung at Joseph's head, barely missing him as Joseph ducked. He parried Joseph's defensive upper-cut, before knocking Joseph's feet from under him. He held his blade to Joseph's throat.

Harlie's face split into a grin. "Gotcha," he said triumphantly.

"Or do you?" Abigail said, arching a brow as Joseph managed to kick Harlie off of him.

Harlie landed hard on his back, the air knocked from his lungs and his sword flying from his hand. It slid a few feet away, and Joseph stood over Harlie.

"Sorry about that," he said, watching Harlie wipe his bloody nose on the back of his hand.

Harlie shot him an evil look. "That was quite underhanded and dirty," he said.

"Well, think of it realistically," Joseph said, helping him to his feet. "If your enemy was about to cut your throat, wouldn't you fight dirty?"

Harlie shrugged. "I suppose so," he said, unable to deny Joseph's logic.

"Great job," Abigail said, patting Harlie on the back. She looked at Joseph. "Now you and I can have a go." She gave a little grin.

Joseph tried to hold in his scowl. He said nothing, only nodded. He wasn't totally thrilled about the thought of having her kick his butt today.

"I'll give you a choice of a weapon," she said. "I'm using my bow and arrow."

Joseph nodded. "I'll use my own strength," he said quietly. He knew this would be less of a battle of strengths like with Harlie, and more a game of wits.

Abigail smiled coldly. "As you wish," she said.

Harlie stepped between them. "On your marks," he said. He waved his hand. "Go!"

Joseph felt like everything happened in a time that was too fast for him. Before he knew what hit him, Abigail loosed an arrow at him, causing him to duck. As he did so, her body was already in motion, spinning to kick his legs from under him. He was on his back with an arrow to his throat in seconds. Abigail's ice blue gaze was cold and heartless.

"Don't try anything," she said quietly, a hard edge to her voice. "The minute my fingers slip from the string of this bow, you're dead." She saw him swallow hard as he relaxed against the ground.

His golden eyes were narrowed as he stared down the shaft at her. "How did you do that?" he whispered. "You moved so fast." He glanced away, a submissive gesture.

Abigail smiled, releasing the tension in her bow. "Years of learning how to outsmart my older brothers," she said, helping him to his feet.

They walked over to Harlie, who was grinning like a fool. "You were faster than usual," he said, nodding at her.

"I didn't feel like dragging it out," she said easily, glancing at Joseph, who was watching her carefully.

Harlie nodded. He didn't seem to notice the looks they exchanged, because he dismissed himself to go back to the barn.

Both Abigail and Joseph watched him go, before Joseph turned his eyes on her. He watched as she picked up the swords, moving to place them back in the stand. She took several steps, and then she suddenly gasped. Joseph was surprised when her knees buckled, and she fell to the ground, dropping the weapons.

"Abigail, are you all right?" he asked, catching her arm and trying to help her to her feet. She was burning under the sleeve of her dress, and he noticed instantly the way she hung her head, her ice blue eyes pained. He sank to his knees beside her when she suddenly burst into tears. "Abigail?"

She shook her head, pulling her arm from his hands so that she could hug her middle. Fierce, burning pain was pulsing through her body; she felt as if her blood was lava in her veins.

"Is there anything I can do for you?" Joseph asked. He could smell the dark magic as it ripped through her. The smell was pungent, like death. He knew that this kind of magic was powerful and very dangerous.

She looked up at him, still trying to fight through the pain. "Just..." She gasped, trying to swallow small cries. "Just help me inside." She curled in on herself. "Before Harlie sees..."

Joseph stood, lifting her small frame easily into his arms. He watched as she threw her head back, gritting her teeth. "You are getting worse," he said quietly.

Abigail released a shuddering sigh as the pain finally began to abate. Once it was tolerable, she relaxed into his arms. She was too weak suddenly to try to argue with him. "We must leave soon," she whispered, resting her temple against his shoulder.

Joseph's wolf eyes were trained on her, waiting for her command.

"We must go tonight," she said, looking up at him. She watched as he nodded. "Bozal is the only one who can undo this."

Joseph pressed his lips together tightly. He didn't think that they would make it to Bozal. "I doubt that we can kill him," he said factually.

Abigail tried to grin wryly. "We must try."

Joseph stood in the entrance hall at the foot of the stairs. He stared pensively out the window at the night sky. He watched as the full moon flashed in and out of cloud cover. He was lost in his thoughts about Abigail. If killing Bozal was the only way to undo her curse, he knew that it was impossible. There was no way that just two of them, no matter who they were and what they were trained to do, could get to Bozal. And, even if they managed to get close, all he had to do was say the word and Abigail was done. It was a losing battle either way.

Soft shuffling made his ears twitch, and he turned his head slightly, pinpointing the sound at the top of the stairs. He drew a slow breath as he saw Abigail staring down at him, her piercing gaze meeting his. She looked like a ghost in her white breeches and tunic and knee-high boots. Her pale blond hair was woven in a braid, and her bow and arrows were strung across her back. Her cloak fell to the floor. She was silent as she descended the stairs, and Joseph felt his heart catch at the way she held his gaze as she reached the bottom step.

"Are you ready?" she asked softly.

He nodded, staring at the silver bow across her back. "Is that..?"

She smiled slightly, nodding her head. "Yes," she said, pulling it from her quiver. "This is Shalamar."

Joseph felt his eyes widen. It was beautiful and unearthly, made of pure unicorn horn. Despite the silver color, it had the texture of a wooden bow, and pure, white horse hair formed a solid cord for the silver arrows in her quiver. It emanated a soft pulse, a pure aura rolling off of it, pushing Joseph lightly. He knew it took much strength to wield this weapon, as the power it exuded was almost overwhelming. He looked up at Abigail as she tucked it back into her quiver.

"Let's go," she said, offering a weary smile.

Joseph let her take the lead, before following her into the snow.

Chapter Three

Snow Belle's feet barely grazed the snow as she galloped swiftly through the trees. She left no trace as she moved carefully. Abigail was a light burden on her back. Joseph followed closely behind, a silent shadow in the darkness. They were covering a lot of ground in a short amount of time, and had yet to encounter any problems.

Suddenly Abigail pulled Snow Belle up to slow her. *'We should stop,'* she said to Snow Belle. *'The forest is unsafe, but we need to rest.'*

Snow Belle eased to a stop, touching her nose to the snow, breathing in its cool scent. *'Yes,'* she said, her voice soft. *'Joseph can scout the perimeter.'*

Abigail slid from her back and rested her hand on Snow Belle's shoulder. She watched as a large black wolf padded quietly through the snow.

Its tongue lolled out of its mouth, and it panted heavily. Its shaggy black coat reflected the light that bounced off the snow. It shook, coming to stand next to Abigail. She noticed the gleam of its pearly-white, razor teeth.

"You should take a break," she said to it.

It licked its lips and laid in the snow. It rested its head on the ground and looked up at her through golden eyes.

Snow Belle looked at him, then at Abigail. *'I don't trust him,'* she said suddenly.

'What?' Abigail said, looking at her.

'I do not trust him,' Snow Belle said quietly as she watched him.

'Why not?' Abigail asked.

'I cannot say for certain, but things that shifted between us at the beginning don't make sense,' Snow Belle whispered.

Abigail watched Snow Belle for a moment. She knew Snow Belle had never read a person wrong, but she could not help but disagree. She looked at Joseph. '*What do you mean?*' she asked. She pulled her saddle and bed roll from Snow Belle's back.

Snow Belle sighed. '*When we touched, his thoughts were momentarily mine,*' she said. '*I couldn't grasp everything, but I saw enough to make me doubt his sincerity.*'

'*Do you think he would betray us?*' Abigail asked.

'*Not intentionally,*' Snow Belle said, dipping her head over Abigail's shoulder. She snorted a sigh as Abigail rubbed her nose. '*I just want you to be careful.*'

Abigail looked over at him. '*I will be,*' she said, even though she knew it sounded unconvincing. She rose after a while and walked over to Joseph, kneeling in the snow.

"Joseph," she whispered, stroking the top of his head lightly.

He opened his golden eyes and looked up at her.

"Would you scout the area?" she asked.

He breathed a heavy sigh and got to his feet. His tail swung slowly back and forth, signaling slight resentment. Abigail watched him trot into the trees. She looked at Snow Belle once he was out of sight. She noticed that Snow Belle's ears and eyes were still trained in the direction he had vanished.

'*What are you doing?*' she asked. She sank into the snow at the base of a tree, pressing her back against it.

'*I was just watching him,*' Snow Belle said, relaxing and turning to lip her.

Abigail could feel sleep tempting her, lulling her into drifting away, when suddenly Snow Belle tensed. '*What is it?*'

'*Listen,*' Snow Belle whispered.

Abigail sat quietly, a soft howl in the distance reaching her ears. '*What is that?*'

Snow Belle's ears were quivering. '*It's the sound of a wolf hunting.*'

Abigail sat forward, rising to her feet. '*Is it Joseph?*'

Snow Belle didn't answer. Another howl made them jump. It was louder and much closer than the first. '*That was.*' She touched her nose to the snow. '*I think we should be prepared to run. It sounds like he is trying to discourage the other wolf, but it is winter. They are starving, and it's coming this way.*'

Abigail threw her saddle onto Snow Belle quickly, pulling it tight. She swung up onto her back. '*What should we do?*' she asked, her breathing quick and ragged.

'*I think it would be wise to find Joseph,*' Snow Belle said, beginning to move into the trees silently.

Abigail scanned the darkness, every muscle in her body tense. She strained to listen for any unfamiliar noises. After a moment, she released a hard breath, realizing she had been holding it. '*Are we getting closer?*'

Suddenly, an unfamiliar howl went up, making Snow Belle start and stumble in the slippery snow. Abigail held tightly to her mane, feeling her heart racing and her body trembling. '*I believe so,*' Snow Belle said, once they regained their composure. She froze as she listened, her body tense and quivering. '*Do you hear that?*'

Abigail shook her head. '*No.*' She couldn't hear anything over the racing of her heart.

'*Something is coming.*'

Abigail pulled Shalamar and an arrow, knocking it. Soft rustling finally reached her ears, and she held on as Snow Belle turned toward the noise. A scraggly-looking wolf suddenly emerged from the trees. It was bone-thin, and a delirious light was in its eyes. It snarled at them, baring razor fangs. Saliva dripped from its lips as desperation filled its golden gaze.

"Go, Snow Belle!" Abigail dug her heels into Snow Belle's sides.

Snow Belle lurched backwards heavily. The wolf lunged at the same time she did, making her rear to avoid his razor teeth. She danced for a moment on her hind legs, before coming down, trying to spear him with her horn. She glanced around for Abigail, who had fallen from the saddle when she reared. She watched as the wolf eyed Abigail as she lay in the snow, a pained look on her face as she tried to sit forward.

Snow Belle attempted to stop the wolf, but it dodged around her, heading straight for Abigail. Instinctively, Abigail reached for her bow. She felt her heart drop into her stomach when her fingers only grasped the thin shafts of the arrows. She glanced around frantically, scrambling backwards in the snow. Despair overwhelmed her when she realized Shalamar was lying on the ground several feet away, the wolf standing between them.

"Snow Belle!" Abigail raised her arm to shield herself, knowing that any moment she would feel the wolf's razor bite.

Suddenly a yelp filled the air, followed by snarling and teeth snapping. Abigail looked up, seeing Joseph holding the wolf down, biting his neck. The wolf struggled against him, but Joseph was bigger and stronger. His pitch-colored hair stood on end as he bit down forcefully, causing the wolf to squeal in pain. Abigail felt stunned as the wolf began to fade, falling still in the snow, and Joseph slid into a crouch, gaining a better grip on his prey. When it seemed thoroughly incapacitated, Joseph transformed. He grunted as he pulled a dagger from his belt and dug it deeply into the wolf's chest. Blood slowly began to stain the white snow, and the light faded from the wolf's eyes as his body went limp.

Joseph stared at the wolf's dead body as he stood slowly. It was several moments before he could tear his gaze away. "Are you two all right?" he said finally.

Abigail nodded mutely as she stared at him. She blinked when Snow Belle stepped toward her, bumping her cheek gently with her nose. She let her hand rest on it, feeling her adrenaline rush starting to fade, leaving her feeling weak.

"Where is your bow?" Joseph asked, looking over at them. He knew if he hadn't arrived right in time, they would be dead. He watched as Abigail's ice blue gaze skirted around the clearing.

"There," she said quietly. She moved to her feet and crossed the clearing to pick up the bow. She felt a surge of warmth fill her as it touched her fingers. It helped to ease the pain that was coursing through her from her fall. She held it tightly in her hands as she turned to face Joseph and Snow Belle.

"Get on Snow Belle," Joseph said, glancing at her. "We can't stay here."

Abigail nodded, walking toward her. She paused as she rested her hand on Snow Belle's mane. "Joseph?"

He turned to look at her, pulling his eyes from the dead wolf.

"Thank you," she said softly.

She watched as a pained expression crossed his face, and he looked away. "Don't thank me," he said softly. "We're not safe yet."

Abigail pulled herself into the saddle, feeling uncertain. Regret had shown plainly in his golden eyes just then, almost as if he wished he hadn't done what he had. She turned Snow Belle to follow after him as he transformed.

'Are you all right?' Snow Belle asked, sensing her discomfort.

She sighed, entwining her fingers in Snow Belle's cream-colored mane. 'I suppose,' she said.

'You're still anxious from what happened,' Snow Belle said.

Abigail nodded. 'Perhaps,' she said. She watched as Joseph wove in and out of the trees, merely a shadow against the forest backdrop.

Snow Belle trotted after him. A gloomy silence began to pervade the cold, night air. After a while longer of trekking through the trees, Snow Belle stopped as Joseph did. He shifted easily into his human form, kneeling in the snow.

"This should be a safe place to make camp," he said. He glanced skyward, seeing faint rays of first light falling between the branches. "We need to rest."

Abigail slid from Snow Belle's back. "I agree," she said softly. She watched his face as he gazed around, feeling caught when their eyes met. She felt uncomfortable as they stared at each other, before she turned and pulled her saddle from Snow Belle's back.

She unrolled her bed roll, sinking down onto it, feeling weariness overtake her. She leaned back against her saddle, which she was using as a pillow, glancing around at her surroundings. Snow Belle settled to her right, and she turned to see Joseph sink into the snow against a nearby tree.

"Will you be all right there?" she asked. She watched as his golden eyes flashed to her in the faint light.

"I will be fine," he said. "I would offer to build a fire, but we are too close to Phoenix and to danger."

Abigail nodded. "If you are cold, you may take my blanket," she offered. She watched as he crossed his arms.

"Keep it," he said softly. "You need it more than I do."

Abigail frowned, staring at him for a long moment. She supposed he thought she wasn't looking, because after a while he rubbed his arms, trying to ward off the pre-dawn chill. She didn't hesitate to rise to her feet and walk toward him. She offered a small smile when he glanced up at her.

"May I sit with you?" she asked.

Joseph's golden eyes narrowed slightly, before he nodded. He was surprised when she sat right against him, throwing the end of her blanket around him. "This isn't necessary," he said quietly, despite the warmth.

Abigail grinned. "I realize that," she said. She let her head rest against his shoulder. "That's why you're keeping me warm."

Joseph snorted a slight laugh. "Oh," he said. He could feel the heat from her body beginning to warm him, and he let the tension her touch brought ease from his body. He could feel the fluttering in his chest beginning to settle, and he relaxed back against the tree. The sun was becoming stronger with every moment that passed, beginning to flood the trees with light.

"Was he one of your own?"

Joseph felt his heart lurch slightly, and he turned his head away quickly. "Maybe he was once before," he said, knowing she was talking about the wolf. "But he had lost himself to the animal inside." His fists clenched tightly in the blanket. "He was only what was left of his dying body," he whispered. "There was no human heart left in him."

Abigail drew a ragged breath. "Does that happen often?" she asked softly. She turned her ice blue eyes up to look at him.

Joseph shrugged. "I have never seen it before," he said thoughtfully. "I had heard stories, but..." He shook his head, sighing deeply. He brushed his thick brown hair from his wolf eyes. "It is something that happens when a man tries to survive by relying on the beast. There is a fine line between our humanity and our animal instincts. When the line starts to blur, there is always a risk." He looked across the clearing. "There are rules to being a shape shifter."

Abigail nodded. She knew some of the rules, but it didn't take much magic for her to transform into the white dove. And what she did was not what Joseph did. He was born with the wolf inside; she could only channel magic to make herself appear different.

"I'm sorry you had to kill him," she whispered. She watched as his golden eyes shifted to her.

"It was the kindest thing I could do," he returned, bitterness in his voice. "We aren't meant for the things that we are forced to do sometimes." He looked away, seeing Snow Belle foraging some feet away. "Humans were never meant to be slaves to animals, and animals were never meant to do humans' bidding." He nodded toward Snow Belle. "Even the bond you share with your unicorn is not something that was intended. It was something that was borne out of necessity, and something that persists because of the imbalance in the world."

Abigail sat up as he looked back at her. She could feel her heart aching at all the pain and suffering that was surrounding them. "I will make Bozal pay," she said softly, despite the hard edge to her voice. She watched as Joseph's eyes changed. "He killed my family. That is how he managed to take Precious." She could feel her brow knit in a scowl. "My brother Shane managed to escape and to save Shalamar, but he was fatally wounded." She shook her head. "It is for that reason that I must kill him." Tears were on the brim of her eyes. "He must pay for what he has done."

Joseph's eyes softened and filled with pity. "I'm sorry," he said gently. "I promise I will help you."

Abigail nodded mutely. She looked up as Snow Belle snorted, looking toward her, sensing her tears. "I appreciate everything you're doing," she said. She watched as Snow Belle slowly made her way toward them. She glanced back at Joseph, surprised to see him smiling softly. "What is so funny?"

He shook his head. "I haven't really done much," he said.

"You've done more than I could ask for," Abigail said quickly. She watched as his smile faded, and she realized suddenly that she would have to appreciate it. She had known from the beginning that he wasn't one to display much emotion, let alone any happiness. It was possible that she would never see that smile again.

"Get some rest," he said as Snow Belle stopped beside them, pressing her nose against Abigail's cheek. "You will need it." He rose suddenly.

Abigail felt her heart drop at the feeling of loss that suddenly swamped her. "Where are you going?" she asked, pulling the blanket tighter around her to try to conserve warmth.

He stretched lightly. "I don't need as much sleep as you do," he said. "I'll stand guard while you rest." He could smell the change in the morning air, and he knew that the road was going to be rough from here on. He looked down at her as she nodded.

"We need to be on the move before dusk," she said. She watched as Snow Belle lay next to her so that she could lean against her.

Joseph nodded. His transformation was seamless as he turned, four paws carrying him into the trees.

'*You are too trusting of him,*' Snow Belle commented softly as Abigail leaned into her. She could feel the sleep on the edge of Abigail's consciousness.

'*He is my protector,*' Abigail said quietly. '*How could I not trust him?*'

Snow Belle blew a heavy sigh through her nostrils. She didn't say anything else, instead transmitting her troubled thoughts to Abigail. She didn't feel any more at ease when Abigail looked up at her, petting her velvety nose softly.

"Everything will be fine," she whispered. "We need him."

Snow Belle fell silent, dipping her head to rest her nose on the snow. She knew it was of no use now. They were too far along to go back.

Joseph dropped to a crouch, letting his nose rest on his paws for a second. He crept forward slightly, seeing movement at the edge of the brush. He knew that, at any second, a small rabbit would come through the brush, right into his waiting jaws. His tail wagged slightly in anticipation. He could hear it hopping, ever so gently, across the brambles, and he rose slightly, ready to pounce.

He felt his heart drop when suddenly the rabbit began to scurry away. He rose swiftly to his feet to lunge after it, but stopped, dropping to the ground and freezing when an unfamiliar scent hit his nose. He felt his hackles rise as he realized it was human, and it was distinctly male. His lip began to curl in a snarl as he rose, moving to where the scent was leading him. His movements were silent as he came upon a cloaked figure crouching in the snow.

The flash of a dagger caught his eyes, and he growled softly. He emerged slowly from the trees, drawing the man's attention. He snarled as he stood, his eyes glittering in the soft light. He wasn't as human as Joseph first thought.

A soft chuckle filled the morning air. "So, he was correct," the man whispered, taking a step toward him.

Joseph snarled, his hackles rising. He crouched low, prepared for a strike.

The man ignored his defensive posture. "Bozal is watching you, Joseph," he said darkly.

Joseph felt his anger prickle at Bozal's name, and he snarled more.

"He is pleased with your progress," the man continued.

This gave Joseph pause. *Progress?* Questions suddenly burned inside him, but he didn't want to risk a transformation. He was vulnerable during the change, and if this other man was a wolf, he would know that and use it to his advantage.

"You know you cannot resist him forever," the man said, reading his confusion. "If you remain friends with *them*," his eyes shifted toward where Abigail and Snow Belle rested, "you'll always be an exile." He tilted his head slightly. "I know you yearn for a pack, and your pack is loyal to Bozal."

Joseph shook his head, his growling lessening. He couldn't believe what this man was saying. Bozal had killed his father and had destroyed the wolf blood line. He had destroyed Phoenix, and all he knew how to do was ruin things. *You're wrong.*

The man suddenly laughed. "I'm not wrong, little doggy," he said condescendingly. "You even carry with you the pack mentality, which allows me to hear your thoughts. You belong with us. Only then can you find the peace that your soul desperately seeks."

Joseph snarled, feeling exposed. He felt like his mind had been compromised, and he suddenly sprang at the man, forcing him back, away from the direction Abigail and Snow Belle were in.

The man leapt back with ease. "Your feelings for her will be your downfall," he said suddenly, his voice amused. "Brother, listen to me. She is but a mortal, destined to die by Bozal's hands. You have great potential; your world cannot exist within hers, just as hers cannot exist in yours. And you know when she finds out who you are, she'll leave you."

Joseph snarled, snapping his jaws. What the hell was this guy talking about? He charged again toward the man, forcing him farther away. He couldn't manage to close in on the man, he was just too quick, but he hated the amused light in his eyes. He hoped he was sending a clear message though: *If I catch you, I'll kill you.*

"So be it, Brother," the man said, leaping up into a tree where Joseph couldn't reach. "You will be ours again." He smirked smugly. "Your heart can only resist the call of the Hunt for so long."

Joseph barked at him, snarled and snapping, wishing he could climb the tree and rip the guy to shreds. He stood there for a long time once the man vanished into the surrounding trees, wishing he had been able to catch him. What had he meant by all the things he had said? Was Bozal really watching him? He must have been if he sent a man to spy.

No, he had to remind himself, not just a man. Another wolf.

A chill fell over him and he shook, his shaggy coat fluttering around him. A crisp breeze suddenly blew through the trees. The smell of ash and fresh meat was upon it. Joseph closed his eyes and turned his back to it. They were close now to Phoenix.

"Joseph."

Joseph suddenly spun, looking for the source of the voice. No one else was in the clearing with him, and his hackles rose. For a moment, he thought he heard...

He shook his head, turning and trotting back to where Abigail and Snow Belle slept. They had to keep moving.

Chapter Four

Abigail opened her eyes and blinked against the fading sunlight. She laid her cheek against Snow Belle's soft coat, and a thought occurred to her. Joseph hadn't come back to wake her yet. She sat up and looked around. She felt a slight chill in the evening air, but then a small fire caught her attention.

She stood and walked toward it. She knelt next to it, warming her hands. She glanced around, her eyes adjusting to the fading light that filtered through the trees. She noticed foot prints and a path that led into the trees. The fire was beginning to burn down into ashes, and she realized it had been burning for a long time. Why hadn't she noticed? The sound of movement caught her ears, and she looked up, seeing Joseph moving through the trees.

Their eyes met, and he offered the shadow of a smile. "Did you sleep well?" he asked as he neared.

She nodded. "We must be moving soon," she said. She glanced up at the fading sun. "Darkness is coming."

Joseph nodded, moving to kneel beside her. He picked up a bundle that he had left next to the fire and unwrapped it. "Here," he said, his golden eyes fixing on her. "You need to eat."

Abigail leaned closer to him, her shoulder touching his. "What is it?" she asked, looking at the cooked meat in the cloth.

"Rabbit," Joseph said, looking down at her. He pulled a piece off and offered it to her.

"Thank you," she said, eating it gratefully. She hadn't been very hungry recently, but the scent of the rabbit made her mouth water. She ate as much as she could stand, before looking at Joseph, who was watching her. "Did you rest at all?"

He shrugged. "I tried to," he said noncommittally. He turned his golden gaze toward the fire, which he was piling snow on to snuff it.

"Will you be able to go on?" she asked, concern in her voice. Joseph glanced at her, seeing her ice blue eyes watching him.

He nodded. "I don't need as much sleep as you do," he said. He rose to his feet once the fire was out. "And besides, there is too much to do to sleep." He looked over at Snow Belle, who was pushing through the snow to find small shoots of grass. "Be sure you have your bow with you at all times," he said, turning his golden eyes back to her. "Bozal has sent spies out into the woods. He knows we are coming."

Abigail's eyes snapped to him. "Bozal?" She felt her heart skip a beat. If he knew already, then getting to him would be nearly impossible, especially if he was tracking their moves.

"He thinks that I am delivering you to him," Joseph said, his eyes falling to the ground. "I caught one of the spies he had sent, and he tried to convince me that I am on the wrong side."

Abigail drew a breath. "Is that what you think?" she whispered. She looked up at him, seeing his eyes shift away from her, to the direction of Phoenix.

"No," he said shortly. He turned away from her and moved toward the trees. "We need to get moving." He changed into a wolf suddenly and trotted into the trees.

Abigail watched him go for a moment, a sinking feeling in her chest. If Bozal was trying to convince him he was on the wrong side, then he was clearly important. She glanced over at Snow Belle, who was watching her. She suddenly understood why Snow Belle said she didn't trust him. She didn't understand the politics of being a wolf, but if Joseph's loyalty meant enough that Bozal would try to make him switch sides, then they were in danger. At any moment, he could abandon them and leave them to their own devices, and take up Bozal's cause. He could become a threat to them.

'I have a bad feeling,' she said to Snow Belle as she pulled herself onto her back. '*Joseph said Bozal's spies are trying to make him come back to them.*'

Snow Belle blew a sigh through her nostrils. '*We need to be on guard. We are close to Phoenix.*'

Abigail nodded, feeling her ease into a lope to keep up with Joseph. They rode well into the night, finally emerging into a field. They slowed to catch up to Joseph as he crested a hill, his tail wagging slowly as his panting fogged the air. Abigail slid off of Snow Belle as she took in the scene before them.

At the base of the hill, the snow was completely melted away. Deep cracks split the dry ground, leading them into a desolate, barren wasteland. Steam spewed from some of the cracks. The carcasses of trees littered the landscape, and a dry heat pervaded the air. Abigail drew a hard breath, trying to become accustomed to the hot, dry air.

"So this is Phoenix," she said, her heart racing in her chest. She could feel her body beginning to tremble with nervousness.

Joseph looked up at her with golden eyes, his expression unreadable. He changed back into his human form, staring at the boiling desert before him.

"It used to be green," he whispered.

Abigail shifted her ice blue gaze to look up at him.

Joseph smiled sardonically. "You didn't think a creature as beautiful as a phoenix came from such a desolate place, did you?" he whispered. Disappointment and longing laced his voice.

Abigail stared at him for a second, before turning her eyes back to the landscape.

"This is the only place on the continent where the Willow Blossom grows," he said. He pointed into the distance. "There is a valley that way. It is where the fire unicorns used to live, before they were turned into black unicorns or driven into hiding in Gandora." He shook his head, feeling his heart sinking. Every day it became worse and worse. "Bozal is destroying my home." He glanced at

Abigail. "It hasn't rained here in years. The people and the creatures are suffering."

Abigail drew a ragged breath. She pulled her cloak from her shoulders and tossed it over Snow Belle's saddle. She pulled her pack from Snow Belle's back, throwing it over her shoulder with her quiver and her bow. "And what of the phoenixes?" she asked, coming to stand beside Joseph.

"No one has seen them in a while," he said. "Bozal tried to capture them and to use their magic of regeneration, but the few he managed to get died."

She watched as he looked down at her. "Let's go," she said, inclining her head. "Let's go stop him."

Joseph nodded. He could feel his body reacting to being so close to his home, and thrill of excitement coursed through him. He remembered this place, more than he liked to, and it seemed as if the magic here made his blood burn. He felt stronger here.

Abigail turned to look at Snow Belle. *'Stay here,'* she said. *'Joseph and I must go ahead. We'll depend on you if we run into trouble.'*

Snow Belle stomped her foot, clearly upset.

Abigail petted her nose and bid her farewell, before turning to Joseph. "I'm ready." She followed Joseph down the side of the hill, sliding the last few icy feet to dry ground. She looked up at Joseph as he glanced over his shoulder at Snow Belle.

'Protect her,' Snow Belle said, lowering her head.

Joseph nodded mutely, before turning away.

Snow Belle touched her nose to the ground, uneasiness filling her. A single flower sprung up from where she had touched the barren ground.

Joseph followed Abigail silently as they wove their way across the steamy plain. It was well into the afternoon when they finally reached the edge, crossing into a dim forest. He looked up at her, watching as she brushed sweat from her face. Her brow was furrowed in what he thought might be pain.

"Are you feeling all right?" he asked.

She glanced at him over her shoulder, her ice blue eyes narrowed. "I'm fine," she said, turning away. "And even if I wasn't, there is no time to stop."

Joseph frowned. He knew that if he was feeling the magic of Phoenix, she was too. Including the increase in the dark magic that she had been cursed with. "We should make camp soon," he said as they made their way into the trees.

Abigail slowed to stop, drawing ragged breaths. Her body was beginning to feel heavy and it was difficult for her to persuade her feet to lift from the ground. She knew it was because of the curse. She could feel her stomach twisting in knots, and she knew Bozal was aware of their presence. He was toying with them.

"Is it wise for us to stop?" she asked after she caught her breath.

Joseph shrugged. "We don't really have a choice," he said, turning his golden eyes on her in a knowing way. "You're too weak to continue for much longer."

Abigail frowned down at him as he knelt to touch the soil.

"This is a good place," he said. He watched as Abigail dropped her small pack and eased to the ground. He noticed the wince on her face, and he pulled the cloth-wrapped rabbit meat from his pocket to offer it to her. "You should eat."

Abigail took it slowly, unwrapping it and tearing off small pieces. "How close are we to Quasar?" she asked.

Joseph looked up, surveying the forest and the sky. "Several days on foot at this pace," he said thoughtfully. "It would have been quicker if Snow Belle had come, but..." He shrugged.

Abigail nodded, looking down at the rabbit meat in her lap. It suddenly appeared unappetizing as she thought about what he really meant. She was slowing them down. She wrapped it back up and handed it back to Joseph.

"Keep it," he said, holding up a hand. "Put it in your pack." He glanced around. "I can always hunt for more." His golden eyes suddenly shifted over her shoulder, and his body stiffened.

Abigail sat forward, grabbing her bow and reaching for an arrow. "Is something wrong?" she asked quietly.

Joseph held up his hand, a clear sign that he was listening, and his eyes tracked something in the darkness that Abigail couldn't see or hear. "I think we're alone now," he said quietly.

Abigail looked around, trying to see anything through the thick darkness that had descended. "What do you think it was?" she whispered.

Joseph eased into a sitting position from where he had been kneeling. "Others," he said simply.

Abigail looked at him, her ice blue eyes confused. "Others?"

He nodded, his golden eyes catching faint moonlight and reflecting it back in a soft glow. "Other demons," he said. "Other creatures."

Abigail glanced around, feeling uncomfortable. "Are we safe?" she whispered.

Joseph shrugged. "Are we ever really safe?" he asked softly. His eyes continued to scan the trees. "We're in enemy territory now. They probably won't bother us, but they aren't what I'm worried about."

Abigail nodded, looking back at him. He could see uncertainty on her face in the darkness.

"You should try to rest," he said. "I'll keep watch."

Abigail nodded, reclining back against her pack. Silence fell over them for a long time. Abigail felt her mind wandering, making her wonder what it was like for him to be here.

He had obviously fled this place for a reason, and she knew it was because of Bozal's cruelties. He was a fugitive in Bozal's eyes, a traitor to the cause. If his father had been forced into joining Bozal, there was no reason why Bozal would let him go so easily. But something didn't really make sense about that, the more she thought about it. She had a suspicion that there was more to Joseph than he was telling her; he was more important to Bozal than he was letting on. She wondered if she was safe with him. If Bozal really wanted him that badly, he would come for him.

It was the soft shifting of Joseph's feet in the dirt that drew her attention, snapping her out of her thoughts. She lifted her head, seeing him reclining on his elbow on the hard ground.

"Why are you so important to him?" she whispered suddenly. She watched as his golden eyes shifted to her.

"What?" he asked, confused.

Abigail sat forward. "Why does Bozal want you so badly that he would send spies to search for you?" she asked. She realized that she should have asked this question sooner. "What do you mean to him?"

Joseph looked away. He was silent for a long moment.

Abigail felt her chest constrict at his silence. "Who are you?" she asked, a hard edge to her voice. She instinctively reached for her bow.

Joseph sat up. He could see her agitation, and it was making him uncomfortable. This is not what he wanted.

"I have told you who I am, and even welcomed you into my home," she snapped, her voice angry suddenly. "You owe me an explanation."

Joseph turned away, his golden eyes trained on the ground. "If I told you the whole story, it wouldn't change anything," he said softly.

"Then explain," she said darkly.

Joseph drew a ragged breath. "My father," he said softly, the words hard pressed to leave him lips, "My father was the last king of Phoenix." He turned his face away. "When Bozal took the kingdom, he told him that if he didn't stay and lead his wolves into battle, he would kill me and my mother."

Abigail was on her knees in an instant. Joseph could see the surprise on her face in the darkness. "You're the son of Jarlath?" she demanded. "Why didn't you tell me?" She felt her chest constrict and her heart skip a beat. Jarlath was a great and renowned warrior. He had led his army into countless battles, and he never failed to bring back a victory.

"Because being my father's son is not what you think it is," he said. "It makes me a target."

"So then, your fighting ability that you showed me," she said slowly, "You were holding back."

Joseph turned to look at her, his golden eyes narrowed. "This doesn't change anything," he said darkly. "I'll still never join Bozal's side."

Abigail's eyes were wide. "This changes everything," she whispered. "You can defeat Bozal. You can take his place." She shook her head. "You are royalty."

Joseph shook his head. "I'm not interested in doing that," he said. "I was too young when Bozal took my father's kingdom, and I know nothing about being a king. The only thing my father ever taught me was how to fight and survive." He rose to his feet, agitated. It was upsetting to think about how his father was tricked and how their people were being treated. He wanted no part of it, only to end the cruelties that Bozal was inflicting on his people.

"Why didn't you tell me?" Abigail asked. She watched as he paced lightly. "Didn't you think that I deserved to know?"

Joseph growled softly. "Don't you think that I knew what I was doing?" he snapped suddenly. "Don't you think that I know that he is searching for me?" His golden eyes were glowing brightly. "I pretty much walk around with a bull's eye on my back." He shook his head, brushing his brown hair from his face. "It was better if you didn't know. Especially when you asked me to join you. I couldn't in good faith tell you about who I was, not when you wanted me to protect you."

"I don't need you to protect me," she said quietly, her voice bitter. Why would a dying man need protection? "I needed your eyes."

Joseph froze. "My eyes?"

"I needed you to bring me here," she said, motioning to the forest around them. "I need you to guide me to Bozal's castle." She held his gaze, ice blue to gold. "You know this place like the back of your hand, and I need that knowledge to help me get close enough."

Joseph was still suddenly. "What about your curse?" he asked.

Abigail looked away. "Of course that was something I did not plan for," she said softly. "But I am still capable and strong, I just need a guide."

Joseph nodded, his hands propped on his hips. "You need to sleep," he said after a long silence. "We have a long way to go tomorrow."

Abigail felt like he had unceremoniously dropped her. She knew he wouldn't answer any more questions, and he was done talking about it. He was back to business, and she sighed, nodding mutely. She lay back against her pack, trying to close her eyes and find some sleep. How could she put aside everything that he had just told her? How could she forget, now that she knew?

The morning came too early for Abigail. She felt like she had barely slept at all, and her body was sore from sleeping on the hard ground. She was initially disoriented when she awoke, glancing around for Snow Belle. Once she realized where she was, she looked around, her eyes finding Joseph. He was crouching a little ways away from her, his back to a tree, his eyes staring into the distance. The sunlight was reflecting softly off his brown hair. She wondered what it was that he was seeing or thinking as she sat up.

She brushed her hands across her face and smoothed stray hairs back. Joseph seemed to be aware of her movement, but he didn't move from where he was sitting. "Is something wrong?" she asked softly. She watched as he drew a shallow breath.

"They've been watching us all night," he said quietly.

"They?" Abigail whispered. She pulled a canteen from her pack, taking a drink of water. She watched as Joseph looked at her, his eyes shaded.

"Lesser demons," he said. "They know who we are."

Abigail swallowed a big gulp of water, feeling it sit heavily in her stomach. "Do you think we're in danger?" she asked, trying to hide her nervousness under a calm façade. There were many dangers she had faced in the past, including other magic users, but demons were different. She had never seen one up close, let alone had to fight one.

Joseph shook his head. "Let's get moving," he said, rising to his feet. "We have a hard day ahead."

Abigail rose too and pulled her pack across her shoulders with her quiver. She felt Shalamar pulsing lightly in her hands, and gentle warmth eased away the stomach-churning. She followed Joseph silently through the trees, suddenly feeling cold eyes on them.

"It's just their presence," Joseph said after a moment, sensing her discomfort. "All dark entities need to feed on fear." He glanced over his shoulder at her. "If you are afraid, you will draw them in."

Abigail swallowed, bracing herself. She offered a small smile. "I'm not afraid," she said, her voice small. "These beasts don't scare me."

Joseph nodded. He forged on ahead.

After a time, Abigail managed to forget about the eyes following them. She could hear them rustling in the background around them, but soon it just became white noise. She kept her attention focused on Joseph, who was calmly and certainly leading her toward the edge of the forest. As the day wore on, Abigail began to notice slight changes in him.

He seemed surer of himself here, as if he knew what he was doing, and he held himself a bit more securely, as if his status as Jarlath's son provided him some sort of protection. She began to realize that this was what he knew; he knew how to live and survive and to fight here. She felt as if she couldn't have picked better in those terms, but she also felt as if she had picked the worst guide in the world. Had she known who he really was, she would not have asked him. She didn't need a high-profile target leading her around, especially not one that Bozal wanted alive.

The thought gave her pause as they were climbing up a hill through thick brush, and she stopped, spluttering as Joseph let go of a thick branch, which swung back and caught her.

"What is it?" Joseph asked, turning when he didn't hear her following. He watched her push the branch out of her way, but she made no move to follow him.

"Is it as they say?" she asked. A sad look was on her face. "Are wolves drawn to their pack?"

Joseph felt taken back at her question, and he crossed his arms. "Yes," he said. "On some level."

"So then a wolf like you," she paused, seeming to gather her thoughts. "You need a pack to lead."

Joseph sighed. He didn't want to talk about these things. He had already divulged to her more than he had wanted, and this was hitting too close to home. "Of course I want that," he said, his voice thick with exasperation. "But I also want to defeat Bozal more than I want anything else."

"Would you choose them, if they asked you?" Abigail's ice blue eyes pierced into him with her question. "If Bozal offered you that, would you take it?"

Joseph felt the wolf inside him growl. Of course he wanted to take it. That was what his Alpha blood longed for. But would he take it over killing Bozal? The wolf inside him snarled darkly. It wanted Bozal's blood first and foremost. That outweighed any other primal need his inner-wolf had.

He shook his head. "My first priority is Bozal's blood," he said darkly. He and Abigail stared at each other for a long moment. He could tell she wasn't pacified, but it was too late now, wasn't it? They were already deep inside Phoenix's borders. There was no going back.

"We need to continue," he said, turning to lead on.

"Promise me," Abigail suddenly said.

Joseph paused, looking over his shoulder at her.

At his beseeching look, Abigail swallowed, looking down at the ground. Her fear was that he would abandon her when she needed his help; that he would allow his instincts to take over. "Swear to me that you will destroy Bozal, no matter what."

She looked up, seeing him staring at her, his golden eyes unreadable.

"I swear it," he said softly. His brow furrowed. "I swear I'll protect you."

Abigail felt her chest constrict. Something intimate and intense was passing between them, through his words. He was giving his word as an Alpha. He would take care of her, and his newly forming pack. She could feel the power behind his promise, and it made her draw a sharp breath.

"Let's go," he said gently, turning.

Relief suddenly flooded Abigail as his eyes turned away, and she took a second to compose herself. What had just happened? She shook her head, continuing after him.

Chapter Five

The afternoon sun was hot as it beat down between the trees, creating a stifling atmosphere. Abigail brushed sweat from her brow as they finally broke through the edge of the trees.

"We're at the base of the mountains," Joseph said, pointing into the distance.

Abigail wrinkled her nose.

Before them rose steep, sharp peaks, shrouded in cloud-cover and smoke. A low, almost inaudible rumble shook the ground they stood on, and Abigail could see previous traces of lava flow. The stench of sulfur was pungent on the air, which was becoming thin and cool.

"Do we have to go over?" she asked, feeling her heart sinking. Mountains were not the easiest thing for her.

Joseph shook his head. "There is a pass," he said, pointing. "It will take us to the other side."

Abigail nodded. She sighed as she wiped her face again with the back of her hand. She noticed that there was dirt smudged across her skin, and she guessed it was probably across her face too. Her body felt weak from the thinning air and the strain of their trek.

"We should camp here," Joseph said, his eyes on her. He seemed to be assessing her condition.

Abigail shook her head. "No," she said. "Let's get to the pass. We can camp there."

Joseph shook his head. "Here is safer," he said, stepping toward her. "The dangers that lurk in the pass will require all of our energy." He watched as her ice blue eyes widened when he caught her hand.

"What are you doing?" she said quietly, unease in her voice.

"I'm pretty sure you won't need these long sleeves," he said. He caught the wrist of her white shirt, giving it a good yank.

Abigail flinched at the sound of ripping fabric. She stood still, though, as he tore the fabric away from her arm. The air was cool on her skin, and she felt relief flood her. Despite feeling better, she leveled a look at him as he prepared to remove the other. "This was my favorite shirt," she said dryly.

Joseph smirked. "Now it can be different."

Abigail rolled her eyes as he tore away the sleeve of her other arm, so that it separated at the seam on her shoulder. She looked down, surveying his work. She felt her heart sink as her eyes drifted over her left arm.

Black tendrils of magic were lacing their way through her veins, and she winced unconsciously when Joseph's fingers trailed over her skin. "It's spreading," he whispered.

Abigail bit her lip, fighting down a surge of despair.

"How did this happen?"

Her ice blue eyes rose to meet his golden ones. "My brother and I, we were in Carmen," she said quietly. "It was after Shane had taken back Shalamar, and we were on our way to the North, to see the king."

Joseph's eyes narrowed as he watched her face.

"We were ambushed as we were leaving the city," she said, her voice dropping to a whisper. "They were Bozal's men, and one of them was a Caster." She let her hand drift to her arm, a grimace coming to her face as her eyes filled with tears. "I was struck with an arrow that was cursed with this dark magic." She shook her head, brushing at her face. "Snow Belle and I went to a healer, but there was nothing he could do. He said he had never seen such evil magic before, and that he didn't know how much more time I had." She looked up at Joseph. "I was there when I lost my brother to this curse."

"I'm sorry," Joseph breathed.

Abigail nodded, brushing away the last of her tears. No words could make any of this go away.

"So even if we kill Bozal, this still won't go away," he said softly. His eyes drifted down to the blackness. "You have to kill the one who put this on you." He wrinkled his nose as the scent of death hit him.

Abigail drew a ragged breath, before turning away from him. She took the torn fabric of her shirt and wrapped it securely around her arm. "Once my purpose is served, it won't matter," she said, a hard edge to her voice. "My life is dedicated to stopping him and protecting Precious and Shalamar."

Joseph watched as she used her teeth to secure the fabric in a make-shift bandage. He felt his heart sink. If the magic was as powerful as they thought, it would spread through her before they reached Castle Quasar.

"This is a fool's mission," he said darkly, watching as she dropped her quiver and pack to the ground. Her ice blue eyes shifted to him warily.

"We still have to try," she said evenly, sinking to the ground. She looked away, toward the mountains. "I can't just give up. I'm the only one left who can do it."

Joseph shook his head, feeling his jaw tighten. Bitterness suddenly swamped him. "You aren't bound by your sense of duty to do anything," he snapped. "You could go to the North and live a perfectly normal life. Go live among mortals and be happy with your family."

Abigail's eyes narrowed, and she pinned him with a glare. "I took an oath," she said darkly. "And I made a promise. I will not let my brothers' deaths be in vain." She looked away, seething suddenly. "Maybe those are things that don't mean much among wolves, but they mean something among men." She watched as Joseph bristled. His shoulders hunched slightly, and a dark scowl came to his face. He was angry.

"You know nothing about me or my father," he snapped. "You don't know what it was like." He was practically growling at her. "How dare you sit there and pretend like you're so pious."

Abigail returned his glare. "At least I didn't run away." She saw sudden, angry words beginning to form on Joseph's lips, but he stopped himself. He shook his head silently, turning and sulking toward the trees. "Where are you going?" she demanded.

"To hunt." He suddenly transformed easily into the black, shaggy-haired wolf, before disappearing into the trees.

His anger was so pungent, he could taste it. Despite being in wolf form, his blood still boiled with rage. His thoughts were drifting vaguely in and out of his wolf-mind, and his human mind was beginning to meld into something different. It was hard to keep hold of human thoughts in his wolf form; they weren't compatible. The wolf saw in only sharp contrasts of whites and grays, and words were foreign and unintelligible. There were only sights and sounds and tastes and smells to lend meaning to things. It was easy for him to relinquish control to his wolf side, allowing his new body to feel the warmth of the Phoenix air filling his lungs.

Soon the scent of a rabbit hit his nose, and he paused, finding the trail. It was easy enough to follow into the trees, but as he neared where it was hiding, he began to feel uneasy. There was a strange, unfamiliar tinge to the scent, one that was uncomfortable to his senses. His footsteps were uncertain as he came to a clearing, and his hackles suddenly raised, a growl forming on his lips. There was indeed a rabbit, but it was dead in the clearing, intestines littering the ground.

There was no sign of the killer, and it made Joseph more on edge. There was no other scent than that of the dead rabbit, and Joseph's eyes shifted around, searching for any other signs of another being. Upon seeing nothing, he turned, slinking slowly back into the trees. The feeling the rabbit had caused didn't abate as he moved back toward the camp, and he shook, trying to rid himself of it. It wasn't until the soft scent of burning flesh hit his nose that he finally understood the feeling.

A howl suddenly filled the forest, followed shortly by a joining chorus.

Abigail felt her body tense. The sad song of wolves filled the air, and it put her on edge. She rose to her feet, pulling her arrows and Shalamar close. She slung her pack over her shoulders. She thought briefly about Joseph and where he might be, before another chorus of howls caused her to jump. Her heart was racing as she realized the wolves were much closer this time. She wasn't sure what to do at first.

She was unprepared to fight a whole pack of hungry wolves. She couldn't possibly hope to injure them, let alone kill all of them, or even enough of them to escape. She notched an arrow as she tried to buy herself more time. She knew that with every second that passed, they were closing in on her.

The rustle of brush made her jump, and she pulled Shalamar taut, aiming into the trees. She held her breath to still her bow as she waited for whatever would emerge.

"We have to go!" Joseph yelled, bursting through the trees. He froze as his eyes took in her armed stance.

For a moment, Abigail had to concentrate on controlling her knee-jerk reaction to loose her arrow. "Sorry," she said, quickly lowering Shalamar. "Is it a hunting pack?"

Joseph shook his head, seeming angry still. "I'm not going to wait around to find out," he said, walking past her. "Let's go."

Abigail followed after him as he broke into a jog. "Are we going into the pass?" she asked.

Joseph nodded his head. "I didn't want to, but we don't have a choice," he said over his shoulder. He began to lead the way up a steep trail. "We need to climb to lose them."

Abigail nodded, following closely behind him. It was relatively easy, until pain began to shoot through her arm and torso. She winced slightly, feeling the pain pulsing with the beat of her heart. She tried to ignore it, but weakness suddenly swamped her as she reached for the next handhold. She felt her body slip, and she gasped, clinging tightly to the rock. A curse left her lips.

"Are you okay?"

Abigail lifted her ice blue gaze to see Joseph crouched on a ledge above her. She nodded her head. "I'm fine," she lied, the pain becoming more intense. She took a moment to assess the fact that he was close, but just out of arms' reach. If the weakness overcame her again and she fell, he couldn't catch her. She pressed her face to the cool rock as nausea washed over her.

A sharp howl made her jump, and she looked over her shoulder, seeing a pack of six wolves swarming the camp below them. Their chorus of howling and yelping sounded like laughter to Joseph as he watched Abigail dangle above them. He could see hunger and something else in their eyes, and he suddenly knew that they weren't just animals. They were Bozal's Hunters.

"Hurry Abigail," Joseph said, urgency overcoming him. He laid flat against the ledge, extending a hand. "Give me your hand."

Abigail swallowed thickly. Her limbs suddenly felt like lead, and she tried to pull herself up to reach him. Pain shot sharply through her, and she paused, shaking her head. "I can't," she whispered. She could just imagine falling and succumbing to the snapping jaws below.

Joseph frowned down at her. "What do you mean you can't?" he asked, irritation in his voice. "You were doing fine a moment ago."

Abigail shook her head slowly, feeling her body begin to shake weakly. "It's the curse," she said, her voice hoarse and strained. "I can't make myself move."

"You have to try," Joseph said. His voice was laced with irritation, but Abigail could see the concern in his golden eyes.

She drew a heavy breath, knowing it was now or never. She would only get worse as her body became more and more taxed, and she swallowed thickly, before clenching her jaw. She just had to work through it.

"Keep your eyes on me," Joseph said, holding her gaze. He watched as she lurched forward, grasping onto another handhold. His heart was pounding hard in his chest. She was close, but not quite close enough for him to reach. He stretched his arm out, seeing her arms shaking. "Come on, Abigail. Just one more."

She could feel her head swimming suddenly, dizziness sweeping her. Her breathing was short and labored, and her heart was racing. She could feel sweat on her brow, running across her cheek. Her arm burned both from the curse and the strain of holding on. She forced herself to keep her eye on Joseph's hand.

"I'm going to jump," she said. She watched as Joseph's golden eyes widened.

"Just get a good grip and pull yourself up one more length," he said. There was fear in his eyes. "If you jump, you might not make it."

She shook her head, keeping her ice blue gaze on him. "I have to," she said. "I don't have the strength to pull myself up there."

Joseph's brow suddenly knit with worry. "Don't," he said, a hard edge to his voice. "You won't make it."

She tried to offer a thin smile. "You'll catch me."

Joseph was stringing together a line of curses in his mind. The last thing he wanted was for her to misjudge and tumble down to the hungry wolves waiting below. He realized that it was too late to argue as she suddenly lurched up, reaching for him. His heart skipped a beat as he realized that she wasn't going to make it, and he felt the air of her hand barely grazing his. All he knew was that he couldn't let her fall.

Her ice blue eyes were wide with fear suddenly. She knew she hadn't jumped far enough. Joseph made a split second decision that he knew would save her life. He slid forward after her, barely keeping a hold on the ledge as he reached for her. He felt the strain in his muscles as his hand wrapped around her wrist, bearing her weight.

"I got you," he breathed, seeing the fear on her face. It only took a moment for him to heft her onto the ledge. He was surprised when she pressed her face against his chest suddenly.

Her fear was radiating off of her, and her body was trembling. Tears suddenly began sliding silently down her cheeks. Her arms were wrapped securely around his waist. Her breath was hot as it blew through his shirt against his skin, and it took a moment for him to realize that she was sobbing softly.

"It's okay," he said gently, unsure as he put his hands on her back. "You're safe now."

She nodded, pulling away from him quickly. "Sorry," she said, wiping quickly at her face, which was heating with a blush. "I'm just being stupid. Thank you."

Joseph nodded, his eyes taking her in. She was still trembling, but he couldn't tell if it was from fear or fatigue. He frowned as his eyes ghosted over her arm, where the blackness was seeping under the makeshift bandage. He pressed his lips together to stop his words. Nothing he could say would make a difference now. All they could do was keep pressing forward.

"Come on," he said, standing and offering her a hand.

She took his hand and let him pull her to her feet. She felt light-headed and sick to her stomach, and the feeling didn't abate as she followed him along a narrow, winding trail. She thought the mountain air would be cooler the higher they went, but it seemed as if it got hotter. She glanced around, wondering where the wolves went to as their howling faded.

"We're close to Olympia," Joseph said, drawing her attention.

"Olympia?" Abigail asked, hearing the strain in her voice. She was breathing hard, both from fatigue and from the thin mountain air.

Joseph nodded. His golden eyes shifted back to her for a brief moment, before back to the trail. "It's the volcano."

"Oh," Abigail breathed, looking skyward. She could see it in the distance, smoke pluming from the top. She frowned as she stared at it. It didn't seem so menacing at first, but she knew that it probably was very frightening to be around when it erupted.

They wound their way down the side of the mountains, night falling over them. There was a faint glow from the active Olympia, and as the winds changed, there was the smell of sulfur. Abigail could feel her body coming to the end of its endurance. It seemed as if, with every step she took, it was becoming weaker and weaker. Her legs were shaking, and her heart felt like it was fluttering in her chest. Sweat was dripping slowly down her temple and her cheeks, and she kept wiping it away defiantly. She was struggling to keep up with Joseph, who had slowed to a crawling pace, when she suddenly tripped and stumbled to the ground.

She felt the rocks grinding into her knees and the palms of her hands, but that pain was miniscule compared to the sudden burning that assaulted her. Her arm felt like it was on fire, and she gripped it with her free hand. It felt cold to her touch, despite the white-hot pain.

"Abigail." Joseph's voice was faint and fuzzy as she looked up at him. Ringing had begun to fill her ears, and she thought she would pass out. "Abigail, listen to me."

She couldn't concentrate on what he was saying as he moved toward her, kneeling beside her. She gazed helplessly into his golden eyes, wishing she could will away the pain. Tears and blackness began to edge into her vision, and Joseph's words were lost on her as she succumbed to the pain.

Joseph caught Abigail as she fainted, falling forward into his arms. His nose wrinkled in disgust as the dead-flesh scent of the curse assaulted his senses. She was getting worse still. Her body felt both hot and cold beneath his touch, and he pulled her into his arms, lifting her easily. Her weight was nothing for him to bear as he carried her to the end of the trail and into the pass.

He felt a chill shake him as the mountain walls rose up around them, casting them in shadowed darkness. The faint glow of Olympia cast little light into the sky, leaving the high walls of Thunder Pass pitch black. He hated that they had to come here in the dark, but there hadn't been much choice. His senses were on high alert as he carried Abigail's limp frame, looking for a safe place to hide. He knew the pass was riddled with hidden dangers, some of which even he would run from. He felt his skin crawl as he remembered the last time he had to come through.

It didn't take long for him to find a small nook, and, after checking to be sure it was free of dangerous vermin, he carried Abigail inside, laying her down gently. He propped her head against her pack, setting Shalamar and her quiver of arrows beside her. He sighed deeply as he slid to the ground next to her, his back against the rock wall.

He cast a wary gaze around, before turning his eyes back to the sleeping Guardian.

Her face was pale, and her blond hair was messy and escaping her braid. She seemed so different suddenly from the strong, sweet girl he had met in the forest. This wasn't the girl he had thought he was guarding. She was becoming frail and fragile, and it frightened him. How could they possibly hope to stop Bozal if she couldn't make it?

He looked away. What the hell were they doing? Going ahead was suicide, wasn't it? But it was a death sentence for her either way. If they tried, she could die, and if they didn't, she would die anyway.

He let his golden eyes drift out of the shallow cave they were hiding in.

What about him? Where did that leave him, if they failed?

He shook his head, putting his hand to his cheek. He didn't like to think about it. He knew Bozal would pull him into his fold. He couldn't stop it or escape it. One way or another, he would win. Bozal always won…

Joseph felt his throat constrict at the thought.

This was so stupid. There was no way to win. And there was no way for him to resist the Call. Even now, just being here, back in Phoenix, was enough to make him restless. It was a restlessness that he couldn't place or explain, but one that he felt more so in his soul. He knew it wasn't him, it was the wolf. The wolf inside was so anxious for the Call of the pack. It looked for it and chased and wanted it more than anything he had ever wanted before.

And it wasn't something he could turn off or ignore. It was innate, and pulsed and flowed with every beat of his heart and every breath he took.

If his wolf wanted it, he couldn't stop it from taking Bozal's offer to take the pack.

He drew a sharp breath, fighting down the sickening feeling in the pit of his stomach. He knew he had to stop it; he had to stop himself from losing control. There were many things that Alphas had a duty to do, and he had to force that part of him to see that his Alpha status had to take a backseat. He needed to convince himself that he was the Alpha of the pack he was leading now; that Abigail and Snow Belle were depending on him to lead them into this land and to help them and protect them.

His golden eyes shifted back to Abigail. He remembered when he had seen her standing there, next to Snow Belle. She had looked like an angel, dressed in white, her pale hair falling around her. He felt his heart flutter slightly as he thought back to that day. It hadn't been that long ago, had it?

She was beautiful. Even now, despite being ill, her beauty still shone through. Her strength, her determination, her will to fight; he thought about their fight earlier. It was respectable, her sheer will to fight and to defeat her enemy. He didn't know much about her or her family, but he knew that, as Guardians, they were sworn to protect not only Shalamar and Precious, but magic itself. And if what she said was true, she was the last one. She had to complete her mission. He wondered if she thought it was as hopeless as he did.

He knew her brothers and her father had been slain by Bozal. How could she possibly hope to stop him if a whole fleet of them had stood against him and failed?

Joseph drew another sigh. They had their work cut out for them. Victory would not be easy.

A soft groan suddenly left Abigail's lips, drawing Joseph's attention. He watched as her dark eyelashes fluttered, revealing piercing, ice blue eyes. She glanced around for a moment, before their eyes met, a clash of blue and gold.

Joseph felt his breath catch. He felt caught in her stare for a moment, and it wasn't until she looked away that he came out from her spell.

"Where are we?" she whispered, looking around.

"We're in Thunder Pass," he whispered, watching her sit up. "Do you feel well enough to move on? We can't linger here."

She turned to look at him, pressing her hand to her forehead. "I think so," she said. She winced lightly, her hand coming to her arm. She looked down, her ice blue eyes widening at the long black tendrils that were winding around her arm.

"It's growing," Joseph said, a frown pulling at his lips. "You don't have much time."

Abigail swallowed, turning her eyes on him. "Then we should get going," she said. "I need to have all my strength when we face him."

Joseph nodded, moving to his feet. He helped her up, before slinging her pack over his shoulders and handing her Shalamar and her quiver. He felt the pulse of magic through Shalamar as her hand brushed it, and it was strange to him. It was hot almost, but he noticed that she seemed to relax once it was in her hand.

"It must have a weakness for other riders," he commented as their eyes met.

She nodded. "It's hard to say," she said softly, looking down at the bow. "It has a mind of its own."

"Just keep it close," Joseph said, turning away from her. "We have to be vigilant. The pass is not safe."

Abigail nodded. She threw her quiver over her shoulder, ignoring the pain in her arm. She followed Joseph as he stepped out into the hot night. They were silent as they walked along, and she could tell that Joseph was listening. Her head still felt fuzzy from earlier, and she tried to shake it off. She knew they were running out of time, too.

She could feel it in her body. She had never felt as weak and vulnerable as she did right then. The thought scared her. Would she have the strength to fight Bozal when they finally met? She could only hope that they could find Precious before that time. She knew if she had Precious, she could defeat Bozal easily. She didn't know if it could remove her curse, but she knew its magic was much more powerful than Bozal's.

She looked up sharply when Joseph suddenly stopped.

"What is it?" she whispered, standing beside him. She looked up at him, seeing his eyes scanning the dark walls of the pass.

"We're not alone," he whispered. His golden eyes were distant. "We're being stalked."

Abigail pulled an arrow from her quiver, knocking it in Shalamar. "Are you sure?" She could feel her heart racing in her chest, causing pain to pulse through her.

Joseph nodded. He scanned the dark ahead, his jaw set.

A low, rumbling hiss suddenly filled the air. Abigail jumped as rocks began to slide down from one of the walls, falling at their feet. She turned quickly, pointing her bow up the rock wall. She felt Joseph shift beside her as the hiss became louder, joined by a clacking sound.

"What the hell is it?" Abigail asked, glancing at him.

He pulled a small dagger from his boot, a scowl on his face. His eyes suddenly widened as a shadow began to climb down the side of the wall.

Abigail turned to follow his gaze, feeling a chill shake her. The shadow was huge, and as it came closer, the hissing and clacking grew louder. She felt her eyes widen as it began to take form.

Large, hairy legs lowered it from the side of the canyon wall, and several gleaming sets of large eyes were clear in the faint light.

"What the—" Abigail breathed.

"Spider," Joseph whispered. He caught her wrist when she made to step backwards. "Be still."

"Are you serious?" she gasped, terror in her voice. If she had been afraid of the spiders they had at home, this one made her want to die. It was twice the size of Snow Belle, and the hissing and clacking were coming from its massive chelicerae.

"They can't see very well," he whispered. His back was rigid and tense. "Their eyes catch movement."

Abigail drew a ragged breath, her arms frozen at her sides.

Its eyes shifted around, searching for them. As its chelicerae moved, Abigail could see venom dripping from its fangs. She gasped when it suddenly opened its massive mouth, brandishing its pointed fangs. It let out a piercing squeal, one that made Abigail press her hands to her ears. It hefted a huge hairy leg from the ground, stepping toward them.

"On my mark," Joseph whispered.

Abigail looked at him. "Are we running?" she whispered.

Joseph looked at her. "You run," he said. "I'll distract it." He looked back at it. "Once you're out of its sight, hit it in the chest with an arrow."

Abigail's brow creased with worry.

"Whatever happens," Joseph turned his golden eyes on her, his brow creased with stern anger, "*Don't* let it get you."

Abigail swallowed hard. She nodded slightly, pulling her bow tight. She watched, feeling her heart pounding as it caught her movement, eight eyes focused all on her.

"Now," Joseph breathed.

Abigail saw the monster look first to her, then its eyes shifted to Joseph, who sprang at it faster than she could move. At first, she wasn't sure what to do, but then she broke into a run as it turned to chase Joseph. She was surprised when he suddenly leaped onto its back, driving his dagger into its body.

It released another piercing squeal as it flailed with Joseph on its back. She had to dodge as it swung its massive, hairy legs around, nearly knocking her to the ground. She tried to move into a position where she could get a good aim at its chest.

"I can't get a good shot!" she yelled, lowering her bow.

Joseph suddenly pulled the dagger from the beast's back, before jabbing it into one of its eyes.

The giant spider suddenly reared back, its squeal painful and agonizing as it thrashed around. Venom dripped from its fangs, which were bared and ready to spear Joseph. It tottered dangerously on its legs, baring a faint mark across its hairy underside.

Abigail gasped, aiming swiftly and loosing an arrow. She watched as it flailed and screamed as the arrow struck home, before it suddenly lurched forward, causing Joseph to tumble from its back. Abigail felt horror fill her as she watched him land hard on his back directly in the monster's path.

"Joseph!"

He couldn't react quickly enough as the spider came down on him, digging its giant fangs into his body. He cried out, before using his dagger to stab at the spider's remaining eyes.

Doing all she could think of, Abigail notched another arrow. She loosed it at the beast, striking it in the head. The spider reared back with the impact, screaming again. It stumbled backwards, its massive weight causing it to crash to the ground. Seizing the chance, Abigail ran to Joseph. She could see his blood littering the ground.

"Joseph!" she gasped, grasping his arm and trying to drag him to his feet.

"I'm okay," he said quickly, letting her help him to his feet. He seemed dazed as he held the wound in his stomach, but he didn't seem to be in much pain. He put his body between her and the spider as it began to lurch to its feet again. "Stay back."

Abigail gasped as the spider saw them and moved toward them. It used a massive leg to knock Joseph to the ground, stepping over him and sinking its fangs into him again. She realized that it was targeting him because it could smell his blood. She could hear him yelling curses at it as it bit him over and over again, causing more of his blood to litter the ground.

She felt nauseous suddenly as she saw the venom from its mouth running down into his wounds. She could see the pain on his face, and for a moment, she felt immobile. She was watching it kill her friend, and she didn't know if there was anything she could do to help him.

Summoning her courage and trying to find anger to steel her, she notched another arrow. She fired it at the spider, hitting it once more in the head. She didn't understand why it didn't die as she loosed another arrow, striking it in the head a third time. She felt her heart sink as it screamed in agony, reeling away from Joseph to bear down on her. It lunged for her, and she managed to roll away from it, surprised by her own nimbleness. She felt pain wrack her as her brain shifted into survival mode, and her body began to move of its own accord, her training kicking in. She thought she felt a dull burning in her good arm, but she ignored it.

She dodged the spider's massive fangs once more, striking it again in the eye, trying to move from her roll to her feet. Sudden dizziness swept her, and her coordination seemed to leave her all at once, causing her to stumble and fall as she tried to regain her feet. She gasped as she realized the spider was standing over her, and she felt Shalamar pulse as she loosed another arrow into its heart.

Finally, the spider stumbled, a squeal fading from its ghastly mouth. It staggered back and forth over her, like a tree in the wind. It uttered a last, low growl, before staggering backwards and collapsing to the ground. It didn't move again.

Abigail felt her chest heaving, her brain fuzzy and confused. She was panting hard, and she tried to sit up as she realized it was dead. She saw Joseph lying motionlessly on the ground nearby, and she staggered to her feet. She felt the world tip heavily, and she swayed like a drunk. She nearly lost her footing, but she made it to Joseph's side, falling heavily to her knees. For some reason, words were hard for her confused brain to supply her with.

"J—Joseph," she managed, leaning over him. She felt the burning in her arm again. This time it was different, and she could feel it spreading slowly through her body. She thought she heard him say something, but she suddenly collapsed. She thought she felt his hands on her arms, but her world began to spin wildly.

"Abigail?" Joseph leaned over her, lowering her to lie on the ground. He grimaced at the burning in his own wounds, but ignored it. He could see where his blood was turning black in the darkness, his body converting the venom to a form that couldn't harm him. It was what made him immune to most poisons, a gift that wolves were blessed with that made poisons ineffective.

He could feel his body beginning to use his wolf's magic to knit itself back together. It was painful, but he ignored it, focusing on Abigail. Her face was deathly pale, and she was too still on the ground.

"Abigail," he whispered, pressing his hands to her face. "Abigail, wake up." He shook her lightly. When she didn't respond, his eyes scanned quickly over her body. He felt the blood drain from his face as he saw the one thing he dreaded.

A deep gash ran across her unbandaged arm. He could see where the edges were beginning to turn to what looked like rotted flesh. He knew that the spider had grazed her with its venom. He touched her wound lightly, lifting it to his nose. The sickly sweet scent of the spider's venom filled his nose, and he gagged.

"Abigail," he breathed. His brow knit with concern, and he pulled Shalamar from her hands. He looked forward, knowing there was still a good distance he had to cover before he reached the open plains. He grimaced as he pulled her quiver and Shalamar across his shoulders, before he lifted her from the ground. His body protested, but with every passing second, he could feel himself becoming stronger.

He carried her quickly through the pass, jogging where he could. He knew time was not on their side as he did the best he could to avoid other monsters that lurked in the pass. He knew that the spider carcass would draw most of them, and he managed to make it in good time to the end of the canyon. He breathed a hard sigh of relief as the mountains and rocks soon gave way to a vast expanse of thin, hard grass and open land as far as the eye could see.

"Hold on, Abigail," he whispered, looking down at her. She groaned softly at the sound of his voice, but didn't wake, and he knew there wasn't much time left.

It was close to dawn before he finally found what he was looking for. Tucked in the grass at his feet, amongst the rocky soil, was a cluster of small silver flowers. He kneeled slowly, lowering Abigail's lifeless form to the ground. He reached for one of the flowers, pulling the petals off of it.

"Abigail," he whispered, pressing his hands against her cheeks. "Abigail, you have to wake up."

Her brow furrowed slightly, and she tried to open her eyes unsuccessfully.

"Abigail, listen to me," he said, propping her against his knees. He could see that her skin was beginning to turn ashen, and she was freezing to the touch. He didn't know if this would work anymore. "Abigail, eat these." He pressed the silver petals to her lips.

She didn't open her mouth, so he had to force the petals between her lips. He closed her mouth, and tipped her head back, trying to help her swallow. He thought she might have swallowed them, but he couldn't tell. She was too still.

He waited a long moment with baited breath. He had only seen one other person be treated with the silver flowers, and the healing had been almost immediate. It felt as if an eternity went by as he waited for her to open her eyes. He felt his heart beginning to sink as more and more time passed, the sun becoming higher and higher on the horizon.

His throat constricted as his heart plummeted to the pit of his stomach. He was too late. Despair filled him suddenly, and he pulled her against his chest.

"I'm sorry," he whispered, his voice pained. He couldn't explain the sudden anguish that swept him.

He had tried.

He had tried to protect her and to keep her safe. He had tried to get her to Bozal, but now...

"I'm so sorry, Abigail," he breathed, pressing his forehead against hers. Her skin was cold to the touch, and it made the heartbreaking feeling worse. "It wasn't supposed to be like this."

He had failed her.

Chapter Six

Abigail felt like she was falling. The sensation jolted her mind, and feeling suddenly overcame her. She could feel burning in her stomach and her limbs, and she wanted to cry. She whimpered, feeling her mind beginning to register the brightness of sunlight. It took another moment before she realized that there was something cradling her, and something pressed against her.

"W—what..?" she breathed. She managed to open her eyes, feeling confused when she looked up right into Joseph's golden eyes. There was such sadness and confusion staring back at her.

"Abigail!" he gasped, his eyes widening in surprise. He seemed unsure of what to do at first, before he pulled her tightly against his chest. "Thank goodness. I didn't think..."

She frowned up at him, becoming flustered at their proximity as the pain in her body began to fade. "What happened?" she whispered, looking around at the open plains around them. "Where are we?"

"The spider poisoned you," he said softly, his eyes on her face. "Gollum spider venom is extremely deadly. I didn't know if you would make it or not." His eyes became angry suddenly. "You scared me."

Abigail felt her heart skip a beat. He was afraid he would lose her? "I wouldn't just die that easily," she said, trying to lighten the mood.

Joseph suddenly sighed. "Of course not," he said, sitting back. "Guardians don't just lie down and die."

Abigail sat up, feeling better now that he had put some distance between them again. Her body still felt weak from the venom. She looked down at her arm, seeing that the blackness hadn't changed. She glanced over at him, her eyes widening as she realized his clothing was stained with black blood.

"Are you okay?" she whispered.

Joseph followed her gaze, looking down at himself. "I'm fine," he said. "My body is much different. I am immune to most venoms and poisons, and the magic that allows me to transform also heals me." His golden eyes shifted to her. "I guess there are perks to being a wolf."

Abigail looked up at him, nodding. Her eyes were distant for a long moment, before she looked away. "It must be nice," she commented.

Joseph shrugged. "It's all there is for me," he said quietly.

"Someday, I want to be something other than a Guardian," she whispered, her ice blue eyes shifting around at the emptiness that stretched in front of them.

"Really?" Joseph's golden eyes were curious and slightly confused as they ghosted over her face. He couldn't imagine that there was much more to life than the things he had already seen and done. He couldn't remember what life had been like before Bozal's reign. All he knew was how to survive in a hostile world.

Abigail nodded. "Once this is over," she paused, feeling a nagging feeling that it wouldn't be much longer for her. She shook her head, trying to dispel the feeling. She had cheated death before, and she had just done it again with the spider venom. If she was meant to die before now, she would have. "I will take Precious and Shalamar back," she said, her voice calm and steady. "And I will destroy them."

Joseph's eyes widened in surprise. "Guardians are the protectors of the magic world," he whispered. "How can you destroy them?"

Abigail looked at him. "Without them, the magic world won't need protecting," she said softly. She pressed her hand to her forehead, feeling exhausted suddenly. "What was once made for good is now the source of the ultimate evil. I don't want to carry this weight anymore. I want to live my life under my own terms, and not live and die alone like the rest of the clan."

"What do you mean?" Joseph asked. He watched as she looked up, her eyes focused on the horizon.

"My mother…she didn't choose to be the mother of Guardians," she said quietly, her eyes shifting to the ground. "She was chosen by the king." She turned her head away. "In the mortal world, being a Guardian is a curse, and being a mother of one, let alone six or seven, is severely frowned upon." She could feel a lump forming in her throat as she thought about her mother. She had hated her husband and her children and everything that they stood for. "My mother hated us just like everyone else did," she whispered, feeling tears threatening to spill from her eyes. "I don't want to be hated anymore."

Joseph felt her words hit him hard. He didn't know what to say as he looked at her. He watched as her shoulders sagged, and he thought he could smell tears. To be abandoned by your family was something he used to think he could relate to since he had been abandoned by his pack, but now it seemed like nothing in comparison to what she had dealt with. His mother and father had loved him and raised him to be strong and to be able to stand up to Bozal when the time came, but her mother had hated her. He didn't know how she was able to be so strong and loving to Harlie.

"Does she live with the mortals?" he whispered.

Abigail shook her head. "She died," she said, her voice hard. "She killed herself after Harlie was born." Joseph saw her clench her jaw. "She couldn't bear the thought of having more of us." She slid Joseph a glance, her blue eyes cold and distant. "She thought we were abominations."

"I'm sorry," Joseph whispered. He watched as she looked away, down at her arm. "I didn't realize…"

Abigail shook her head. "I don't want to talk about it anymore," she whispered. "We need to keep moving."

Joseph nodded, rising to his feet. "Do you feel well enough?" he asked. He watched as she nodded, standing slowly.

She staggered back slightly. When he reached for her, she waved him away. "I'm fine," she said. Once she gained her balance, she reached for Shalamar and her arrows. "Let's go."

Joseph nodded, sighing as he led the way. He had no idea that she hated being a Guardian as much as she did. It didn't make anything more clear to him as to why she felt she had to stop Bozal, but it made him have even more respect for her. He felt his heart twist, and he glanced over his shoulder at her. Was it possible that one little blonde girl could be so strong?

His thoughts suddenly shifted back to the spy in the woods. Could he learn to make her his pack, and forget about Bozal's offer? He had been devastated when he thought she would die, and he couldn't even imagine what he would do if she did die. How would he carry on? Could he even hope to do what she was trying to do? He didn't think he could. He wasn't as strong as she was, and he couldn't force himself to be as determined as she was.

But then, what if they did it? What if they defeated Bozal, and she did destroy Shalamar and Precious as she intended? Then where would they be? The thoughts were alarming enough to make him stop.

Abigail, lost in thought, nearly ran into the back of him. "Joseph?" she asked, slightly startled. "Joseph, what's wrong?"

He turned to face her, his golden eyes on her ice blue ones. "What happens after this?" he asked quietly. "After all this is done?"

Abigail frowned. "What?" she breathed.

There was an expression in his eyes that she couldn't place; one that unnerved her. "When everything is right again, where will you go?" he asked.

She shook her head. "I hadn't really thought that far," she said quietly.

Joseph was quiet for a moment, before he nodded and turned away.

"Is that it?" she asked, following after him as he continued to lead the way.

He nodded.

A few moments of silence passed as she followed him across the hard, barren fields. She noticed that the grass was stiff and weed-like, and the ground was littered with rocks. Was it like this in the rest of the land?

"How close are we?" she asked, looking up at Joseph.

The sunlight was hard as it glinted off his dark brown hair. He turned slightly, looking over his shoulder at her, his golden eyes more alive in the bright sunshine. He had shed his thin, long-sleeved shirt in favor of the sleeveless shirt he had on beneath it.

"Once we reach the end of the plains, we'll be able to see Quasar," he said. "It's nestled against the Lake of Fire."

Abigail frowned, tilting her head. "Lake of Fire?"

Joseph nodded. "It's extremely hot," he said. "The water boils, and no one can survive if they fall into it."

"Oh," Abigail breathed. She was beginning to feel taxed again, even though they had only gone a short way. She was breathing hard and beads of sweat were rolling down her face.

"Can you make it?" Joseph asked, arching a brow as he glanced back at her.

"Yeah," Abigail breathed, hefting her quiver and Shalamar. "I don't really have a choice, do I?"

Joseph's eyes narrowed slightly, hiding a hint of humor. "Guess not."

Chapter Seven

The sound of heels on marble drew a set of amethyst eyes. A golden scepter glinted in the candlelight. A giant, blood-red ruby sat atop the scepter, twinkling with the soft movements of his hands as he stroked a fat, grey cat. He blinked, staring thoughtfully as the approaching soldiers kneeled before him. He leaned back in the throne, stretching lightly. He had been so bored, waiting for Abigail and King Jarlath's son.

"They are close, my lord," one soldier said, his head bowed low.

"Good." Bozal rose slowly from where he was sitting. The cat leapt from his lap, yowling at the soldiers as it disappeared. Bozal's voice was low and threatening as he stepped down from the dais. "I want them both alive, but take them separately." He stepped toward the soldier who had spoken, watching as he bowed lower to the floor. "No need for the Guardian to fill our Alpha with her nonsense." His amethyst eyes bored into the soldier's head. "Now go."

The soldier nodded, him and his companion rising swiftly. Their transformations were seamless as they both transformed into wolves, hightailing it from the room.

Bozal's nose wrinkled in disgust as he turned back to his throne. The fat grey cat suddenly reappeared, meowing softly, curling around Bozal's ankles. He bent and picked up the cat, petting it softly as he moved back to his seat.

"I hate those damn dogs," he said quietly, resting the cat in his lap as he settled back into the cushioned throne. He listened to the cat purr loudly. "Once I have Jarlath's son, though, no one can stand against my wolf army." He grinned. "I have a feeling Joseph will not be able to resist our offer, eh my pet?"

The cat mewled softly, closing its eyes happily.

Abigail was falling behind. She could see that Joseph was trying to slow his pace for her, but it didn't feel like she would ever catch up. Her legs felt stringy and uncoordinated, and her feet felt like lead weights. The pain in her arm was increasing with every step, and she could see that the black tendrils were reaching nearly to her wrist. She shivered at the thought of how far they had spread across her torso. She felt her endurance and her resilience waiver as they came to a sharp escarpment.

"Do we have to climb that?" she breathed as she stopped beside Joseph.

He nodded, watching as she sank to the ground. "Unfortunately." He offered a slight smile. "But there is a small trail."

Abigail felt some relief flood her. "I just need a minute," she said, looking up at the blue sky. Phoenix was much hotter than Gandora, and it was difficult for her to imagine that it would have been much easier even if she had been well. She winced as the searing, white-hot fire began to spread through her once more. She noticed that it seemed to be more painful when she thought about facing Bozal.

"I'll carry you," Joseph said, drawing her gaze. He could see the pain etched in her ice blue eyes. It had been constant, something he was used to seeing on her face. The only comforting thing was that he knew it wasn't getting worse.

At his suggestion, Abigail's face blanched. "That's not necessary," she said, sounding almost offended. She watched as he stepped toward her. She didn't want him to think she was that weak. She knew she hadn't really been holding her own, considering everything that had happened since they arrived in Phoenix, but she wasn't weak. She didn't need him to treat her like she was broken.

"You won't make it on your own," he said, holding a hand out to her. "Let me help you." He thought she would protest, and she stared at his hand for a long moment, before her eyes softened, and she took his hand. He pulled her to her feet. "Climb on my back."

He hoisted her onto his back, holding her legs around his hips. She was a light load, even with her pack and bow and arrows.

"I'm not too heavy?" she whispered. Her breath was hot against his neck, and he tried to ignore the goose bumps that rose across his skin.

"No," he said shortly. "I've carried you farther than this."

She wrapped her arms around his neck, resting her cheek against his shoulder. She felt very conscious of the way their bodies were pressed together, and she wondered if he could feel the blush that was heating her cheeks. She was grateful for the chance to rest, however, and she tried to calm her pounding heart.

They began their climb along the trail in silence. Abigail was surprised at how well Joseph could navigate it, as he seemed to know where to step, despite the slippery, gravelly footing. He moved along the thin trail as if her weight was nothing.

"Thank you," she said, finally breaking the silence.

She heard Joseph draw a sharp breath. "There is no need to thank me," he said quietly.

"Well, still," she said, lifting her head to look up the escarpment. "I've been so useless."

Joseph grunted what she assumed was meant to be a laugh. "I'm used to it."

Abigail was momentarily surprised, not sure if he was joking or if she should be offended. She held her tongue as they neared the top. "You can let me down," she said. "I can make it the rest of the way."

Joseph paused, before slowly lowering her to the ground.

Abigail was surprised by the care with which he let her slide off his back, his hands lingering on her hips to steady her. For a moment, she felt flustered, and she was glad that he wasn't turned toward her.

"Be careful," he said, holding his arm out to keep her away from the edge while she oriented herself. "It's steep and slippery."

Abigail nodded, looking down at the gravelly trail. She followed slowly after him, her feet sliding underneath her for a few steps. Once she gained her balance, she was able to follow him more quickly. She could see the blue sky beginning to arch over the top, and she felt a sense of victory as the end of the trail became visible. She was so ready to reach the top that she slipped when Joseph suddenly stopped in front of her.

She felt irritated for a second, before she saw the look on his face. "What is it?" she asked.

Joseph held a hand out to her, suddenly turning. "Go back," he said quickly, ushering her in the opposite direction. "Go, quickly!"

Abigail didn't understand what was happening. She turned too fast, her feet sliding from under her. She felt Joseph catch her wrist, keeping her from plummeting over the steep edge. She was having trouble understanding what they were running from, when suddenly a white wolf landed in the trail in front of them.

"Melanie, stop!"

The ragged sound of Joseph's voice caught at her. He knew this one? He must have known all of them.

The white wolf was snarling angrily, keeping them from escaping down the trail. Abigail didn't need to look to know that they were trapped. She pulled Shalamar from her back, knocking an arrow. She took aim at the wolf, but she realized too late that it was too close for her to sight properly. She released her arrow as it sprang at her, but it dodged it, narrowly avoiding a fatal strike. She felt her heart stop as the wolf collided heavily with her.

Joseph felt time freeze as he saw Abigail fall from the corner of his eye. He turned his back to the brown wolf he was preparing to square off with, diving for her. He wasn't fast enough.

He could only watch helplessly as she fell to a ledge that jutted below. His heart dropped to his stomach as she hit the rock, sprawling across it. He couldn't react quickly enough as the brown wolf and the white wolf both fell on him, and his human body was no match for their teeth. He tried to fend them off, but he felt the white one close its jaws around his throat, cutting off his air flow.

This wasn't the way he had pictured things going. He never thought he'd die by the hands of his own comrades.

Darkness followed quickly.

When he finally started to come to, Joseph instantly felt the pain in his throat. It was sharp, and it was hard for him to draw a breath for several moments. He pressed his hand to his neck, feeling the wolf inside him snarl. Sneak attacks were low, especially for the people he had once known so well. A sharp pain caught in his chest, sadness seeping over him. How could they betray him like this?

Once the pain registered and began to fade, he realized he was lying on a hard stone floor. He opened his eyes quickly, looking around. His heart dropped as he realized it was the cold floor of a dungeon. How long had he been unconscious?

He grimaced suddenly.

Abigail...

His wolf whined softly in response to her name, and he felt his heart sink. He hadn't really seen how far she fell, but there was no way she could have escaped injury. And it was impossible that the wolves had tried to get to her. They had only been trying to separate them. What use was she to Bozal, anyway? She was fighting to destroy him, and he had nothing to offer her.

The sound of footsteps suddenly interrupted his thoughts, and he sat up quickly. He looked toward the door as a shadow fell across it. It was a heavy wooden door, and faint light spilled in from underneath it. A key grated heavily in the rusty lock. The door swung open slowly, an ominous feeling suddenly filling the dungeon. Joseph knew his hackles would be raised at this point. He unconsciously bared his teeth and growled low as a tall figure entered the cell.

"Joseph." A smile accompanied angry amethyst eyes. "You have returned home."

Joseph didn't know what to say. His feelings were so intense that it left him speechless for a moment. This was the moment; he finally got to see his father's murderer in person. He thought he might have something good to say, but nothing came, save for intense, gut-wrenching hatred.

"What?" Bozal asked, his voice soft and deceptively gentle. "No words?"

Joseph felt his hands fist suddenly. He didn't move as his golden eyes bored into Bozal's amethyst ones. "I'll kill you."

Bozal laughed suddenly. "Kill me?" he drawled, stepping closer to Joseph. "Why would you do such a thing? Am I not the one who gave you and your weak father power?" He was close enough to Joseph that he could smell the musty scent that reminded him of old bones and old, untouched tombs.

"You didn't do anything for my father," he hissed angrily. "You stole what he worked his whole life to create, only to destroy it." He had unconsciously moved into a kneeling position.

Bozal laughed, waving his hand. "Never mind what I did back then," he said dismissively. "It is what I want now that matters."

"And why should I give a shit about what you want?" Joseph hissed, seconds from changing into his wolf form and tearing Bozal to pieces.

Bozal grinned, turning his back to him. "Because," he said, drawing a small orb from his pocket, "I control your little Guardian's life."

Joseph felt his whole body still. His brain did a sudden turn, and his eyes widened. "Abigail," he breathed. His eyes hardened as he turned back to Bozal. "Where is she?"

Bozal grinned wickedly, holding the orb in the palm of his hand. It began to glow suddenly, swirling into a cloud. Joseph's eyes widened as he suddenly saw her lying against the rock, motionless. There was blood trailing around her.

"She is alive, little doggy," Bozal said tauntingly, suddenly closing his fist around the orb, causing the cloud to vanish. His amethyst eyes were pleased as Joseph leaned forward, his golden eyes begging for a command. "I will give you a chance to save her."

Joseph felt his heart racing, his chest heaving with his rapid breaths. She was still alive, but not for long. He could still get to her and take her out of Phoenix. He could still help her...

"What must I do?" he whispered, lowering his eyes to the ground. His wolf snarled fiercely at the forced submission, but he couldn't do anything else.

"Pledge your loyalty to me," Bozal said, stepping toward him once more. He leaned in, waving his hand.

Joseph jumped as a piece of parchment paper swirled in front of him.

It was a contract.

He watched as Bozal's amethyst eyes studied him, waiting for his decision. He didn't want to, but what else could he do? There was only one way to save Abigail.

He lowered his head, his eyes on the conjured contract. He knew entering into a deal with a being as powerful as Bozal was dangerous, and he knew he would have to do things he didn't want to, but it was worth it. It was worth it to save Abigail's life.

"Simply sign here," Bozal waved his other hand, a quill forming. He grinned as Joseph reached for it.

Joseph winced as the pen moved of its own accord, piercing his finger. He watched as two drops of blood fell onto the contract. He couldn't look at Bozal as he laughed, the contract vanishing suddenly.

"Now bring her to me," Bozal ordered suddenly.

Joseph's eyes snapped to his face. "You said you would keep her alive," he said, fear creeping over him.

"But I never promised I would let her go," Bozal laughed. He pointed to the door of the dungeon. "Now go!"

Joseph couldn't resist the command. He felt his body moving of its own accord, and he felt hopelessness sweep him. What had he done?

There was pain. Much, much pain.

She couldn't think past it as she struggled to open her eyes, hoping she could make sense of what had happened to her. She felt her heart ache as the wall of the escarpment rose up above her, the reality hitting her. She thought she vaguely remembered Joseph trying to catch her, but she wasn't sure what was real and what she had imagined as she stared at the sky.

She tried moving, but incapacitating pain left her immobile. Tears filled her eyes.

Was this the way it ended? Was this really what was to become of her?

She lifted her hand slowly, fighting back a sob at the ache that crawled through her. The black tendrils had reached her finger tips now. She guessed that was part of her inability to move; her curse was reaching the point that it was leaving her in too much pain to move. She guessed that it gave Bozal much pleasure to watch her die this way, but she wondered why he hadn't bothered to bring her to his castle, where he could kill her on his own terms.

She wondered if Joseph had managed to escape. She closed her eyes as she realized that it wasn't likely. Bozal wanted him.

By now her tears were sliding across her face to moisten the parched ground below her. She could see that the sun was low on the horizon, and she knew it would be dark soon. She felt grief overwhelm her. That was her final resting place; she knew she would die there, on that ledge.

After several moments of crying, she decided that the least she could do was pull herself together. She forced herself to stop crying, hearing her father's voice in her head. He would be so disappointed if he saw her like this. He hadn't trained her to just give up and die like this. She was stronger, and she could find a way to survive. She gritted her teeth as she rolled onto her side, biting her tongue to silence her pained cry. Her eyes widened at the blood on the ground, and she guessed that was why the pain in her head was so intense. She brushed her fingers across her skull, feeling sticky blood and a knot.

It took her last bit of strength to force her body into a sitting position. She knew she was hurt badly, but it was a good sign that she could sit up. Her head swam with the change in position, and a dull throb pulsed through her temples. She leaned against the wall of the escarpment, stretching her legs in front of her. She could feel her toes wiggling inside her shoes, and she knew her motor functions were still good. She glanced around, her eyes landing on her quiver, which had spilled her arrows during her fall, and Shalamar, which was a few feet away.

She clenched her jaw as she reached for Shalamar, grasping it easily.

The bow pulsed lightly, filling her with warmth. She felt the aches in her body ease slightly, and her spirit lifted some. She could do this. She could find a way off this ledge.

The sound of rocks sliding down the trail suddenly caught her ears, and she used her arm to shield herself as they fell over the edge, hitting her. She turned her eyes quickly to the top, thinking she saw movement.

"Hello?" Her voice was hoarse and hard-pressed to leave her throat. She swallowed thickly, trying again. "Hello!" Her heart was pounding as she waited for an answer. Was someone passing by that could help her? The thought of rescue made her stomach flip-flop.

"Abigail!"

She felt her heart jolt hard in her chest. "Joseph?" Her voice was barely a whisper, one she knew he couldn't hear. "I'm here." She couldn't understand the relief that flooded her when she saw him kneeling over the edge of the trail. She felt tears suddenly flood her eyes.

"Are you all right?" he called.

She nodded her head quickly. "I'm okay," she said, unable to stop her crying. She wiped quickly at her face.

"Stay still," he said. "I'm coming to get you."

Abigail felt her heart sink when he disappeared, and she held her breath as she waited for him to come back. The seconds seemed eternal, and she was starting to think that she was imagining things and that he wasn't really there, when suddenly a rope fell over the side, uncurling beside her. She looked up as Joseph used it to rappel down to the ledge. Once his feet hit the ground, he was beside her, kneeling.

His golden eyes were filled with worry. "Are you sure you're okay?" he asked.

Abigail nodded. She took his hand as he stood and offered it to her. He pulled her slowly to her feet, causing her to whimper with pain. Once she was up, she felt lightheaded, and she swayed suddenly. Aching numbness trickled down her spine.

"Careful," he breathed, wrapping his arms around her to steady her. "Are you sure you're fine?"

She nodded her head quickly, bracing her hands on his arms. She couldn't speak, her voice locked behind her clenched jaw.

"Can you hold on to me?" he asked, searching her face. He could see where the blood had stained her pale blonde hair, and dirt smudged her face and clothing. He could tell she was in a lot of pain; she was just too stubborn to admit it. He watched as she drew a ragged breath, before nodding her head.

"Yes," she breathed, her voice ragged.

Joseph didn't question her, knowing their window of time was closing quickly. The longer they lingered, the darker it got, and the worse she would be. He kneeled and scooped her onto his back.

"Hold on tight," he said, wrapping her legs around his middle. He hooked her ankles together. "Keep your feet like this."

She nodded mutely against his shoulder, her arms tight around his neck. She gasped when he easily began to climb up the rope. It felt like an eternity before he reached the top, and she breathed a ragged sigh once they were safely on the trail. She thought that he would set her down, but he surprised her by putting his arms around her legs, holding her in place.

"Where are we going?" she whispered, watching as he began to ascend the trail. "How did you escape the wolves?" There were suddenly a lot of questions rolling around in her fuzzy mind.

Joseph was silent. With every step he took, Abigail could feel tension building inside her.

"Joseph," she said, her voice somewhat stronger, "where are you taking me?" She watched as he bowed his head slightly, shame suddenly coming over him.

"I'm sorry," he whispered.

Abigail felt fear hit her hard suddenly. She knew where they were going, the realization hitting her like a sack of potatoes. "Put me down," she said, pushing against him. "Put me down now!"

Joseph shook his head. "I can't," he said, his voice surprisingly hard.

Summoning strength she didn't realize she had, Abigail began to flail against him, kicking and punching. She cried out when he dropped her suddenly, causing her to land on her back, but she tried to recover quickly. She rolled onto her side, trying to will the pain away as she tried to drag herself away from him.

He hadn't escaped and come back for her, he had joined them.

Despair seeped through her. Snow Belle had been right. He did betray her.

"I won't go!" she yelled, anger and pain coursing through her. "I won't let you hand me over to him!"

Joseph didn't move as he watched her. His golden eyes were sad as she turned and glared at him. "I don't want to," he said softly. "But it's the only way to keep you alive."

Abigail shook her head. "What are you talking about?" she demanded. "Betraying me and giving me to him is going to keep me alive? Are you insane!" She wished desperately that she had arrows. Shalamar was pulsing gently against her back.

"He was going to kill you," Joseph said, looking away toward the castle in the distance. His golden eyes were unreadable, and his jaw was set.

Abigail felt dread suddenly overcome her. Her ice blue eyes widened with terror as she stared at him. "What have you done?" What promises had he been forced to make in order to keep her alive? "My life isn't worth what you just did."

Joseph's golden eyes shifted to her, a hard expression on his face. "It is to me," he said, advancing on her. "You'll thank me someday." He transformed seamlessly, mid-step, growling as he lunged at her.

She raised her arms to block his teeth, but she was no match for his wolf strength. She dug her fingers into the fur around his neck as his mouth closed around her throat, blocking her air flow. She tried in vain to push him off of her, but the damage was done. She couldn't breathe. She flailed and gasped, desperately trying to draw air into her lungs as his weight pressed down on her. She thought she saw sadness in his wolf eyes, but her vision was fading quickly.

Abigail's mind was fuzzy and disoriented as she struggled to wake up. She turned her head slowly, feeling the achy pain across her back, as well as the burning that always assaulted her. Her eyes flew open as she realized that she was comfortable, cool sheets pressed against her skin. She tried to comprehend what she was seeing as her ice blue eyes widened in shock.

She was lying in a big, four-poster bed. Crisp, white sheets were pulled over her. A pillow cushioned her aching head. Her clothes were lying nearby on a boudoir, folded neatly and clean. She tossed the sheets back slowly, easing her bare feet to the polished floor. The hem of a silk nightgown brushed her knees as she stood. She tried to push her thoughts past the disorientation in her head, looking around the room. It was quite large, with a chair and table, and an attached bathroom.

Where was she?

A window caught her eye, and she moved toward it, pulling back the curtains. She felt her heart drop when she saw how small it was, merely a slit in the stone wall, and realization began to dawn on her. She must be in Bozal's castle.

She felt extremely uncomfortable suddenly, and she rushed to pull on her clothes. She noticed that her quiver and Shalamar were nowhere to be found. She expected as much, though. She pulled on her boots quickly, before looking around the room. There had to be something she could use to help her escape. She ran to the bathroom, digging through the things there. She was dismayed to find only soap, scented bath oils, and a hair brush. She gritted her teeth as she walked back into the bedroom.

What was his game? How long did he plan to keep her here? And why had he allowed his servants to tend to her?

She began to pace the floor, feeling the aching burn in her limbs become worse. She froze as she heard footsteps in the hallway beyond the door. Her heart skipped a beat in her chest, making the pain worse. Her ice blue eyes narrowed as a key clicked in the door lock. The door swung in slowly, revealing a heavily armed soldier.

"You are requested," he said, his voice deep. His eyes were trained on her in an unseeing way.

"And if I refuse?" she countered. She felt dizziness sweep her, and she held her arm tightly, trying to fight down the burning. She could feel that it had spread to her stomach, and the pain made her toes curl.

The soldier's face didn't change. "Then you will be taken before our lord by force."

Abigail wanted to resist. She had no desire to see Bozal or to die today, but she knew she had to pick her fights. A struggle now would leave her useless later.

Bowing her head, she walked calmly toward the soldier. She could feel her body trembling both from fear and pain. She followed the soldier's orders as he directed her where to go, following closely behind her. The walk to the throne room seemed to last for an eternity, every step she took becoming more and more painful. By the time they reached the doors, she was blinking back tears and fighting to keep her knees from buckling under her.

She winced, her body trembling harder as the doors were pushed open, revealing a dimly lit throne room. She flinched when the guard pushed her forward, nearly causing her to lose her footing. She glanced around quickly, seeing that there was no way out. She swallowed thickly as her eyes landed on the man seated before her.

"Ah, Princess Abigail," he purred, rising to his feet. The grey cat leapt from his lap with a yowl. A vicious grin was on his face. "How do you feel?"

Abigail clenched her jaw, her breaths heavy between her teeth. She was shivering fiercely, and she wondered how she was still standing despite the pain. She wrapped her arms around her body, trying to hold herself together.

"You're sick," she said angrily, despite the way her voice trembled.

Bozal laughed softly, his amethyst eyes narrowing. "I couldn't make it easy for you," he said, stepping closer to her.

Abigail felt as if white-hot irons were being shoved into her as he came nearer. Blackness was eating at the edge of her vision. She knew she was on the verge of collapse. She tried to hold his gaze as he stopped before her, and she lifted her chin in a defiant gesture.

"You're much stronger than your brothers," Bozal commented darkly. "I didn't think you would make it this far."

Abigail felt the mention of her brothers cut her heart like a knife. Bitter anger fueled her, lending her strength. "I'm not done with you yet," she hissed, her ice blue eyes narrowed dangerously.

Bozal laughed again, the sound grating to Abigail's ears. "Nor I with you, little Guardian," he said. He reached out slowly, pressing his fingertips to her shoulder.

Abigail expected to feel more burning pain, but instead, she suddenly felt numb. The pain was instantly gone, and it made her knees threaten to buckle. She hated the way Bozal sneered at her.

"Is this what you want, little Guardian?" he asked tauntingly. "To be cured?"

Abigail wanted to slap his hand away, but she found she couldn't move her body. She glared at him. "I would rather die first."

Bozal's amethyst eyes didn't register surprise. Clearly he had expected her answer. He shrugged lightly, before removing his hand.

It was unbearable as feeling surged back over her, and she gasped, falling to her knees.

"You can't hope to defeat me," Bozal said frankly. "You'll be dead in days." He grinned, sadistic humor in his amethyst gaze. "This curse has served me well." He turned away from her. "I will be sure to use it on Harlie."

Abigail felt her heart stutter in her chest, fear washing cold over her. "Leave my brother out of this," she breathed, feeling as if her chest was going to burst open. "He has nothing to do with you."

Bozal looked at her over his shoulder, the action condescending. "I know how you Guardians are," he said. "Always persistent, little pains in my side." He shook his head. "I can't have him interfering. Besides,"

∽ 84 ∽

he shrugged, "My wolves are already on their way to slaughter him, as we speak."

Abigail shook her head, tears coming to her eyes despite her desire to fight them down. "No!" she gasped, bowing her head. "I'll do whatever you want!" She felt pathetic as she recalled her conversation with Joseph. This is how he trapped them. Desperation was overwhelming her.

Bozal turned to face her, genuine interest on his face. "And what, little Guardian, do you have that I could possibly want?"

Abigail was shivering fiercely now, tears dripping down her cheeks. There was only one thing he needed her to do; it was all very clear now, why he had allowed Joseph to bring her here.

"You can't use it, can you?" she whispered, looking up at him. Her ice blue eyes were challenging. "You can't touch Precious."

The expression eased from Bozal's face, melting slowly into displeasure. He didn't say anything as they stared at each other.

"I can purify it," she said, her voice steely. "I can remove the spell."

Bozal stepped toward her. "You aren't a caster," he said darkly. He held out a hand, clenching his fist tightly.

Abigail felt as if he was squeezing her heart, and severe pain wracked her. She almost wished that she was dead. She didn't know how much more she could take.

"I was taught!" she gasped. She heard his footsteps freeze, and she fell to the floor, writhing in pain. She gasped harshly as the pressure was suddenly released.

"You're lying," Bozal said angrily. "Only powerful casters have the ability to remove such curses." He stepped to stand over her. "Don't toy with me, little Guardian."

Abigail could feel her heart breaking. "It's because of Snow Belle," she whispered. She looked up at him from where she lay on the floor. "My bond with Snow Belle allows me to channel Charlotte's powers."

Bozal's amethyst eyes widened in shocked surprise. How had he not known that she could do this? His game had simply been to toy with her and make her miserable before he killed her, but this was unexpected.

"Get up," he commanded.

Abigail moved slowly to sit, feeling the pain lessening some. She looked down at her clenched fists to see black tendrils winding around her fingers.

"You will break the curse for me," he said, his amethyst eyes dangerous. "And then I will spare your wretched brother's life."

Abigail nodded, rising shakily to her feet. She watched as he waved to the guards, who stepped forward.

"Remove her to the dungeons for the time being," he ordered, waving his hand. "I must prepare."

Chapter Eight

Abigail pressed her face against the cool stone of the dungeon wall. Tears were sliding slowly down her face. Her bodily pain was minimal now, but her heart was hurting in more ways than one.

What had she agreed to do?

She couldn't just hand over the power that she was trying so hard to protect. Bozal would use it to destroy her and the rest of the world. He wouldn't stop. All of this that she was doing, she knew it was only to buy herself and Harlie some time. Bozal wouldn't let them live long, especially now that he knew about what their bonds with their unicorns afforded them. He would know that if she could break the curse, she could certainly replace it.

She wiped slowly at her tears.

And then there was her oath. She had sworn her life to this cause. She had made a promise, before her family at the sacred shrine that she would lay down her life before she would allow Precious and Shalamar to fall into evil hands. She was breaking everything that she believed in; every ideal that she had ever fought for meant nothing now.

But it was worth it, wasn't it? Harlie's life had to be worth something!

She couldn't let the last bit of her family slip away. She couldn't let Harlie be killed like this. She couldn't...

Her heart twisted painfully, and she shifted against the wall. She couldn't let this be the end for her.

Joseph pressed his back against the wall, watching as guards passed each other in the corridor. Surprisingly, he still knew this castle like the back of his hand and it was easy to sneak to the dungeon where they were keeping Abigail.

He had heard the other guards talking about her. He knew what she had done, the deal that she had made. He looked down at his finger, a small spot still there from the deal he had been forced to make. It was a painful reminder of the fact that he had sold his soul to Bozal. Bozal's wish was his command, no matter what it cost him.

He looked up as the corridor cleared, before slipping into the dungeon passageway. He shut the door quietly behind him, seeing easily in the darkness. It was easy to find her cell.

He pressed his hands against the door, finding it was unlocked. "Abigail?"

The door swung open easily, faint light falling across her small body. He grimaced when he saw how the black tendrils were wrapped around her hands and arms and curling up her neck. Her eyes were focused away from him, but her jaw was clenched. She didn't move.

"What do you want?" she whispered darkly.

"I heard about what you did," he whispered, shutting the door behind him and moving toward her. Despite the anger rolling off of her, it made him feel better to be near her.

"So?" she countered, the muscle in her jaw flexing tighter. "It's none of your concern."

"You don't have to do this," Joseph whispered, kneeling beside her.

She shook her head, pinning him with an icy glare. "Loyalty to my family is not something I take lightly," she hissed. She turned away, anguish suddenly covering her face. "I can't let Harlie die." She shook her head, looking down at her hands. "Not like this."

Joseph swallowed thickly. "I can help you."

Abigail rounded on him suddenly. "You're the reason we're in this mess," she snapped. She watched as his golden eyes widened, uncertainty in them. He looked like he was afraid of her. "If you hadn't brought me here, none of this would be happening."

Joseph's eyes were pleading. "Don't you see what he did to us?" he asked. "He was going to let you die there, on that ledge. If I hadn't done this, you—" He couldn't find words as he shook his head. "I did what I thought was best." He looked away. "Just like you."

Abigail's ice blue eyes widened slightly. Harlie was her family; of course she would lay down her life for him. But she was nothing to Joseph, right? Only a traveling companion; certainly no one to be important enough to swear allegiance to Bozal.

She shook her head, looking away. "You don't know me," she whispered. "You threw your freedom away for a stranger."

Joseph leaned toward her. "I would have done it for you for less," he whispered. He watched as she looked at him, her eyes widened with surprise. "I brought you this far, I won't have your blood on my hands knowing there was more I could have done."

Abigail wanted to scoff, but the way he was staring at her stilled her. His golden eyes were glowing lightly in the faint light, a reminder of the fact that he was different than she was. It made her look away.

"So why did you come here?" she asked quietly, letting her chin rest on her arms. "What can you possibly do for my brother?"

"I can get to him first."

Abigail looked up at him, hope on her face. "Are you sure?" she whispered.

Joseph could see the uncertainty in her eyes. "I have to try," he said, trying to give her a grin. When she turned her ice blue gaze to the floor, Joseph felt his heart sink. He knew what she was thinking.

"Bozal will still make me unlock the curse," she whispered. "You must take Harlie somewhere safe." She shook her head. "Don't bring him here to try to free me."

"Why not?" Joseph demanded.

Abigail held out her arms to expose the black tendrils. "He'll kill me once I have served my purpose," she whispered. "I'll be dead soon." She looked up at him. "You won't get back in time."

Pain crossed Joseph's face for a brief moment. "We'll come back for you." His voice was sure and strong. "I promise."

Abigail offered him a sad smile. "Don't make promises you can't keep." She was surprised when Joseph leaned closer suddenly, catching her chin in his hand.

"I don't break promises," he whispered softly, his golden eyes searching hers. He was close enough that Abigail could smell the scent of his skin, and his breath ghosted across her face. He didn't seem to notice when she drew a sharp breath, a blush springing to her cheeks. "I *will* come back for you."

Joseph was silent as he ran through the trees. He could smell the scent of the pack ahead of him, and he ran harder, knowing he had to catch up to them.

Soon he could see the trail they had left behind. Their paw-prints were shallow in the snow, and he saw that there were only three of them. He wondered why Bozal had sent three wolves to kill one boy. He came to a stop as a familiar scent caught his nose.

"Joseph."

He turned, not surprised to see Snow Belle step from the trees. He noticed that her sides were heaving, and her eyes were wide.

"Where is Abigail?"

Joseph lowered his head. *"She was captured."*

Snow Belle snorted, her nose wrinkling in disgust. *"Captured? How can this be?"* She stepped toward him. *"You were supposed to protect her."* She advanced on him angrily.

Joseph's lip curled in a snarl.

"I knew you couldn't be trusted." Snow Belle lowered her head, her horn sharp and menacing.

"She's safe for the time being." He growled low, crouching slightly in case she struck out. *"Right now, Harlie's life is in danger."*

"How do you expect me to believe anything you say?"

A chorus of howls suddenly echoed in the distance. Snow Belle's head shot up, her ears forward. She recognized the sound of hunting wolves. Her eyes flicked back to Joseph, who was staring toward the sound as well. She winced when he suddenly threw his head back, giving a corresponding howl.

"What are you doing?" Snow Belle's eyes were wide with the fear of a prey animal.

"I can stop them." Joseph leapt away from her with a snarl, plunging into the trees toward the others.

He ducked as branches whipped at his fur, hearing the howls of the others becoming stronger. He knew he was catching up to them. He sent up another howl, one that he knew would stop them momentarily, giving him enough time, hopefully, to catch them. It wasn't long before a single howl answered him back, and he suddenly broke through the trees to find them.

Three sets of yellow eyes stared back at him, snarls on their faces. A dark brown wolf stepped forward, hackles raised defensively.

Joseph wasted no time, knowing that it was fight or flight now. He needed to take control. He leapt at the wolf immediately, slamming his body into the others. He was much bigger than they were combined, and it was easy for him to pin the wolf to the ground. The dark brown wolf offered submission immediately, knowing he was no match for Joseph's size and strength. His golden eyes were shifted away, and he bared his neck, his tail tucked tightly against his body.

Joseph held him there a moment longer, stealing glances at the others, his teeth bared in a commanding snarl. He saw that their heads were bowed low, their eyes watching him carefully. The white wolf wasn't among them, and it made his heart drop in disappointment. It didn't matter though.

He knew he had control now.

Stepping toward them, he began to snap and snarl, herding them away from the direction they had been going. They each whined low, clearly distressed at being stopped from completing their mission, but none could challenge him. They knew him instantly as their Alpha.

Once they began moving away, Joseph began to feel a sense of relief. Maybe his plan could work. Maybe he could just take them back to Phoenix.

A sense of power and rightful belonging surged through him as he led the three wolves through the trees.

Maybe he did have what it took to defeat Bozal and to rise against him with his father's army.

A strong sense of hope was beginning to well inside him, and he was certain the others could feel it too.

Joseph!

His body suddenly slammed to a halt of its own accord. He wasn't sure what was happening, as he found himself becoming a slave to a voice inside his head.

Kill Harlie. Kill the Guardian.

Joseph shook his head, trying to fight the invasive feeling, but his body turned, snarling at his followers to come. He began to run against his will toward the castle. He snarled and snapped furiously, trying to shake the control he was under, but it was useless. He didn't have any control over himself any more.

He knew it was Bozal.

Panic and dread filled him, and he threw his head back, sending up a harsh howl into the wind.

Snow Belle whinnied loudly as she broke through the trees into the clearing before the castle. She could see servants moving about the courtyard, and she ran into it, whinnying and rearing. She looked around frantically.

Where was Harlie?

She dodged the waving arms of the servants trying to calm and subdue her, turning and running toward the barn. She heard the echoing whinny of her brother, the Dream Catcher.

"Abigail?" Harlie appeared from inside the barn, his eyes darting around the courtyard to find his sister. His face blanched when his eyes landed on Snow Belle.

She whinnied frantically to him, coming to a stop before him, dancing in place.

"Snow Belle, where's Abigail?" he asked, walking toward her. He lifted his arms to soothe her, placing his hands on her withers. "Easy girl, easy." He gasped when Snow Belle turned to him, touching his temple with her horn.

Thousands of images and places flashed through his mind, sewing together a story. He saw images of Abigail and Joseph, felt Snow Belle's distrust of the shape-shifter, and even saw the images of the night Abigail and Snow Belle were attacked. Like a flash, the scenes were gone, leaving him with feelings that were jumbled and confused. He looked into Snow Belle's eyes, knowing what she was running to warn him about.

The wolves were closing in.

"Let's go," he said. He checked the sword that was at his back, before running into the barn and throwing open the Dream Catcher's stall door. He swung easily onto Catcher's back, grasping his cream-colored mane in his hands.

At Snow Belle's lead, Catcher ran after her, around to the back of the castle, where a secret exit was located. It led into the woods beyond the castle, and it would serve for a time to distract Joseph and his hunters.

"Snow Belle, take me to Abigail," Harlie called to her. He watched as she glanced back at him, throwing her head in compliance.

He felt his heart twist. Why hadn't she told him that she was sick? He could have helped her. He was just as capable as she was.

The knot in his stomach twisted tighter, burning with anger as he thought about Joseph. She should have never trusted him.

He leaned into Dream Catcher's mane, willing him to run faster. They weren't bonded, and he couldn't hear Dream Catcher's thoughts the way Abigail did, but they had a unique relationship. They were synced on a level that made bonding the next logical step. He should have had his ceremony by now and been accepted as a true Guardian, but his father and brothers' deaths had kept those things from happening.

His closed his eyes, fighting down the worry for his sister. She had told him to postpone the ceremony until after they secured Shalamar. But now, there didn't seem like there would be a ceremony. Or anyone to be there to celebrate.

The thought made his heart ache.

They had to save Abigail.

Joseph snapped at the wolf that ran next to him, baring his fangs. He was furious.

Not only was Harlie not at the castle, but the servants seemed to have been alerted to his arrival. He ignored the wound to his shoulder as he ran with his pack. He had succumbed to the voice inside his head, but he was hating every minute of it, and fighting it the best he could.

When his pack mates would run too close, he would lunge viciously at them. He wanted to channel all the rage he felt into tearing into one of them, but his body was on a different course than his mind.

They wove through the trees, following the trail of the unicorns. Joseph wasn't happy about the fact that there were two of them now, but he didn't have any other choice but to pursue. He could only hope that Snow Belle and Harlie reached Phoenix before he did, and that Harlie had a chance to escape.

Harlie looked up as Snow Belle whinnied. He knew the wolves were close behind them, and he felt his breath catch when he saw Snow Belle stop ahead.

"Why are we stopping?" he asked as the Dream Catcher came to a stop beside her. He watched as she tossed her head, and he felt his mouth go dry.

Before them was the expanse of the river that separated Gandora and Phoenix. Close to them, on the side that belonged to Gandora, the water was frozen. It was a thin piece of ice, floating atop a deadly, cold river. Beyond that, on the Phoenix side, the water was boiling, so hot that it would kill a man in seconds.

Harlie shook his head. "We can't get across that," he whispered. He looked at Snow Belle, seeing her watching him. The Dream Catcher nickered to her, before turning his eyes on Harlie as well.

Harlie knew what they wanted.

You must cross.

He shook his head as he slid from the Dream Catcher's back. "I can't cross this," he said, leaning over the out-cropping they stood on to look down at the river. "It's impossible."

But it was the only way to Abigail, and they all knew it.

Snow Belle lowered her head, whinnying softly to him. Her brows were knit together, worry clear on her face.

"I know, Snow Belle," Harlie said, turning to her. "We'll find a way." He reached out to pet her. "We'll get her back."

Suddenly the sound of howls began to fill the woods around them. Harlie cursed inwardly to himself, before drawing his sword. He watched as the Dream Catcher turned, putting himself in between the wolves and Harlie. He was massive, much bigger than his sister, and his coat shown sky blue in the sunlight. He tossed his head, his cream-colored mane flipping across his neck. Snow Belle joined him as the wolves grew closer, their howls louder on the wind.

Harlie felt his heart jump when a huge black wolf stepped through the brush first. His fangs were bared, and his golden eyes were searching the clearing. Once they landed on Harlie, a snarl was ripped from his throat. Three more wolves soon joined him, each of them snapping and snarling.

The black wolf gave a silent cue to the other three, who began to fan around them. Harlie knew that they probably could hold their own, but they were still outnumbered. He raised his sword as the black wolf took a step forward, their eyes locking. He knew that he was the target.

A sudden flash of eyes appeared across his memory, and he felt his hands grip the sword tighter. His jaw clenched as anger came over him, and he stepped in between Snow Belle and Dream Catcher.

"Am I what you want, Joseph?" he asked, holding the black wolf's gaze. He watched as the wolf crouched slightly, snapping at him. "Well come on then."

Joseph suddenly lunged at him, a signal to the others to pounce.

Harlie raised his sword, swinging at Joseph as he tried to pin him to the ground. He watched as Joseph leapt back, barely dodging his blade, before rushing forward again. Harlie raised his sword to block Joseph's attack, feeling his massive, furry body slam him to the ground. He knew he was no match for Joseph's strength, and he used his arms to block Joseph's giant teeth.

He glanced around frantically, trying to figure out how to escape with his throat still intact. He was surprised when the Dream Catcher suddenly appeared, using his shoulder to throw Joseph to the ground.

Harlie rolled quickly to his feet, running to grab his sword, which had been knocked from his hands. He caught movement out of the corner of his eye, and he barely managed to lift the blade as the third wolf lunged at him. The air was knocked from his lungs as the wolf's body slammed into him.

His mind couldn't register the shock as he felt himself falling. He could see Dream Catcher and Snow Belle rushing toward him as he went backwards over the out-cropping, but their movements seemed slow in comparison. He knew that a cold death waited below for him.

Joseph felt his heart skip a beat as one of his pack mates fell into Harlie. Inside of his wolf body, his human heart was screaming as he watched Harlie and the wolf fall over the edge of the cliff. His mind didn't want to comprehend what was happening, but at the same time, he felt the controlling curse lift from his limbs.

He tore his body away from Dream Catcher's horn, rolling to his feet to run to the edge. His body transformed seamlessly, and his human hands caught him on the edge as his knees hit the ground.

"Harlie!"

His breaths were ragged as he stared over the edge, no sign of Abigail's brother, save for a break in the ice. He could feel his body trembling, and sudden pain assaulted him as he remembered the wound the Dream Catcher had inflicted. He pressed his hands to stem the bleeding, his eyes never leaving the frozen waters below.

"Harlie! Answer me!"

He could feel his emotions getting the best of him, his eyes becoming misty. What would he tell Abigail? How would he explain to her what he had done? He bowed his head as his strength left him. How could he tell her that he was the one responsible for her brother's death?

Footsteps behind him made his head snap up, and he moved to a crouch as Snow Belle and the Dream Catcher advanced on him.

'My boy,' the Dream Catcher's voice was full of sorrow as he

stepped to stand beside Joseph, his eyes searching the waters. He rounded angrily on Joseph. *'What have you done!?'*

Joseph didn't move. "I couldn't stop," he whispered, unafraid of the massive unicorn. "I don't have control over my actions. Bozal controls me." He bowed his head. "Just kill me." He leaned forward against his hands, feeling anguish overcome him. "Kill me now, please. I can't possibly explain to Abigail…"

The Dream Catcher lifted his head, his cream-colored mane falling still against his massive neck. He was exquisite, a sight to behold as he glared down at Joseph.

'I will not kill you,' he said. *'You will live with this.'*

Joseph clenched his fists in the dirt, shutting his eyes tightly. There was nothing he could say. He knew that the Dream Catcher held the authority to do as he saw fit. No one could touch him now in Gandora without the Dream Catcher's permission.

Unicorns were strange creatures, with laws and magic that were far beyond his comprehension.

'Come, Snow Belle.' The Dream Catcher turned, leaving Joseph kneeling. *'We must do what we can to save the princess.'*

Joseph looked up suddenly. He wanted to try to help, but what more was there that he could do? Bozal controlled his actions, and he knew he would just be in the way. He sank back to the ground as Snow Belle and the Dream Catcher vanished into the trees. He was to be Bozal's toy, for the time being.

Chapter Nine

It was so cold, it took his breath away.

He opened his mouth to gasp for air, but cold water filled his lungs instead. He was like a lead weight, sinking down into blackness. The cold had numbed his body to the point that he couldn't tell if his arms and legs were moving or not. It had taken over so fast that at first he felt pain, but now he felt nothing. Nothing except cold, numbing blackness.

He knew this was the end; his mind was beginning to fade into a comforting warmth. He began to wonder if he was crossing to the other side, into the spirit world. A glimmer of hope at seeing his family again caused more warmth to shoot through him.

This had to be it.

This was the moment of death, certainly.

He tried to move against it, feeling still as if he was in water. He realized the feeling had returned to his limbs, and he paddled as hard as he could. He was surprised when he realized that he wasn't gasping for air like before.

Confused, Harlie opened his eyes, surprised to see himself wrapped in bright, glowing wings. He was nestled safely inside a cocoon, and he felt the feeling of being in water begin to ease away. After a moment, once he stopped feeling like he was floating, he felt his body being lowered gently to the ground. His mind still felt foggy and confused, and he drew ragged breaths, the air precious in his lungs. He rolled to his back, trying to take in the creature before him.

It was bright, glowing with a red and gold intensity that reminded him of flames. Long, flowing feathers bloomed in its tail, and it flapped long wings. It had the body of a bird, but its head was covered in deep red scales. It cocked its head slightly, huge green eyes piercing him with a cat-like stare.

'You could at least thank me,' it snapped unceremoniously, its voice gravelly and deep.

Harlie used shaking arms to prop himself into a sitting position. "Thank you," he whispered, unable to tear his eyes away from the creature. "What are you?"

Offended, the creature snaked its head, snapping its beak and flapping its wings angrily. 'I am a phoenix, you dull human child,' it said bitterly. 'Obviously our kind has been gone for too long. You have forgotten us.'

Harlie's eyes widened and he gasped, bowing his head. "Please forgive me, Great One," he said quietly. "I have never had the fortune of being able to see one such as you."

The phoenix pressed its wings to its side, arching its neck haughtily. 'Only the worthy may lay eyes upon us.'

Harlie kept his eyes downcast. "And why is it that you have deemed me worthy, Great One? Not only have I seen you, but you saved me."

The phoenix ruffled its feathers. Harlie glanced up as it took a step toward him.

Its body was massive, much larger than he was. When it stretched its wings out, they were longer than at least three of him. Its beak was massive, and its eyes were piercing, both into the seen and the unseen.

'You are a Guardian.' Its voice was matter-of-fact, as if Harlie should have known why.

Harlie looked up at it. "I'm sorry, I'm afraid I still don't understand," he said. "My sister is a Guardian as well; why not go to her instead of me? She is much more capable than I am."

The phoenix lowered its head so that it could look at him with one giant eye. 'Your sister is brave, but she lacks the one thing you have.' It blinked, turning its head so that its scales caught the light. 'You are innocent to the world.'

"Innocent?" Harlie asked, confused. He shook his head. "You must have me confused with someone else. I know of the world and the people in it."

The phoenix rounded on him, capturing him in a mesmerizing stare. *'Your sister carries much pain and bitterness in her heart,'* it said. *'You know nothing of the burden she carries alone, or of her resentment. Your heart is still pure.'*

"Well what good does that do us?" Harlie asked. He looked down at the ground, seeing for the first time that it was Phoenixian soil, but instead of rocks and barren weeds, deep green grass and wildflowers were blooming all around them. He realized it was the magic of the phoenix's presence.

'I have been watching you mortals for some time now,' the phoenix said. *'Frankly, my kind is disgusted with your behavior. We are tired of the people in this land suffering, and we are tired of hiding from this sorcerer, Bozal. Now is our time to rise up, and to right the wrongs that we allowed. We have never been afraid of Bozal, only indifferent. And our indifference has cost the land and the magic that we tend.'* The phoenix lowered its body to the ground. *'You will come with me, and we will rescue your sister and take back this land from his monstrous rule.'*

Harlie rose shakily to his feet. He didn't know that he was ready to do what the phoenix was asking. Could he bring a battle to Bozal?

The phoenix turned to gaze at him. *'When the time is right, we will not fight alone. Now come.'*

Harlie did as it commanded, and climbed onto its back. It was bigger than the Dream Catcher, and under its feathers it was burning, emitting heat like an unkempt flame. As the phoenix launched itself into the air, the heat from its body warded off the chill from the wind.

Abigail closed her eyes, pressing her face against the cold stone wall. She couldn't move her body. She couldn't make her limbs work to even stand, and it hurt to try to even move from her sitting position.

Her breaths were labored and shallow, and she knew that she was nearing the end. She could feel the curse, spreading like a poison throughout her limbs. It was sapping her last bit of strength from her body. She was beginning to wish that it would just end; that Bozal would stop toying with her and just kill her.

Harlie...

She felt her chest constrict and tears welled in her eyes. She was ready to give up. There was nothing left that she could do, and she knew Joseph would be too late. Bozal would use her to unlock Precious, and then she would die. No one could save her now.

A small cry escaped her lips as fierce, blinding pain shot through her. She felt as if someone was twisting her body in half, and she gasped harshly as the pain passed.

A shadow appeared suddenly in the doorway of the cell.

"It is time."

Abigail forced her eyes open, gritting her teeth. She couldn't lift her head as she watched Bozal walk toward her.

His amethyst eyes glittered delightfully in the darkness. His smile was fanged. "I must admit, Abigail," he said, kneeling beside her, "it is quite the pleasure watching you die slowly in this manner." He grinned wider as she pinned him with a deadly stare. "Killing you will be much more fulfilling than killing your brothers."

More tears welled in her eyes. She wanted more than anything to stand right now and drive a knife through his heart. She would have preferred a swift death, not because it would have been over sooner, but because it would have given Bozal less satisfaction.

She didn't have the strength to utter words, and she blinked, feeling tears sliding down her cheeks. She closed her eyes, trying to block Bozal out of her mind.

Instead, his harsh laughter only filled her ears, making her head pound. She couldn't concentrate on what he was doing as he stood beside her, the sound of voices fading through her mind. She knew that she was slipping further and further away. She felt her strength suddenly give out, and her body collapsed to the floor. She couldn't focus as she laid there, her eyes staring up to the ceiling.

Her breathing was too shallow, and she could feel how labored her heartbeat was in her chest.

"Nuh uh, little Guardian." Bozal's voice somehow still managed to slice through her fading mind. "You aren't going to slip away from me yet."

Abigail vaguely thought he crossed into her field of vision, but she couldn't be sure. Everything felt like a dream; one that she would wake from soon and forget. She couldn't feel him lifting her hands to press against the cool glass of Precious's crystal ball.

She felt the remainder of her life force draining slowly away, and she faded into black silence.

Bozal watched as Abigail collapsed to the floor. He loved watching people suffer.

He took Precious from the guard in the doorway, feeling it pulse against him. It seemed as if it was trying to repel him, and it glowed an ugly red. As he carried it toward Abigail's prone form, it pulsed harder, easing from red to blue.

Bozal felt satisfaction fill him. Precious was working, sensing the Guardian's presence.

He knelt slowly beside her, brushing her blonde hair from her face. "You were a fool to think that I would spare you," he whispered. He could feel her life force leaving her with every breath she breathed. Her ice blue eyes were staring, unseeing, into his face and ragged, barely-there breaths blew between her lips. "And you are a fool to think that I won't kill the last remaining Guardian."

He set Precious on the floor beside her, watching as it swirled a deep, ocean blue. He knew it sensed release, and the energy inside of it swirled more and more fiercely.

"Use your remaining strength to unlock Precious," he whispered. He lifted her wrist, which was cold and lifeless, placing her hand against the crystal.

Bright light suddenly immersed them, forcing him to shield his eyes. A wave of power burst from Precious, nearly causing him to be knocked backwards. Waves and waves of warm energy began to roll off of it as the light faded.

Bozal lowered his arm, excitement making his heart race.

This was it. This was the moment he had been waiting for.

He lifted Precious slowly from the floor, Abigail's hand sliding from it. He laughed at her as he held Precious in his hands, its power swirling dark green inside the crystal.

"Fool!" He laughed harder. "This world will be mine."

He rose slowly from where he knelt next to her, his maniacal laughter drowning out the frightened scampering of his soldiers. He held Precious tightly to his chest, summoning its power. His body began to morph, growing and changing, absorbing Precious into his chest. Insurmountable strength filled him.

Harlie could see Castle Quasar coming into view. He held tightly to the phoenix's back, his body shaking.

He didn't know what to expect or how they would defeat Bozal. He was afraid and anxious. He just wanted to get Abigail out of there and go home. He pressed his face into the phoenix's feathers, trying to use the warmth to ward away his chill.

'What is our plan?'

The phoenix turned its head slightly, its eye catching him in a stare. *'You don't need to be frightened, Harlie,'* it said. *'We will stop him.'*

Harlie frowned at the phoenix's response. He looked back at the castle. How would they even get inside?

A sudden rumble filled the air as they flew around a tower, one that made Harlie jump. He nearly lost his balance as the phoenix suddenly twisted away from the castle.

'What was that?!' He clung tightly to the phoenix's neck as it righted itself.

The phoenix circled back around. *'There.'*

Harlie gasped at the sight below.

A massive black dragon burst through the roof of the castle, sending rocks and beams showering over the land. It roared loudly, the sound piercing through the air like a knife. Harlie pressed his hands to his ears, feeling the phoenix beneath him flinch as well. It twisted through the air away from the dragon.

'What the hell is that?'

The phoenix let a cry escape its throat. *'Bozal.'*

The dragon suddenly turned, sensing their presence. An evil glimmer filled its yellow eyes, and it flapped into the air, its wings massive. It made the phoenix look like a mouse as it flew toward them.

'Hold on.'

The phoenix suddenly rocketed through the sky, soaring higher and higher into the clouds until they were hidden.

Harlie held tightly to its neck. *'How can we possibly hope to kill him?'*

The phoenix twisted in and out of clouds. *'You will have to strike him down,'* it said.

Harlie gasped as a shadow suddenly overcame them, and the phoenix let out a cry as it banked away from the dragon's gaping jaws. Harlie heard a low, rumbling growl escape from the dragon's mouth, and he turned, looking into massive yellow eyes.

'Look out!'

The dragon suddenly lunged at them, swinging a massive paw. It caught Harlie and the phoenix just right, sending them plummeting through the sky.

Harlie couldn't see anything as the world spun around them, closer and closer on each turn. His heart was in his throat as the phoenix banked at the last moment, managing to keep them from crashing to the ground, but unable to stop from colliding with it. Harlie yelled as he was thrown from the phoenix's back, before slamming into the hard ground. He rolled over and over several times before finally coming to a rest some feet away from the phoenix.

Pain shot through his body as he looked up, struggling to get off the ground. He tried using his arms, but severe pain shot through his wrist. He knew it was broken.

"Phoenix!" he gasped. He watched as the phoenix flapped against the ground, struggling to right itself as well.

The black shadow suddenly descended on them again, and Harlie scrambled to his feet. "Phoenix!" he gasped, watching as the dragon slammed into the ground. The force of the impact felt like an earthquake, and sent him sprawling across the ground a short distance from the fallen phoenix.

"Phoenix," he called, watching as it turned its head, its deep green eyes filled with pain. "You must fly."

The phoenix shook its head. Its wing was badly broken, bones jutting in different ways. 'No,' it said.

Harlie gasped when bright light suddenly began to surround it.

'You must kill Bozal,' its voice was fading as the light brightened immensely, before fading quickly away.

Harlie could only stare at the bright red bow and single arrow that were lying on the ground. He managed to get to his feet, running to snatch it up as the dragon barreled down on him. He barely managed to dodge the dragon's massive paw again as it tried to crush him.

"I'm not the archer in the family," he whispered to himself, feeling hopelessness surge through him. He cursed, his eyes traveling over Bozal's bared underbelly.

He wasn't even sure where he was supposed to strike Bozal to be effective, and he only had one shot. His eyes searched frantically as he tried to stay under Bozal's body.

A blast of wind suddenly surrounded him, and he knew Bozal was taking flight. If he managed to become airborne, Harlie knew he had no chance. He notched the arrow quickly, feeling his wrist protest. The pain was intense and numbing, but he ignored it, lining up a shot to where he thought Bozal's heart should be. He only had one chance.

The wind became stronger, and Bozal began to lift into the air.

Harlie said a quick prayer, before swiftly pulling back the arrow, sighting down the shaft like Abigail had taught him, and loosing it. He held his breath as it slipped between his fingers and found its target.

A sudden, screaming cry was ripped from Bozal's dragon throat, and he flailed backwards. Light began to emanate from where the arrow struck him, forcing Harlie to shield his face. The sound of a thousand flapping wings suddenly filled the air, drowning out the dragon's roaring. The songs of the phoenixes began playing as the light grew brighter and brighter, until it surrounded Bozal.

Harlie fell to his knees, the light too bright for him to stand.

An explosion suddenly rocked the air, waves of magic pulsing down into the earth. The light faded as soon as it had appeared.

When Harlie opened his eyes, he was surprised to see a grassy meadow surrounding him. His breathing was shallow as he took in the scene around him.

Hundreds of phoenixes fluttered down around him in a showering of glittering pieces, landing easily on the ground. Flowers were sprouting anywhere they landed, and the sky began to turn gray and cloudy.

A single phoenix stepped forward, deep green eyes on Harlie.

'Thank you,' it said, lowering its head in a bow. 'Thanks to you, our *home is safe once more.'* It stepped toward him, its magic seaming his wrist back together.

Harlie felt his knees buckle beneath him as he tried to comprehend what had just occurred. He stared around him at all of the phoenixes before turning his eyes back to the one in front of him. He watched as a single piece of glitter fell before him, and he picked it out of the grass. His eyes widened when he saw that it was a shard of glass.

'Your arrow struck Precious,' the phoenix said, lowering its head to study the glass shard. *'It has been destroyed.'*

Harlie looked up into the phoenix's eye. "So then, the magic it held?"

'Gone. You and your family are free from your oaths. There is nothing to protect.'

Harlie's heart was racing in his chest, his mind suddenly filled with possibilities. That's what they had wanted all along, wasn't it? Their freedom was what Abigail had been fighting for. Abigail...

"What about my sister, Great One?" he whispered, feeling his heart aching. He knew she was out there somewhere, possibly still sick. He knew that she would still be bound by her curse.

He watched as the phoenix crouched low to the ground, signaling for him to leap on his back.

'We will find her and I will heal her.'

Lightning suddenly began to strike in the distance, and thunder rumbled across the plains. Harlie lifted his head as a single rain drop landed on his cheek.

Chapter Ten

J oseph ran swiftly through the forest, breaking through the trees and onto the open plain. He had managed to cross the river, by finding a fallen tree to cross over, and he was racing toward Bozal's castle. He had seen the dragon burst from the stone walls in the distance, and he knew Abigail was in danger, or worse. He hoped he could reach her in time.

The landscape was flying past him as he pushed himself faster. He wasn't expecting the sudden wave of light and magic that besieged him, and it knocked him to the ground. He whimpered as it pressed down on him before slowly fading away.

When he opened his eyes, he felt his heart catch.

There was grass growing beneath his paws.

Sudden elation caught at his heart. Could it be?

He ran faster toward the castle.

Once he reached it, he slid to a stop. The sky was cloudy and overcast suddenly, and thunder echoed in the distance. He transformed into his human form as rain began to pound the ground. Covering his head with his arms, he ran into the castle, which was demolished and empty. He guessed that Bozal's servants and the wolves must have fled when he transformed.

He made his way around the fallen ceiling and walls, feeling at a loss. He remembered this as his home, but now it was destroyed. He tried not to take in all the damage as he moved toward the dungeons. As he came upon the door, he felt his heart stutter.

Blackness fell through the doorway, and as he stepped inside, he could see that the damage to the castle was allowing water to seep in. It was dripping slowly from the ceiling, soaking the floor.

He walked toward the cell that he knew Abigail had been kept in, feeling his chest constrict.

The door was open.

"Abigail?" he called softly, moving toward it slowly. "Abigail, can you hear me?" He stepped into the doorway, his wolf eyes adjusting to the dim light.

His breath caught hard in his throat, a lump blocking him from taking a breath.

Her body was motionless on the floor. Her hand was outstretched at her side, and her golden hair fanned about her head.

Joseph ran to her, collapsing to his knees beside her.

Her ice blue eyes were staring up at him, unseeing.

"Abigail?" he whispered, brushing her hair from her face. She was cold to the touch, and her lips were blue. He felt tears blur his vision. "Abigail, no."

He bowed his head as a sob wracked him.

He hated that he had let this happen to her. He had only wanted to protect her, but he had failed her, and in so many ways. He had let Harlie die, and he had let her die. He scooped her into his arms, pressing her against his chest. He hadn't realized how much this girl had meant to him; how much he had come to care for her. His heart was breaking as he held her there in his arms.

After several long minutes, he felt his anguish slow, and he gazed down at her. "You didn't deserve this," he whispered, seeing where his tears had graced her cheeks. "You should have had better."

He stared at her for a long time, feeling the silence weighing on him. He stood slowly, lifting her body from the floor. If nothing else, she deserved a proper burial. He carried her body, which was light and barely anything pressed against his chest, into the corridor. As he neared the courtyard, a sudden cry caught his attention. He looked up, his eyes widening as he saw a phoenix drop to the ground, Harlie sliding from its back.

Joseph froze in the courtyard, thinking his eyes were deceiving him. The rain was soaking them.

"Abigail!" Harlie yelled, running toward them. A bolt of lightning and the crack of thunder echoed behind him as he reached Joseph. His eyes took in Abigail's limp form, and his face paled.

"What have you done?" he whispered, his eyes meeting Joseph's. Bitter fury filled him. "What did you do to her?!"

Joseph shook his head, relinquishing her body to Harlie as he shoved him away. "She was already gone when I found her," he said. "There was nothing I could do."

Harlie knelt to the ground, watching as the rain dripped from her face. Despair was quickly taking over his heart, and his own tears mixed with the rain. "No," he breathed, sobbing softly against her neck. "No, no, no." He held her tightly to him. "Please don't go."

A soft sound made him look up suddenly. The phoenix was standing over them, shielding them from the rain. It lowered its head close to her body. A single tear slipped from its eye, landing heavily against her cheek.

Harlie met the phoenix's gaze. "We were too late," he whispered. He watched the phoenix's gaze soften, and he looked down at her. He could see where the black tendrils from her curse stained her skin, and it made his heart ache more. He pressed his forehead against hers. "Why didn't you tell me that you needed me?"

Abigail was floating. That was the one thing she was sure of, and she cast her eyes around, trying to see through the haze that surrounded her. She didn't know where she was, but, strangely, she didn't feel upset by that fact. If anything, she was calm and collected, and she finally felt like her old self again.

She straightened her body, touching down onto the gray haze, her feet bare. She looked down at the knee-length, white gown she was wearing, and she frowned. She couldn't remember owning anything like that.

"Welcome home, Daughter."

Her head snapped up, her heart leaping at the sound of the voice. "Father?" she breathed. Her ice blue eyes widened as a figure approached through the haze, materializing into a tall, broad-shouldered man.

He smiled happily, dark blonde hair cascading around his shoulders. His green-blue eyes were filled with delight as they landed on her.

"Father!" Abigail gasped. She ran to him, throwing her arms around his middle. Tears filled her eyes. "I have missed you so much!" A choked sob escaped her throat.

He wrapped his arms around her, pressing her against him. "And I have missed you, Abigail," he said gently.

Abigail breathed deeply, his familiar scent enveloping her. Tears continued to slide down her cheeks. "Every moment since you left us, I haven't stopped thinking about you," she whispered, burying her face in his chest. "And Harlie..." She felt her heart lurch at the thought of her younger brother.

She pulled herself away from her father, wiping at her tears. "Harlie." She looked up into his eyes, seeing him smiling down at her. "I can't leave him."

Her father nodded, his smile widening. "I thought you might say that," he said gently. He caught her arms in his hands. "I'm so proud of you, Abigail. You never gave up, and you never sacrificed your beliefs."

Abigail felt her heart ache. "Really?" she whispered. She had wanted for so long to hear her father say that to her. She had always known it, but he had never said it to her.

"Of course," he said, drawing her into a hug. "We miss you every day that we are apart. *I* miss you."

"Oh Father," Abigail said, more tears in her eyes as she pressed her face into his chest once more. "I wish I could stay, but…"

He held her at arms' length, a gentle smile on his face. "Do what you must," he said gently. "When the time is right, we will all be together."

Abigail nodded, pulling away from him.

"Now go, Daughter," he said. "Take care of him for me."

"I love you," she whispered, watching as he began to fade into the gray again. She thought she heard her words whispered back to her, but he was gone before she could determine if that was the case.

Sudden darkness began to surround her, and the sickening sensation of falling came over her. Her body suddenly felt like lead, and she thought she screamed, but she couldn't tell if it ever left her lips.

The falling stopped with a jolt, and she drew a ragged breath. Pain coursed through her, her lungs burning as her chest muscles strained to draw in air. She blinked her eyes, cold rain stinging her skin. She turned her head slowly, her neck aching at the motion.

"H—Harlie…" Her voice was hoarse and hard-pressed to leave her lips. She winced as she realized that he was holding her tightly in his arms.

"Abigail?" Her eyes found his face, focusing slowly. She saw that there were tears streaming down his cheeks.

"Harlie," she breathed. "Why are you crying?"

He smiled, despite his tears, cradling her head. "I thought you were dead," he said. "You died, Abby."

Abigail blinked slowly, her foggy brain making her feel drugged. "I…I think I was, too," she whispered. Tears filled her eyes suddenly, her father's scent coming to memory. "I saw Father." She looked back to Harlie. "He said he was proud of me."

Harlie's face broke into a bitter-sweet smile. "I'm proud of you, too."

Abigail smiled back at him before shifting her eyes away. She glanced around, feeling as if something was missing. She wasn't sure what it was, until she saw the black wolf running through the rain, away from them.

Joseph.

Abigail sat silently in a lounge chair, staring out the study window into the night. It had been several months now since Bozal's defeat, and things were starting to be normal again.

When Harlie shot the arrow that pierced Bozal's heart, it had struck Precious, shattering it into a million pieces. It had been impossible to retrieve them all. She had found Shalamar, and brought it back with her to Corona, where it was safe. Harlie had finally had his initiation ceremony, and he had been bonded.

Abigail smiled as she thought about it. She knew that the Dream Catcher loved Harlie dearly, but he had let Harlie go, recognizing the strength of the bond between his boy and the phoenix. Aithne had gladly accepted Harlie's bond, and they were inseparable. This worked well for them as Guardians, because, as the phoenixes began to return to Phoenix, it allowed them a way to monitor their progress.

The land had finally become lush and beautiful again, and phoenixes were a welcome sight, flying high in the skies about Phoenix and Gandora. Even the mortal kingdom had celebrated their return by means of a festival to honor them. The king, however, had not thanked Abigail or Harlie for their help. He did not even invite them to participate in the celebration.

Abigail sighed, rising from her seat and walking across the room to the balcony. Light snow had begun to fall, coating the land in a peaceful calm.

It was all right that the king didn't acknowledge them. There was a mutual respect that they held for each other; one that meant that the king would leave them be, and they would do their duties to protect his kingdom. But things were so peaceful now, Abigail didn't know if the king would ever need their protection again.

The thought was both sad and happy. It meant that they could live their lives the way they wanted. Abigail knew that Harlie would always be immersed in the magic of the phoenix's world. It was an innate part of what Aithne was as a phoenix, and it was an integral part of their bond; Aithne was the keeper of the magic and Harlie was the Guardian. She knew Harlie would always live in the magic world.

But where did that leave her?

She wasn't crazy about the magic, save for her bond with Snow Belle, but she often entertained the idea of moving to the mortal kingdom. She could start a new life there, possibly fall in love, find a husband... Things that she never knew she wanted were suddenly all around her.

She drew a ragged breath as she looked out over the forest from her balcony. Her options weighed heavily on her all the time.

She looked up at the moon, feeling its light shining down on her face, the cold air crisp as it blew across her skin. She was beginning to feel tired. Turning away from the moon, she started to turn to go back inside, when a shadow caught her eye.

Looking down into the tree line, she gasped when she saw a pair of golden eyes staring up at her. She thought she could make out a figure behind the eyes, but it was too dark among the trees to tell.

Could it be?

Abigail turned and ran out of the study, down the stairs and into the courtyard. She tried to tell herself she hadn't, but she had thought about Joseph every day since the last time she saw him, running through the rain. She constantly wondered where he was, what he was doing, if he was okay...

Harlie had given her a report several days ago that he had taken his rightful place as the king. He had brought all the wolves back together, and was helping them rebuild their kingdom.

The news was wonderful to hear, but she wished she had heard it from Joseph, himself.

Her heart was beating out of her chest as she ran, barefoot, across the snow, toward the tree line. She broke through the first line of brush, feeling her heart drop to her feet.

There was nothing. Not even a sign of anyone having been there.

She tried to fight down the crushed feeling that was welling inside her. It didn't really matter if he had come to see her or not. They didn't really know each other, and he shouldn't have meant anything to her.

She felt unexplained tears gathering in her eyes as she turned back toward the castle, and she wiped at them quickly. She walked slowly back inside, glancing over her shoulder, hoping beyond hope that he would be there.

Once she was back inside, she made her way to her bedroom, her heart feeling heavy. She took one last moment to look out the window, before she crawled into her bed. She drifted soon into a warm slumber.

Beneath the silvery moon, a lonely howl drifted through the still night.

Part Two

The Soul of the Shifter

Chapter One

Abigail woke to the sounds of screaming.

She was disoriented as she rolled out of her bed, her feet hitting the floor hard as she knelt down and pulled her bow and arrows from under her bed. She didn't know what was going on, and the sleep was fading fast from her mind. As she stood and stepped into her boots, her ice blue eyes widened at the orange glow that was filling the loft of the barn where she stayed.

"Snow Belle!" she yelled, running and sliding down the ladder to the ground floor. The horses were whinnying and screaming themselves, panic filling the air. Her eyes quickly found Snow Belle's stall, where her noble head hung over the door.

Her eyes were wide with fright as Abigail ran to her, throwing open the door. *'Quickly,'* she said, prancing as Abigail pulled herself onto her bare back. *'The city is on fire.'*

"Fire?" Abigail gasped. She leaned into Snow Belle's mane as she ran from the barn, bursting through the doors.

The sight that greeted Abigail was enough to make her stomach turn. All around them people were fleeing. The sky was lit by the flames that licked from one house to another, buildings crackling and burning all around them. Women and children ran past them, the sounds of their wailing filling the night.

Abigail's heart dropped to her feet. What the hell was happening?

She held on as Snow Belle turned, racing up the street. *'We must find out what is happening,'* she said.

Snow Belle tossed her head as she surged up a hill. As they crested it, a sharp cry left Abigail's lips.

Down below, it was clear what was happening. A force of soldiers and wolves were clashing in a battle. The wolves clearly had the city guards outnumbered, and they were easily slaughtering everyone in their wake. Abigail felt her brain screech to a halt.

"Wolves?" she breathed.

What did this mean?

Were these Joseph's wolves, or had someone else taken control of them? Were they looking for her? What was the reason for this massacre?

Tears filled her eyes as she watched the battle rage. "Snow Belle, we must get out of here," she said. She pulled an arrow from her quiver as Snow Belle turned, charging down the street. "We can't take the main entrance, we must find another way."

'There is another way out,' Snow Belle said, galloping along the cobblestone street. She slid to a halt as they reached the end.

A group of men was standing there. Their eyes sparkled in the night as they caught sight of Abigail and Snow Belle. They were wolves.

Abigail wasted no time in loosing arrows, striking one easily. He fell to the stone, his body rippling as it shifted into his wolf form, arrows protruding from his side. Abigail knew there was the only way to end the fighting; the wolves needed to be killed, not simply injured.

Snow Belle launched herself away from their pursuers, charging down the street the way they had come. Abigail's mind was racing as she clung to Snow Belle's mane.

'Are these Joseph's wolves?' Abigail loosed another arrow, watching as it caught the wolf in the chest, causing him to crash to the cobblestone. It did little to slow their attackers as he struggled to his feet.

She hadn't thought about Joseph since they had come here to Carmen. She had been trying to forget about him. It had been easy for them to come to live here, among the mortals. It had been somewhat difficult for her at first, but once she found the job at the barn, she settled right in. No one knew who she was, and she was grateful for a chance to start over.

No more chasing after demons in the dark. No more fighting to protect her family. No more near-death experiences.

'I have no idea,' Snow Belle said as she leapt a fence into a field.

The sounds of their howling became louder as the battle and the burning city faded into the darkness.

'We have to lose them,' Abigail said.

Her heart leapt into her throat when she realized that one was gaining on them. His glittering eyes were blood-thirsty as he lunged at Snow Belle's heels. With a gasp, Abigail loosed an arrow, watching as it pierced the wolf through the eye. He fell heavily to the ground, his injured cries spurring his pack mates into a frenzy.

Abigail realized then that she couldn't stop them, but she could hurt them.

It was easy for Abigail to drop several wolves with her arrows. She gasped in surprise when more suddenly appeared in front of them, and Snow Belle snorted, slamming to a halt. Abigail clung desperately to her neck as Snow Belle dashed back, charging back toward the city.

"We have to lose them!" Abigail gasped again.

'We may be able to hide in the city,' Snow Belle said. Her hooves were hard on the stones as she leapt back onto the main road.

Abigail held on as the main gate suddenly came into view. She felt her stomach turn as she saw wolves ripping out soldiers' throats. The streets were slick with blood. Rage suddenly gripped her as they came upon a group of men being besieged by the wolves.

'We must help them!'

In a fluid motion, Abigail swung from Snow Belle's back, colliding heavily with a wolf. It snapped and snarled as she tangled with it, crashing hard into the stone. She rolled free of it, seeing it struggle to its feet, fury in its glimmering gaze. Quickly, she pulled a knife from her belt, preparing for a strike. She lunged at the wolf as it leapt at her, sinking her blade into its heart the way she remembered Joseph doing so.

The wolf yelped, falling to the cobblestones. It didn't move as Abigail yanked her knife from its chest. She looked up, seeing the soldiers were following her example, driving their swords into the wolves' hearts. Once the danger wasn't so pressing, one turned to her.

"Thank you," he breathed.

Abigail recognized him as the one she had saved. She shook her head as she wiped her blade on her pants. "Don't thank me," she said. Snow Belle stepped toward her and she pulled herself easily onto Snow Belle's back. She watched the soldiers' eyes widen as they took her in, sitting on her white horse.

"Who are you?" the soldier asked.

Abigail wound her fingers into Snow Belle's mane as she tossed her head. "That's not important," she said. She pointed into the distance. "Help your fellow soldiers." She held tightly as Snow Belle launched into a gallop through the gates. They were alone as they flew down the main road, away from the city.

"We must go home," Abigail said, watching Snow Belle toss her head in agreement. "Something is terribly wrong."

Snow Belle galloped long into the night, cresting a hill as the rays of the sun began to brighten the horizon. Abigail felt her heart twist as the forests of Gandora began to glitter in the morning light. It had been nearly six months since she had been here; since she had come home. She could see through the protection spell that had been cast over the lands, castle Corona standing tall in the distance. Her thoughts immediately turned to her brother.

Was he okay? Did he know what was happening? What about Aithne? Did the phoenix know? How had this been allowed to happen?

She tried not to let it, but every time she thought about Aithne, her mind always turned to Joseph.

There hadn't been any word from him for a long time, not after he took control of his father's kingdom once more. Harlie said that things were well in Phoenix, and that the wolves and the other creatures were once more in balance. But that didn't tell her anything she really wanted to know. She wanted to know about Joseph.

Was he okay? Did he miss her? Did he know that she was gone from Corona?

Her thoughts turned back to the night she thought she saw him in the trees. Her heart twisted a bit at the thought. Did he think about her every day, the same as she did about him? She remembered hearing howls sometimes, late at night, after the castle had fallen quiet. But there was no way to know if it was him.

But none of that made any sense if it was his wolves that attacked Carmen.

She gave Snow Belle a gentle squeeze. "We must hurry."

Snow Belle's certain steps allowed her some comfort as they drew closer to home. She felt the quiver shifting against her back, and she frowned, remembering the familiar pulse of her bow, Shalamar.

After Precious had been destroyed, the magic of Shalamar never seemed to wane. It continued to pulse and it seemed to call out to her. Harlie couldn't sense it when he held Shalamar, but Abigail could. She knew Shalamar had chosen her. She hadn't brought the magical bow with her to Carmen, knowing it would be safer with Harlie, and she missed it now as the shadows of the forest stretched over them. Memories of a flight for their lives flashed through her mind's eye, and she glanced over her shoulder. She knew, for now, the danger was past, but she couldn't keep herself from wondering if she was ever really safe.

Abigail could feel the cold from the land, the scent of snow on the wind. A thrill raced through her body as Snow Belle wound her way through the forest, this stretch of woods familiar and different at the same time. The cold burned Abigail's lungs as they crossed the magical border, and it filled her with joy. She hadn't realized how much she had missed being here. The spell that Snow Belle had been forced to wear to hide her true nature began to fade away, and she arched her neck proudly. It didn't take long before they were into the stretch of woods that Abigail knew like the back of her hand. The road to the castle gate was unchanged.

She heard yelling as the guards at the gate recognized her and allowed her entrance. Pleased and excited greetings of servants and other residents of the castle met her ears as Snow Belle took her inside. Her smile was broad across her face as she was welcomed by her people.

A female servant with dark hair approached her, her brown eyes kind. "My lady," she said, bowing. "We are so glad to have you home."

Abigail slid from Snow Belle's back, allowing the girl to take her bag. "Where is my brother?"

The girl nodded toward the castle. "He is inside," she said. "Shall I go to him?"

Abigail shook her head, climbing the steps in leaps. "I'll find him." Her heart felt heavy suddenly as she disappeared inside.

She ran up the stairs toward the study, knowing he would probably be there. Her guess was correct as the door was propped open. She frowned as the soft sound of voices echoed through the door. She was silent as she walked toward the door, peeking around the corner.

Sunlight was beaming in through the window. The curtains were thrown open, and the light fell across a desk where a blonde-haired boy sat. Abigail frowned at the worry lines etched on his face. He was studying hard whatever was in the book before him, and he seemed to become frustrated, as his jaw clenched after a moment. He read another page, before drawing a ragged breath and sitting back in his chair. He looked up at a young woman who stood before him, his words soft and unintelligible as he spoke to her.

Moving slowly, Abigail stepped into the doorway, her heart twisting in her chest as she pulled her knife. She watched as his eyes shifted to her, widened in surprise. The woman turned slowly, the Wolf King's emblem becoming clearer on the front of her tunic.

"Abigail?"

"What is this, Brother?" she demanded softly. Her eyes never left the woman.

Harlie rose swiftly to his feet, frozen when he saw the distrust on her face. His jaw tightened at the blade in her hand. "There is no need for violence, Sister," he said carefully.

"Like hell there is!" Abigail suddenly snapped. "Carmen has been attacked, reduced to ashes by the comrades of the one who stands before you." Her ice-blue eyes were furious as she watched the woman. "I should kill you where you stand."

Harlie suddenly rounded the desk, stepping between them. "What are you saying, Abigail?" he asked, confusion on his face. He turned to the woman. "Is this true?"

The woman gritted her teeth. "If this is the news your sister brings, then yes," she said evenly. "It would seem that our king has carried through with his threats."

Harlie's blue-green eyes were suddenly filled with sorrow. "Why would he do this?" he whispered.

"What is going on?" Abigail asked. Her stance never eased, and her eyes never left the woman.

Harlie sighed, easing himself to sit at the desk. "Things were fine for a while," he said quietly. "After you left, it was easy for Aithne and me to keep things peaceful. With the return of the phoenixes, the land has been plentiful and beautiful. The animals and the magical beings have flourished." He pounded his fist on the desk. "But recently things have changed."

"Is it Joseph?" Abigail moved toward the desk. She felt her heart twist in her chest.

"Yes, Guardian," the woman said, drawing Abigail's cold gaze.

"And you are here on what business?" Abigail demanded. Nothing about this meeting was sitting well with her.

"I am Our King's right hand," the woman said. Her amethyst eyes were suddenly haughty. "I have heard much about you, Guardian, but you are not what I expected."

Abigail gritted her teeth, bitter anger filling her. What had been happening since she had been gone? And why would Joseph have this woman as his right hand? Abigail decided then that she couldn't stand the sight of her.

"Sister, this is Melanie," Harlie said softly. "She brought warning that Joseph has assembled an army."

Abigail felt her heart catch in her throat. She remembered that name. How could she ever forget the white wolf that had tried to kill her? It took every ounce of strength to focus on her brother's words. "An army?" she breathed.

Harlie nodded. The desk before him was empty, save for the book.

Abigail's eyes widened as he slid the book toward her, taking in the words written there. It talked about the old laws of Phoenix and about what was legal in regards to standing armies. She frowned as she read the old law. What did this mean?

Abigail felt her heart catch as she realized what this meant. Something was going on with Joseph. Worry consumed her suddenly.

Harlie was watching her carefully. "I thought I could handle it, but he's getting out of control," he said. "He has a standing army of wolves, numbering in the thousands. He is breaking many of the old laws..." He ran a hand through his hair, knowing Abigail would know the punishment for Joseph's crimes. "I couldn't be sure, but I thought he might do something stupid." He looked to Melanie. "This confirms it."

Abigail frowned, shaking her head. "I don't understand," she whispered. She was having a hard time wrapping her mind around what was happening. How could the Joseph she knew do this?

Harlie sighed. "Clearly he's pushed his army into the north, attempting to take control."

"What?" Abigail breathed. She felt as if she had been hit in the chest. "Why? How can this be? How could he have moved his force through Gandora unnoticed?"

Melanie's jaw clenched as she avoided Abigail's gaze. "We are borne of a cunning spirit," she said softly.

Abigail felt fury fill her suddenly. Before Harlie or Melanie could stop her, she had slammed Melanie into the wall. Melanie's amethyst eyes were unconcerned as Abigail held her there.

"If you're so cunning why didn't you stop him?" she demanded. She could feel tears filling her eyes. She lowered her voice to a whisper only Melanie could hear. "Did you think you were cunning when you shoved me off that cliff?"

Melanie's eyes did flash to her then, wide with surprise.

"Abigail, stop," Harlie said quickly. He was beside her, grasping her hands gently. "Melanie has been my contact since Joseph began this whole mess. She is on our side."

Abigail released Melanie, watching as she smoothed the front of her tunic, drawing a slow breath and tucking a strand of her brown hair behind her ear. She brushed at her face, feeling her heart breaking. Had she done this? Was Joseph killing innocents because of her?

"Have you tried to talk to him?" Abigail asked, feeling a tightening fist in her chest as she looked to Harlie.

"He refuses to see me."

"Refuses to see you?" she asked, incredulousness filling her voice. "He can't refuse to see you." She felt disbelief and anger filling her. Her brother was a Guardian.

"He has," Harlie said. "He made it very clear that I was not welcome in Phoenix."

Abigail was stunned. "And Aithne?" she asked. "Did he not have an influence?"

Harlie clenched his jaw. "Joseph tried to kill us," he said. "He didn't care who we were."

Abigail shook her head. Surely this wasn't true. She watched as Harlie looked out the window.

"I don't know what to do," he said softly. "I have needed you to come home to help me, but I didn't know how to find you to tell you." He looked back to her. "If we don't stop him, he'll take more cities, not just Carmen. He'll bring his war here to us, too. I don't think he has perceived us as a threat yet, but if he does, there will be hell to pay. He'll take all of Gandora."

Abigail straightened slightly, knowing what must be done. "We will stop him," she said, her voice hard.

"I have come here to offer my assistance," Melanie said, looking from Abigail to Harlie. "I will lead you into the palace."

Abigail glanced to Harlie, seeing his sea-green eyes were worried as he nodded.

"What is your plan?" he asked.

The night was long and cold. Abigail couldn't find rest as she lay in her bed, waiting for the sunrise.

Her thoughts were plagued with the screams of the people of Carmen. Could their quest really even wait until sunrise? There would be nothing left of the city by sunrise.

But she knew there was nothing she could do. They didn't have access to an army, only the people that lived with them in the castle, and that was hardly a force. She closed her eyes tightly, fighting down tears.

How many lives would be the cost of her failure?

Guilt plagued her. If she hadn't left, this never would have happened. She shouldn't have ever abandoned her brother and her rightful place. Because of her, there was a war brewing. How many more people would die because of her?

All she had wanted was a normal life; to be someone other than a Guardian. She wanted to find something that would curb her obsession with Joseph. She craved the companionship of another human being. She wanted a relationship, something that was lasting and meaningful. She wanted to be loved by someone who would accept her for what she was. But she knew she would never find that among mortals. She had met many brave men during her time away, but none who could turn her thoughts from golden wolf eyes.

After having been there for a while, she had come to see that they really had lost touch with the magic world. They didn't really seem to know that there was anything out there, other than what was here, and the stories they told about Gandora and Phoenix were ludicrous nonsense. Abigail wanted more than anything to show them that they were wrong; that there was nothing to fear from the unicorns and the demons that inhabited the lands, but she knew it was a fool's errand. Besides that, she didn't want to draw attention to herself. She hadn't wanted them to know who she was or what she was capable of.

But what had gone wrong with Joseph? Was it because of her? Or was this always Joseph's plan? Had he tricked her? Was he even really who he had said he was?

She turned restlessly onto her side, staring out the window at the bright moon. Part of her felt terribly betrayed once more. She had thought that she had come to terms with everything that had happened, but now she wasn't so sure. Every time she thought she was coming closer and closer to finding ease to the restlessness in her soul, something always caught her, bringing her back to where she started. It had been so easy before, when she knew who the enemy was and what she had to do. When she thought that she wouldn't make it, that there was no future beyond Bozal's death. But now, it was so complicated, and it caught at her heart.

She recalled the nights she had spent, pining away for the wolf-boy from Phoenix. She saw his eyes in her dreams, and heard his lonely howls in the darkness. She wanted to go to him, to find him in the forest and to see him once more, but she never could. He was too elusive; he kept his distance as a wild thing would.

The pain of his avoidance was what finally drove her to leave Corona. She could never bring herself to tell her brother or anyone else about how she really felt. The pain finally became too much for her to deal with, and so she left. It had been sudden and unwarranted; she and Snow Belle fled in the dark, unbeknownst to Harlie and the servants.

But strangely, she hadn't been able to outrun her memories. Joseph still haunted her, even in her new life in Carmen. So she just got used to it. And for a while, her new life had been a good distraction.

She hadn't wanted another war. She didn't want any more pain or suffering or fighting.

Tears were welling in her eyes.

She didn't want this life.

Chapter Two

T he sun was barely over the horizon as Abigail swung onto Snow
Belle's back. She looked over as Harlie swung onto the Dream
Catcher's back, grasping his creamy mane in his hands. The Dream
Catcher whinnied, tossing his massive head, rearing slightly with ex-
citement. He leapt forward into a gallop, Snow Belle racing after him.

Abigail looked up as Aithne's shadow fell across them. Another
movement in the brush caught her eye, and she turned to see a white
wolf weaving through the trees. She gritted her teeth, memories
and unwanted feelings assaulting her. Part of her hated the sight of
Melanie, but part of her knew that she was their only hope. Without
her, there was no way they could possibly reach Joseph on their own.

She knew that they all could sense the danger ahead. She felt
Shalamar pulse against her back, filling her with familiar warmth.
This scene felt so familiar, yet so foreign at the same time. Her stomach was twisting in knots as the unicorns carried them through the
forests of Gandora.

They paused to take several breaks during the day, reaching the
border of Phoenix well into the night. For some reason, the journey
had seemed longer the last time Abigail had taken it. But there were
a lot of things that had been different then. She tried to block out the
memories that were assaulting her.

"We should press on," Abigail said, looking to Harlie. She tensed
when Melanie shifted into her human form beside her.

Harlie was silent as he looked ahead, the plains of Phoenix stretching before them. They were green, the grass flowing in the night
wind. Deer-like creatures could be seen in the distance.

"We are close to Quasar," Melanie said quietly. Her eyes were glittering in the darkness as she looked up at Abigail. "It might be wise to rest."

Harlie nodded, sliding from the Dream Catcher's back. "Melanie is right," he said, stepping up to Snow Belle. "We need all our strength for when we face Joseph."

Abigail scowled, her heart racing in her chest. She didn't want to rest. She wanted know what the hell was going on.

She could see, though, that she was the odd man out, and she slid from Snow Belle's back, landing softly in the grass. She took a moment to stretch and ease the pains from riding from her body before she sank down to sit in the grass.

A shadow fell across her, causing her to narrow her eyes as she looked up. Melanie's eyes were glowing brightly as she eased to sit beside her.

Abigail could tell that Harlie trusted Melanie, but she couldn't say the same. Everything about Melanie rubbed her the wrong way, including the fact that Melanie was tall and beautiful. Joseph must have seen something he liked in her if he chose her to be his right hand.

"I'm sorry that I cannot drop dead like you wish me to," Melanie said suddenly. Her voice was soft, cutting through the night.

Abigail gritted her teeth, turning her face away. She wasn't sure what to say. She knew she couldn't deny her feelings.

"If it pleases you, Our King has only ever had nice things to say about you," Melanie continued. "He regards you very highly." There was a condescending tone to her voice that Abigail didn't like.

Abigail turned to look at her, hearing the edge to Melanie's voice. "Does that bother you?" she quipped. "I'm sure you wish that I had died that day."

Melanie's amethyst eyes suddenly sparkled with mirth. "I was only following orders," she said quietly. "I'm sure you can understand that."

Abigail scoffed, rolling her eyes.

"I couldn't imagine why a little blonde girl would capture the attention of Our King," Melanie continued. Her voice suddenly softened, bitterness lacing it. "But now that I have seen you with my own eyes, I can see what he has seen."

Abigail felt her heart catch. "And what do you see?" she asked softly.

Melanie let a small grin slip across her face. "You are strong." She moved slowly to her feet. "He needs your strength to guide him."

Abigail watched her turn and walk away, feeling her mind reeling. What had Joseph been saying about her? And what had he confided to Melanie? And why? Who was Melanie to him?

She closed her eyes, leaning back into the grass, her heart aching. She hoped that everything could be right again.

The soft sound of Harlie's voice roused her from a light sleep some time later.

"It's time," he said, kneeling beside her.

Abigail rose mutely, leaning into Snow Belle's neck as she watched Harlie with the Dream Catcher.

'Will you and Catcher be okay?' she asked.

Snow Belle tossed her head. *'The dark magic here is not as strong as it used to be,'* she said.

The last time they had come, it had been too dangerous for Snow Belle to traverse the plains of Phoenix. The unicorns that had once been here had been transformed into shadow unicorns. They had since vanished from Phoenix, but Abigail was certain that their spirits still haunted this place. She knew there was an enchanted grove where they still remained. The legend among mortals was that at the place where the sun set was where the shadows lived; not only the shadow unicorns, but the *others* as well.

Abigail looked over as Aithne swooped down, landing with a graceful bow. The grass suddenly became alive with flowers under his feet, and he glowed softly in the night. Magic sparkled around him, and his green eyes were alive and bright. She guessed that he drew strength from this place.

He leaned toward Harlie tilting his head, and Abigail could tell they were speaking with one another. Harlie's blue-green eyes were focused intently on Aithne. After a moment he looked over to her.

"Aithne said it would be safer to fly ahead," he said.

Abigail looked from him to Aithne, before looking down at Snow Belle, who had turned her head to gaze at the phoenix. *'You and Catcher will stay behind?'*

Snow Belle's deep brown eye shifted to her. *'It will be safer for you to be with Aithne,'* she said, though there was a certain unhappiness in her voice.

Abigail nodded, before looking to Harlie. Shalamar pulsed softly against her back as she walked toward her brother and the phoenix. Melanie was standing nearby, waiting for instructions. She looked up at Aithne.

"Is Joseph expecting us?" she asked. She watched as Aithne lowered his head, bringing his eye level with her. She didn't know if she would ever get used to the heat that rolled off of him in waves. She fought the urge to step away from him.

'He knows we are coming,' Aithne said.

Abigail frowned at Harlie. "We cannot hope to sneak up on him," she said softly. "He must have spies watching our moves." She glanced to Melanie, feeling distrustful.

"I will bring you into the castle safely," Melanie said, her voice defensive. "The rest is up to you. I cannot say if he has spies watching us or not, but I will make sure you have your chance to see him."

Harlie nodded. "He may know that Aithne and I are coming, but he may not know that you are with me, Abigail," he said. He walked toward Aithne, climbing onto his back. He held out a hand for her. "You may be our secret weapon."

Abigail clenched her jaw as Harlie pulled her up behind him. At first, Aithne's body was searingly hot, but as he launched himself into the air, the heat became comfortable and bearable.

The plains of Phoenix stretched for miles beneath them. Melanie was but a white speck as she shifted into her wolf form.

Abigail felt her heart lurch in her chest. This was her first time to fly with Harlie and Aithne, and she wasn't sure she liked it. She had never been one to be afraid of things, but watching the ground below them disappear made her heart race in her chest. She held tightly to her brother's back as Aithne whirled up into the clouds, twisting with the winds that caught under his wings.

She was in awe as he suddenly broke through the clouds, the moon large and bright in the sky. She felt she could almost reach out and touch it, and she gasped as she took in the masses of bright stars surrounding them.

She had never seen the sky so beautiful and so close before. For a while, all her troubled thoughts of Joseph were gone as Aithne coasted through the clouds.

The soft, barely audible sound of footsteps drew his attention. His ears swiveled to capture the sound, and he lifted his large, black head, his lips curling in a snarl. He could see a man approaching him. As the man reached the steps of the dais, he kneeled slowly. He seemed uncomfortable at the position he was in, but he kept his eyes downcast.

"The Guardians are coming, Your Highness," he said, bowing his head. "They are approaching from the east."

The man winced as his snarling increased, and he rose slowly to his feet.

His wolf-mind heard the words the man was speaking, and in some way they made sense, but the scent of the man made his wolf heart race with spikes of fear. His tail was low, and he lowered his head, baring his fangs in a silent gesture to the man to leave. He watched as the man rose to his feet, leaving the room quickly. Once he was gone, visions of a girl, pale and with hair yellow as the sun, flashed before his mind's eye. He remembered her, fragmented though the memories were.

His heart felt heavy for unexplained reasons, and he returned to where he had been lying, curled behind the throne on the dais.

He let his head rest against his massive paws, and a soft whine escaped his lips. The animal inside him didn't understand the world around him, and his human heart was beginning to slip away. His hackles bristled when another human entered the room, carrying a silver tray.

Her eyes were downcast as she moved quietly and slowly toward him. "Your dinner, Highness," she said, kneeling on the steps of the dais, setting the tray down slowly.

Joseph snarled at her, seeing her hands shaking and sensing her fear. He instinctively rose to his feet as the scent of fresh blood hit his nose. He moved slowly toward her, his snarling growing more intense. He watched as she winced with his movements, taking the lid from the tray and rising quickly to her feet.

Her movements made him stop, and he let out an angry bark as she stood over him. Frightened, she turned and ran from the room. Joseph thought to chase after her, the scent of blood and the thrill of the chase echoing in his mind, but the food before him was more pressing. His stomach was empty from letting the earlier meals go to waste, and he walked toward the tray, grabbing the slab of meat in his jaws.

The taste was wonderful to his mouth, and he retreated to his hiding place behind the throne. He consumed the meat in peace, licking his lips and paws in a moment of contentment. He sighed as he rested his head on the floor, sleep on the edge of his mind.

Visions began to dance through his head, mostly snapshots of the forest, the scents of the snow being replayed in his dreams. Animals scurried before him, and he whimpered slightly in his sleep, chasing after them. A white rabbit in particular caught his attention, and he ran through the brush after it as it dodged for cover. It leapt into a tight tangling of trees, and Joseph pursued it, breaking through the heavy sticks into a clearing.

He whimpered softly in his sleep, his lips curling slightly.

As he gazed around the clearing, he could see a shadowed figure on the far side. He knew he should be afraid, but for some reason, he wasn't. His body relaxed as the shadow came closer, the soft smell of freshly-fallen snow washing over his senses. His eyes took in the sight as a single ray of light fell across her face.

Her piercing, ice blue eyes looked right into his, no fear to be found. She came closer to him, until she was but a step away, and she kneeled slowly before him. Her eyes never left his, and, strangely, he couldn't look away either. Something about this one, this human girl, was familiar, and he lowered his head submissively, whining softly as they stared at one another.

"Joseph."

Her voice was like a jolt to his system, and he jerked, feeling something happening to his body. He was losing the animal quickly, and he whined as he fell to the ground. His mind didn't know what to call it, but his body knew the feel of it, and the wolf faded into the back of his mind as his body transformed.

He suddenly gasped, his eyes flying open, the dream evaporating from his consciousness. He drew long, labored breaths as he looked wildly about the room, feeling almost as if he was drowning. The cold air stung his bare skin as he realized that he was no longer in his wolf form. He was confused and disoriented as he lay on the floor.

Abigail.

His mind supplied him with a name, and for a moment, he could remember her. He could remember what she looked like, the soft scent of her skin, how light she felt in his arms. But the memory faded quickly, other voices covering it with noise.

Kill her. Kill the Guardian.

Joseph grimaced, pressing his hands over his ears, trying to block out the whispering. Pressure was building inside his head, causing a dull ache that traveled down his spine.

Kill her, son of Jarlath. Kill the Guardian and her brother. Take back what is yours.

"No," Joseph whispered. "No, I can't."

She is going to stop you. She is going to take away what rightfully belongs to you. Kill her.

Joseph drew his knees to his chest, trying to bury his face. He wished he hadn't come back to his human form. He had been trying to avoid it, to avoid sleeping. Every time he fell asleep, he dreamed of her, and when he dreamed of her, he always transformed back. The transformations were painful now. All of the memories came rushing back, all of the time he had spent, wishing she would come back. And the voices...

Since she left, voices had plagued him. He couldn't escape them, and they constantly whispered in his mind. There was no escape from them. None...

He tried to force his body back into his wolf form, but he didn't have enough strength to transform again. Desperation came over him, and he tried to crawl away from his hiding place behind the throne. Maybe if he could move fast enough, he could escape the whispering.

She'll stop you.

She'll force you to give up what belongs to you.

She'll kill you.

Kill the Guardian.

Joseph couldn't take much more of it, a frustrated cry left his lips as he pressed his hands to his head. "Make it stop!"

The sound of sudden, hurried footsteps was barely audible as he collapsed on the dais steps. He looked up as guards and the servant girl from earlier rushed to his aid. He couldn't really hear their voices over the whispers inside his head. He barely registered the feel of a blanket being wrapped around his naked body. He was disoriented, and he closed his eyes as the guards lifted him from the floor and carried him from the room.

Abigail closed her eyes as the ground raced to meet Aithne's feet. She felt the jolt as he landed on the ground, but it wasn't as bad as she expected. She looked up at the castle on the hill, an ominous feeling overcoming her. It was still dark, and they were hoping they could sneak in undercover. The mist rising from the Lake of Fire blew across their path, shielding them from the eyes of the guards on the castle walls.

Harlie turned and looked to her as he slid from Aithne's back. He caught her as she slid down behind him. "Aithne will be our eyes from the air," he whispered.

Abigail nodded, straightening her quiver and pulling out Shalamar. She watched as Aithne lifted easily into the air, leaving them in the shadows. He was a beautiful blur of red light as he vanished into the skies.

"This way," Harlie whispered, leading her toward a gap in the wall.

Abigail wrinkled her nose as she saw the sewage water running through the opening. She wasn't keen about having to go in this way, but Harlie pressed on, and she followed his lead. The stench was terrible, and she covered her mouth to keep from gagging.

"Was there no other way?" she whispered.

Harlie chuckled lightly. He glanced over his shoulder at her. "It was this or walk in the front door," he said. "And we wouldn't make it far the other way."

Abigail nodded, looking ahead to where the tunnel opened. Moonlight flooded into the end of the tunnel. She was so distracted by it that she gasped when she stepped down into the water up to her knees. Disgust filled her for a brief moment, before she saw Harlie ahead of her, scanning the opening.

"Come on," he whispered. He waved his hand for her to hurry.

Once they exited the tunnel, Harlie helped pull her onto steady, dry ground. She felt disgusting, but her heart suddenly began to race. They were inside the walls of the castle now, and guards were on alert all around them. She looked up, seeing heavily armed guards on the wall above them. Ahead were more walls and keeps, with guards standing on them as well. She wondered where all the citizens were, but the thought was fleeting as Harlie ran ahead, scouting the area. He kept an eye out as he motioned her to come to him.

They somehow managed to sneak unnoticed around the small city and the castle, until they were standing in the shadows of a tower. Abigail looked up, seeing how tall it rose into the sky.

"Where are we?" she whispered, looking at Harlie.

Harlie moved slowly around the base of the tower, pressing his hands against the bricks. "This is where his personal chamber is," he whispered. "Melanie knew of a secret door here."

Abigail felt her heart lurch suddenly. They were just going to barge into Joseph's bedroom at Melanie's suggestion? It didn't sit well with her at all. "This doesn't feel right, Brother," she whispered.

"You must trust me," Harlie said. He grinned victoriously when he found the door and managed to push it open.

Abigail's heart was racing as they stepped into the darkness of a stairwell. She stopped him as he began to ascend the stairs. "What are we doing here? He'll throw us in jail! Or worse!" She shook her head. "Melanie is his right hand! How do you know we can trust her?"

Harlie shook his head, seemingly surprised by her outburst. He drew a slow breath as he seemed to gather his thoughts. "We need to put a stop to this," he said quietly. "Melanie has helped us come this far." His sea-green eyes were pleading. "You must trust me."

Abigail felt her heart sink as she followed her brother up the stairs. The last thing she wanted was to think that her brother was being fooled, but she couldn't shake the unwelcome feelings she had about Melanie. But maybe that was where they were different; Abigail preferred to work alone.

The walk seemed eternal as they wound up the stairs. She didn't know what she was expecting to see when they finally arrived, but her rolling thoughts didn't prepare her for what she did see. She came to a halt as they came to the top of the stairs. Faint light could be seen through the seams of the door, and Harlie pressed his hands to it, pushing softly. Abigail drew an arrow as Harlie moved into the room.

Her eyes widened as she followed behind him, seeing that they were in a closet. Clothes hung on racks around them, and candlelight flooded into the closet from the bedroom. Abigail felt her heart lurch in her chest as the scent of Joseph's clothes caught at her. She had expected the sudden, gripping feelings that were constricting her as she pushed her way from the closet. She watched as Harlie rounded the corner into the room, confusion on his face.

"He's not here," he whispered, glancing back at her.

Abigail's ice blue eyes shifted around the bedroom. It was clean and looked untouched, the bed made. There was a candle lit on the night stand, and another sitting on the desk in the corner, where papers were lying. Abigail walked toward it, touching it gently. A fine layer of dust was covering them.

"I'm not sure he's been here in a while," she whispered. She glanced over her shoulder, seeing that Harlie was making his way down the hall into the living area.

"I'm going to look around," he said, crossing the living room into a study. Candles were lit in the study as well, illuminating books that were left out around the room. They were strewn around the room, each one open to a different page.

Harlie felt confusion swamp him as he looked at them. They were all on dark arts and dark magic. He paused at one in particular, picking it up. A painted image of a demon snarled up at him. Harlie felt his heart sink. What was Joseph getting into?

Chapter Three

Abigail watched Harlie vanish into the next room. She turned her eyes back to the sitting room, seeing how untouched it looked. Where was Joseph? It didn't seem like him not to be here. It didn't seem like him to leave things untouched and left out.

Part of her wanted to see him as she gazed around. She felt some intimate connection to him from seeing where he lived, and she also felt she was trespassing. She knew they shouldn't be there. She knew *she* shouldn't be there; she should be finding a way to stop his army. Anything that she had to say to Joseph would be along the lines of if he didn't stop, she would kick his ass. She sighed as she turned away from the polite little sitting chairs and table. She put her arrow back into her quiver, her eyes scanning the room.

She frowned when she suddenly noticed that the bedroom door was cracked open. She walked toward it, feeling her heart skip a beat as she walked through it, following the stairs down to another door, which was flung open. She peered around the frame of the door into the hallway. As she looked up and down the empty hall, she noticed that, aside from the single wrinkle in the carpet, the hallway was spotless and deserted. She frowned as she stared at the wrinkle.

It was out of place, considering the condition of everything else in the castle. She stepped slowly into the hallway, her eyes scanning around quickly. Darkness submerged her, and she moved silently through the castle. She didn't see any signs of any servants or guards, and it was easy for her to follow the corridor to two large doors. She wondered if the emptiness was Melanie's doing.

Her heart lurched as she made her way to the doors, which were pushed open slightly. She drew a sharp breath as she stepped inside, letting her eyes adjust to the moonlight flooding in from a glass spot light above a dais.

A single throne sat atop it.

She couldn't turn her eyes away from the throne before, her mind supplying her with images of what it must have looked like before. She wondered what Jarlath, the great king of Phoenix, had been like; what Joseph must have been like as a child. She felt her heart ache as she stepped closer to it. Where was Joseph?

A snarl suddenly caught her attention, and she jumped, pulling a short sword from the hilt at her belt. Her eyes widened as a massive black wolf rose from behind the throne, eyes glittering bright gold in the darkness. As it stepped toward her, she saw the moonlight glint off razor fangs. Her heart caught in her chest as it moved through the bright rays of moonlight.

"Joseph?" she whispered. She felt bitterness fill her suddenly as she stared at him.

The wolf lowered his head, his snarling increasing. He stood at the top of the dais, mere feet from her.

Abigail knew she was in danger. Joseph was fast, much faster than she could ever be, and he was in leaping distance from her. She slowly tried to take a step back, wincing when Joseph snapped a bark at her, almost commanding her not to move.

"It's me," she whispered, feeling her heart twist. "It's okay. It's just me." She lowered her sword. "I need to talk to you. You must stop all this madness." Her thoughts turned to the innocents he had murdered.

He continued to snarl as he moved down the steps, out of the moonlight and into the darkness. His paws were massive, and his claws ticked lightly on the cold stone. As he came closer, Abigail realized that he was much bigger than she remembered, standing easily to just above her hip. His body was solid muscle and black fur as he came closer to her.

"Please, Joseph," she whispered. "It's just me. It's Abigail. Don't you remember me? Can't you just talk to me?" She felt tears welling in her ice blue eyes. Did he really hate her so much?

She gasped when he whined softly suddenly, his body beginning to ripple in an unnatural way. She realized he was transforming, and she stepped back. The transformation seemed harder for him, and it seemed more painful as his body melded back into human form. Her ice blue eyes widened as he suddenly became solid before her. She didn't know how to react initially, until she saw him sway lightly in the darkness.

"Joseph!" She stepped forward quickly, dropping her sword as she reached to catch him as he stumbled forward. Her breath caught in her chest as his body pressed against hers. How many nights had she lain awake, wishing for this?

"Abigail." His voice was a soft whisper, the sound of her name almost strained on his lips. His dark hair fell across his face, brushing against her cheek. "I...have missed you..."

His words were so soft, Abigail almost missed them. They made her heart ache, and she closed her eyes as she pressed her hands against his head, her fingers weaving into his hair. She felt his arms curl around her, his hands pressing against the small of her back, holding her close.

"I have missed you," she whispered, feeling her heart racing as tears filled her eyes. It couldn't be true, what Harlie said about him. He had to have been mistaken. Her thoughts were racing with all of the possibilities, with how right it felt to be here, with him, like this. He couldn't have been the one who sent those wolves to attack Carmen. There had to be some other explanation.

She felt Joseph's grip on her tighten slightly, and she felt him draw a sharp breath. She gasped when he suddenly shoved her away from him. She was stunned as she saw his golden eyes narrowed angrily.

"I should kill you where you stand," he ground out suddenly, his jaw clenched. "Guardian filth."

"What?" Abigail breathed. She felt blindsided, and she glanced around, realizing her sword was lying on the floor. "Joseph? What's wrong? Why are you doing this?"

Fury flashed across his eyes. "You're here to take away what rightfully belongs to me," he snapped. "I'll kill you first."

"What are you talking about?" she asked, the confusion and hurt mingling inside her. It was suddenly clear that Harlie had not been mistaken. He had sent his forces to attack Carmen. She knew she had to push the pain aside, but she just couldn't seem to bring herself back, despite the fact that her instincts were telling her to fight or run. "Why did you attack Carmen?"

"Because this world will belong to me," he growled, his golden eyes filled with delight. "Those mortals will bow down before me." He suddenly tensed, anger on his face. "But you're here to kill me, aren't you? To try to stop me. Well you won't have that satisfaction, little Guardian wench." He suddenly transformed quickly, catching Abigail off-guard.

She lunged quickly for her sword as he jumped at her, his jaws aiming for her throat. She narrowly avoided him as she rolled across the floor, ending in a crouch. Her sword was lifted to guard her face, and her ice blue eyes were narrowed dangerously. No matter how she felt about him, she couldn't overlook this. He was killing innocent people.

She rose to her feet as Joseph leapt toward her once more, swinging her blade. She heard him cry out as the steel met his flesh, leaving a gaping wound.

"Abigail!"

Her head snapped up as Harlie appeared in the doorway to the throne room. "We must go!" she yelled, crossing the floor quickly. She tried to ignore Joseph's pained whines as they ran from the room. He was lucky that she didn't finish him off.

"This way," Harlie said, leading her back to the tower. "To the balcony."

Abigail took the stairs two at a time, listening as Harlie slammed the door shut behind them. She fought down her feelings as she burst into the room, throwing open the balcony doors.

Harlie was soon beside her. He pressed his fingers to his lips, a sharp whistle piercing the air.

Aithne was like a flash of lightning as he swooped from the clouds, landing easily on the balcony railing. Abigail wasted no time in swinging onto his back, Harlie climbing in front of her. She drew a sharp breath as Aithne launched into the air, barreling into cloud cover as the sound of yelling could be heard from the guards below.

As the cold night air clawed at her face, Abigail felt the tears finally begin sliding down her cheeks. It was as Harlie said; something was wrong with him. He had obviously recognized her, but something was terribly, terribly wrong. Why was he doing these things? What had changed in him?

It didn't make any sense.

Abigail slid slowly from Aithne's back, her knees weak as she hit the grass. She collapsed momentarily, looking up as Harlie moved to help her.

"Are you hurt?" he asked, his blue-green eyes wide with concern.

She shook her head, leaning forward into the grass for a moment. She couldn't force her mind to accept everything that was happening. She couldn't make the hurt in her heart go away. And she couldn't ignore the fact that she had watched Carmen burn while its citizens were murdered in cold blood.

"What did he say to you?" Harlie asked, kneeling in front of her. He watched as tears slid silently down her cheeks.

"He said he would kill me," she whispered. "That he wouldn't let me stop him or take what is rightfully his. That he would make the mortal kingdom bow down to him." She brushed the back of her hand across her eyes, sitting back on her heels. Her eyes met her brother's. "I don't understand why this is happening."

Harlie frowned deeply. "Something isn't right with him," he whispered. He knew how they felt about each other. He had seen the way Joseph had looked at her that day. He could never know for certain what had happened between them during their time together, but he knew Joseph cared deeply for her. He also knew she cared for him, too.

He could remember nights of passing by her room, hearing her crying through the door. He could remember standing in the window of the study, seeing her standing barefoot in the cold, waiting. He could remember hearing howls on the wind outside the castle in the dead of the night.

He caught her hands, pulling her to her feet. "We will make him stop," he said, holding her gaze. "We will make him see reason again."

Abigail's ice blue eyes narrowed with worry, but she didn't say anything. She knew it was hard for Harlie to see her this way. He wasn't used to seeing her tears, and she wasn't used to showing her emotions like this. Was she becoming soft?

"Let's go," Harlie said, ushering her toward the unicorns, which were waiting at the edge of the grass for them. "They will be pursuing us. Melanie can only give us so much time."

Joseph whimpered and snarled as he writhed on the floor, pain filling him.

The gaping wound to his side was slowly knitting itself back together, but it still burned like hell. He forced himself to his feet, trying to pursue Abigail and Harlie, realizing quickly that they were long gone. He collapsed for a moment in front of the door that led to his chambers, hearing footsteps closing in on him.

His body shifted easily into human form as a soldier kneeled beside him. "It was the Guardians," he said angrily, his hands bloodied from his own wounds. "Gather a force and bring them to me."

The guard nodded, taking his small force with him as a single figure lingered behind the rest.

"Highness, are you all right?"

Joseph gritted his teeth, using the wall to brace himself. "Get away from me, wench," he snapped, his eyes barely skimming over Melanie. "I don't need help."

She was silent as she stood beside him. Her heart was racing in her chest. She had barely been able to help Harlie and Abigail escape. Her amethyst eyes watched her leader as he steadied himself, turning his golden eyes on her.

"You are walking a fine line, Melanie," he said softly, his voice dangerous. "Don't think your pandering ways have gone unnoticed."

Melanie felt her heart catch in her chest. She tried to keep her face schooled, and she lifted her chin slightly. "I know not of what you speak, Highness," she said, keeping her eyes downcast.

Joseph's movements were quick as he suddenly rounded on her, backing her into the wall. "Let me be clear then, Melanie," he said darkly. "As my right hand, it will be your job to taste the blood of my enemies."

Melanie's eyes flashed to his face.

"*You* will kill the Guardians," Joseph whispered. "And you will be thankful that it is their lives I seek and not yours."

Melanie realized she was trembling as silence fell over them and Joseph stepped away from her. This was not the person she remembered from when they were pups. Joseph had become some monster, some blood-thirsty animal she didn't recognize. She knew their friendship kept her mostly immune to his cruelties, but she also knew he would find ways to punish her for her treason. For a long moment, she couldn't move as his words rattled inside her brain.

"Why are you still here?" he suddenly snapped.

Melanie jumped at the sound of his voice, bowing her head. She scurried away quickly.

Joseph felt a dull headache pounding against his skull as he watched her go, his rage ebbing away slightly. He knew it was like a tide, though; he had little control over it, and it would come surging back. He could hear the vague whisperings of the voices again, and he winced against it.

You didn't listen, Joseph.

We told you she would come.

You should have killed her when you had the chance.

She will kill you if she catches you first.

You should have listened to us.

Kill the Guardian, and the world will be yours.

Joseph growled softly, moving toward the castle entrance. He transformed seamlessly, sending a sharp howl into the air as he joined his pack in the search for the Guardians. The others answered his call with a chorus of wolf-chatter, finding him easily in the night.

The grass was cool as it whipped against his face, the wind burning in his lungs. He felt a surge of strength as he ran with the pack, and he turned his head, watching as the smaller wolves snapped at one another. He ignored the gaze of the white wolf running beside him. Images passed like words between the pack members, everything controlled by his movements. A snarl tore from his throat as the image of a blonde girl began to shift between them.

He pushed them faster, the desire to taste her blood on his lips coursing through him.

Abigail leaned into Snow Belle's mane as she raced through the trees.

'Are you sure it was wise to split up?' she asked.

Abigail nodded. *'Joseph wants to kill me,'* she said. *'He'll follow my trail first.'*

Snow Belle snorted. *'And Harlie?'*

'He needs time to stop what Joseph started,' she said. *'No one in Gandora or Phoenix can afford a war with the North.'* She wasn't so sure there was any way to stop it now, though. The mortal king would bring down his wrath upon all of them.

'And in the meantime, we are supposed to just be on the run?' Snow Belle's voice was irritated. *'This is a fool's errand.'*

Abigail threaded her fingers into Snow Belle's mane. *'We just need to buy Harlie and Aithne time. And we need to find a way to stop Joseph.'*

Snow Belle leapt easily over a fallen tree as she made her way through the forest. She made a sharp turn around a tree, feeling Abigail cling to her neck in surprise.

'We should be leading him away from our home,' Snow Belle said, pushing hard through the snow.

Abigail flinched as the sound of howls echoed around them. She knew they were crossing paths, and she leaned in to Snow Belle's neck. It didn't take long for the sounds of the wolves to fade into the distance and for the plains of Phoenix to form on the horizon.

"Hurry Snow Belle," Abigail whispered, her ice blue eyes fixed ahead. "We need to reach a safe place."

Snow Belle's feet were barely crossing the grassy plains of Phoenix when suddenly a sharp howl filled the air. Abigail turned, seeing that the pack had found them. She sat up quickly, pulling Shalamar and an arrow from her quiver. She loosed one quickly, reloading and loosing another. She watched as two of the wolves running at Joseph's side fell to the ground, the others passing them up.

"They're gaining on us!" she gasped, seeing that they were still catching up. "You must go faster Snow Belle!"

Snow Belle's feet barely touched the ground as she lunged forward, her stride lengthening into a full gallop. The wind whipped against Abigail's face, and she could hear Snow Belle blowing hard as she drew breaths through her nose. Abigail knew they couldn't go far this way. Sure, Snow Belle was not weak or unfit, but she wasn't invincible. The only thing that would save them was if Snow Belle could suddenly sprout wings.

Abigail looked over her shoulder, lining up another shot. She sighted straight down the arrow, seeing a white wolf in her line of fire. She drew the string back, knowing it would be an easy shot. She heaved a sigh as she prepared to release the arrow.

At the last moment, she aimed to the left, striking down the wolf beside her. She watched as Melanie's head snapped to the side. A chorus of howls and chatter filled the air. Abigail knew that she couldn't strike Melanie, despite the way her heart twisted with rage. It was easy for her to strike down another, his squeal filling the air as he fell.

Joseph's eyes were bright as he surged past his comrades. His teeth were bared in a deadly snarl as he gained on Snow Belle with each stride he took.

'Abigail,' Snow Belle's voice was strained. *'You must stop him.'*

Abigail looked down at her, seeing thick lather forming on her neck. She was getting tired. She could feel Snow Belle beginning to slow, her breathing labored. She could feel tears crowding her eyes.

'I can't.'

Abigail couldn't muster her strength as she turned back to see Joseph and two other wolves running them down. They were close enough now that she could see the glittering of his eyes and hear the soft growl coming from his throat. She gasped as he took several more hard strides, before lunging for Snow Belle.

The world spun as Snow Belle's legs locked together, tangling her in a dangerous crash. The ground was hard as Abigail was thrown over her shoulder, slamming into it. For a moment, she saw stars. Pain shot through her, causing her to gasp hard for a breath. It took a long moment for her to realize that she was lying on the ground on her back.

Snow Belle's pained whinny brought her back to herself, and she pushed herself to her feet, despite the pain. Horror streaked through her as she saw the wolves taking turns snapping at her. Her pure white coat was stained with blood, and she was limping from her back leg. One wolf was lying on the ground, her horn having pierced through his heart. Joseph and the other wolf closed in on her, lunging for the kill.

"No!"

A white blur suddenly shot across the grass, slamming into the other wolf. Snarls and yelps filled the air as they tangled in a deadly fight for a moment. Abigail's eyes were wide when the other wolf suddenly fell heavily to the ground, Melanie's teeth digging into his neck. She watched as two golden eyes suddenly turned on Melanie as she released her pack mate.

The fury in Joseph's golden eyes made Melanie shrink to the ground in fear. She knew that he would kill her for her betrayal. Her eyes darted past him to Abigail, who was scrambling for an arrow.

Joseph's fury was only curbed from her to Abigail when her arrow struck true, sinking deeply into his flesh. His lips curled in a deadly grin as his attention turned to her.

Melanie could feel his thoughts, knowing he would deal with her once he slaughtered his prey.

"Is this what you want, Joseph?" Abigail suddenly yelled, pulling another arrow from her quiver. "I'll make this quick." Her anger was too fierce to let her feel upset about what she was about to do.

Snow Belle was too important. The lives of the mortal people were too important. His cruelty had been escalated to a level that she couldn't overlook.

Her hands were steady as she sighted down the shaft of the arrow to where she knew his heart was beating quickly in his chest. She was on the brink of letting go, when suddenly Joseph's body began to ripple. She gasped as she realized what was happening. Killing his wolf body was one thing, but killing his human body... She knew she couldn't do it.

"Joseph!" She watched as he fell to the ground, the rippling intensifying. A harsh cry left his wolf lips, before his body suddenly twisted and morphed. He was still for a moment as he lay on the ground, his body heaving with his ragged breaths. Blood was staining his clothing as the arrow protruded from his very human body.

He was slow to move, his dark hair falling across his face as he winced in pain.

"Abigail."

His voice was a soft whisper, and he continued to breathe hard. It took a long moment for him to lift his head, his golden eyes fixing on her.

"Don't move," she ground out, tightening her grip on Shalamar. "If you come near me, I'll kill you."

"Please, Abigail," he breathed, his eyes pleading with her. "You must help me." Desperation came over his face, and he pressed his hands to his temples. "The voices...just make them stop..." Pain was suddenly etched across his face. "Please, Abigail, the voices. They're so loud!"

Abigail's ice blue eyes widened as she stared at him, watching as he collapsed to the ground, writhing in pain. What was happening? He was hearing voices? What voices? Concern came over her, and she lowered her bow, running to his side.

"Joseph." She fell to her knees beside him. "Tell me what's wrong," she gasped, feeling terrified as she watched him claw at his head. "What's wrong with you?"

He suddenly snarled in an animalistic way, turning his golden eyes on her. They were bright and intent, focused on her face. Abigail fell back as he suddenly began to morph again, his mouth growing into a muzzle filled with razor teeth. She couldn't tear her eyes away from his, his golden orbs piercing into her as his body materialized into solid muscle covered in thick black fur.

She was trembling as they stared at each other for a moment.

I will kill you.

The thought was like spoken words as it filled Abigail's mind. She couldn't make herself move as he suddenly lunged at her.

The smell of fear was pungent as it filled Joseph's nostrils. The beast inside him craved what he was about to do, but something was causing him to hesitate. Listening to his pack mates' thoughts about this blonde-haired girl had stirred him to madness, but now that he was here, alone, standing over her, the scent of her skin suddenly caused him pause.

Abigail.

Her name was like a jolt to his system, and it caused him to wince, sinking to his belly before her. His eyes held hers as he lay before her, ice blue to gold. He whined softly as he stared up at her.

Did she know how much he needed her? How hard it was for him to cower here before her like this?

Another whine escaped his throat as he stared at her. He felt so confused. His human mind was spilling into his wolf brain, filling him with feelings that he couldn't understand or comprehend. But at least he could hide here from the voices; for some reason he couldn't hear them when he was like this.

He watched as she moved into a crouch, slowly reaching forward her hand to touch his nose. His body began to tremble despite the strange desire he felt to let her.

It wasn't right.

Letting her be this close wasn't right.

He suddenly jumped up, snapping at her as he did so.

He knew she wasn't a wolf. Her human scent, though familiar, was still very human, and it made him snarl. Wolves and humans couldn't interact peacefully.

He snarled at her, watching as she stood slowly, her ice blue eyes wide with fear. Her fear was heady and spurred him on as he lunged at her, his golden eyes focused on her throat.

Abigail fell back, screaming as Joseph lunged for her. She expected to feel his fangs tearing into her flesh, and she gasped when an angry bark filled the air. Instantly, she knew where it came from as Melanie's body collided with Joseph's. Fear filled Abigail for a different reason.

Melanie was barely half Joseph's size, and she was no match for him. Within seconds of her attack, Joseph had her pinned to the ground, sinking his teeth into her with unbridled rage. Abigail felt tears fill her eyes as she suddenly realized that Joseph would tear Melanie apart in front of her, and there was nothing she could do to save her.

"Joseph, stop!"

Her voice sounded foreign to her as Melanie's cries filled the air and Joseph's snarls darkened. Melanie's white coat was quickly becoming stained red with her blood, and she was fading quickly.

The world seemed to slow suddenly as bright light suddenly flooded around them. Abigail couldn't tell what was happening at first, but she was surprised when the fighting slowly ebbed away, Joseph collapsing heavily to the grass. Abigail shielded her eyes with her arm as she stared up from where she fell back in the grass. Her heart was twisting painfully in her chest and tears were filling her eyes.

'You are safe, little Guardian,' a voice like chimes filled her mind.

Her ice blue eyes widened as the light began to fade, leaving a burning crimson phoenix in its wake. Confusion and gratitude suddenly came over her.

For a long moment she couldn't move as she stared into the phoenix's golden eyes. As she gained some semblance of mind, her thoughts turned bitter.

'You could have come sooner.'

The phoenix lowered its head, following her gaze to where Melanie lay in the grass. She was breathing slowly, soft groans whispering past her lips with each breath.

Sorrow filled Abigail as she moved toward Melanie and Joseph.

The phoenix angled his head, his golden eyes shifting to Joseph's body. He was lifeless on the ground. 'He will awaken after a while,' the phoenix said. There was sorrow in its voice as it turned its head, taking in all of the casualties.

"Snow Belle!" Abigail leapt to her feet, running to her side. Her white coat was stained with blood and her legs were twisted in an unnatural way. "Snow Belle."

Snow Belle lifted her head lightly, her brown eyes filled with pain. She breathed a pained sigh.

Abigail looked up at the phoenix, feeling her heart twisting. "Will they be all right? You can heal them, can't you?" She heard the desperation in her own voice.

The phoenix lowered its head, its gold eyes skimming over Melanie. 'There are ones who are more powerful than I,' it said, looking back to her.

Abigail followed its gaze, seeing that Joseph was beginning to stir. "You can heal Joseph too, can't you?" she whispered.

The phoenix was silent for a long moment.

Abigail felt her heart sink as she looked back to the phoenix. "Can't you?" she breathed.

The phoenix looked at her, its golden eyes unreadable. 'The curse he is bound by is beyond my healing powers,' it said. It fluttered its wings, sending waves of heat cascading over her. 'But I can take you to one who can touch the curse in his mind.'

"And Snow Belle and Melanie?" Abigail rose from beside her beloved friend. "They will be healed?"

The phoenix nodded. Just as he did so, the lights of more phoenixes began to fill the air. *'You and I must go,'* it said. *'He will do as the curse commands and will not stop trying to kill you.'*

Abigail nodded, sparing a glance over her shoulder at Snow Belle as the light of the phoenixes engulfed her. She soon disappeared from sight with Melanie, leaving only Abigail and Joseph and the phoenix behind. Her ice blue gaze shifted to Joseph one last time as he whimpered, his golden eyes fluttering suddenly.

They were out of time, and she climbed quickly onto the phoenix's back, holding to his feathers as he launched himself into the air.

Chapter Four

Joseph blinked slowly, his eyes adjusting to the light that was filling the sky. He rolled slowly to his feet, shaking his shaggy coat. Pain filled him at the arrow that was still jutting from his side, and he used his teeth to pull the offending object from his flesh. He glanced around as the momentary pain subsided, trying to remember what had happened. He lowered his head to the bloodied ground, catching the scent of the Guardian and a phoenix. His lips creased in a snarl.

Images came to his mind of the chase and the fact that he had been about to kill Abigail, until Melanie had intervened. Something inside of him stirred, causing him to growl sharply.

You must kill her.

The thought was sharp and poignant, translating easily with an image of him standing over her body, her blood dripping from his lips.

His golden eyes traced the sky for signs of the phoenix, before he sighed. There was no way to know which direction they had gone.

Another foreign thought invaded his mind, images of a sorceress deep in the woods forming.

He lifted his tail and turned, recognizing the scene.

'*How much time do we have?*' Abigail asked as she leaned against the phoenix's neck. His warmth kept the cold wind from chilling her deeply, and it seemed as if they had been flying for some time. She was hoping that focusing on her task would help keep the guilt away.

Melanie had selflessly offered her life to save Abigail's. How could she ever repay that debt?

'Joseph will have to cross the plains on foot,' it said. *'It is a day's trek on foot to Lady Arianna's forest.'*

'How can we be sure that he will follow?' Abigail asked, her eyes skimming the ground below.

'He is bound to obey,' the phoenix said, flapping its great wings and banking into a turn.

'How do you know so much? Can you see his mind?' Abigail asked.

The phoenix turned its head to glance back at her. *'Aithne sent me to take care of you, little Guardian,'* it said. *'The bonded Guardian told Aithne of what he discovered when you foolishly snuck into the Wolf King's castle.'*

Abigail sat up suddenly, her heart skipping a beat. *'And what did he discover?'* Harlie hadn't said anything to her about finding any information.

'If what the Wolf King has been reading about is any indication, it would appear that he has been bound by a controlling curse,' the phoenix said. *'It would seem that a remnant of Bozal is still trapped inside him.'*

Abigail gasped. "Bozal? How can this be?" She felt fear and helplessness overcome her. Bozal was still inside Joseph?

The phoenix glanced back at her. *'That is all I know,'* it said.

'We must hurry to Lady Arianna,' Abigail said, holding tightly to the phoenix. *'Are you certain she can help us?'*

'If she cannot help you, then she may tell you how to help yourself.'

Abigail frowned at the phoenix's answer, but she steeled herself. She would do whatever it took to help Joseph.

She could tell that he was still there. He was trapped inside his own body. She thought back to what he had said to her. He was being driven mad by Bozal's voice inside his head. But the way he said her name...He was still in there.

The sun was high in the sky as Harlie and Aithne swooped down over Carmen. Harlie's eyes widened as he took in the devastation. The city had been completely razed. Aithne swept down low enough that Harlie could see people trying to pick through the ashes.

There were cries of alarm and uncertainty as Aithne landed atop the city wall. Harlie slid from his back, leaning down as a small crowd began to gather.

"Who did this to you?" he called. He could see that the remaining citizens were dirty, covered in ashes. Most were women with tear stains down their cheeks.

"It was the wolves," one woman cried, cradling her child to her chest. "They killed our men and destroyed our lives."

"Who are you?" a man yelled, stepping between them. He wore the garb of a soldier.

"I am a Guardian," Harlie said, stepping closer to Aithne. He climbed onto Aithne's back, holding onto his feathers as he flapped his wings.

Aithne wasted no time in rising into the air, carrying Harlie away from the destruction. The scent of burning wood was still heavy on the air, even as Aithne spiraled higher and higher.

'We must go to the king,' Harlie said.

Aithne glanced back at him, his piercing emerald eyes catching Harlie's. 'He will not listen,' Aithne said. 'There is too much to be avenged, and mortals cannot possibly understand the ways of immortal beings.'

'If he pursues, Joseph's army will destroy him,' Harlie said, his heart heavy. 'He cannot try to retaliate.'

A soft cry escaped Aithne's mouth. He said nothing, but his feelings still touched Harlie's mind. They both knew that the mortal king, King Alabaster, was foolish. He was too prideful and arrogant, and he would not heed their warnings. He would try to march against Joseph anyway. Many lives would be lost before the king saw reason.

Abigail held tightly to the phoenix as it swooped down into a grove of trees. She felt her heart drop into her stomach at the feeling of falling, her adrenaline coursing through her as the phoenix touched down on the land. It gave a small cry, bowing low to the ground as she slid slowly from its back.

'This is it?' she asked, her ice blue eyes scanning the trees.

Humid mist was hanging in the air, casting a haze over the forest. Abigail could feel magic in the air, the thick mist blocking her view.

'This is where she can be found,' the phoenix said, turning away from her. 'I must take my leave of you, little Guardian.'

Abigail turned quickly toward it. "But how do I find her?" she asked, feeling abandoned suddenly.

'She will find you.'

Abigail felt her heart drop as the phoenix suddenly flapped his wings, vanishing into the clouds. She watched after it for a long time, before drawing a ragged breath and turning back to the trees. She forged ahead on foot, hoping that there would be some sign of where she was supposed to go. She could feel Shalamar pulsing lightly against her back, lending her some comfort.

The daylight was beginning to wane when she finally stopped, brushing her golden hair from her face. She was breathing hard, and sweat was beading on her brow. She had been pushing her way through the thick brush, feeling as if she were going in circles. She was certain that she had passed through this same patch of trees once before.

Despair was beginning to overwhelm her, and she pressed her back to a tree, sliding to the ground. She cast her ice blue eyes around as the sounds of creatures of the night began to fill the air.

What was she doing there?

She had been searching all day, and still there was no sign of the enchantress.

"What am I doing here?" she whispered softly, pressing the back of her hand to her forehead.

She knew she was running out of time. Joseph would be closing in on her soon. But was it even worth it to be here? What could Lady Arianna do for her? Could she really even help Joseph?

A soft, warm wind suddenly began to blow through the forest, stirring the mist around her. She lifted her head, feeling a strong presence suddenly moving toward her. She rose quickly to her feet, notching an arrow in Shalamar. Whispers of voices suddenly began to fill the forest around her, and she felt her breath catch in her throat.

"Am I what you seek, little one?"

Abigail spun, raising her bow as a feminine voice filled the air. She couldn't see anyone, and she gritted her teeth, her heart racing. "Lady Arianna?" She cast her eyes around, a shadow beginning to part through the mist.

"Tell me why you have come, Guardian."

Abigail's ice blue eyes widened as Arianna's form became clear. She was beautiful, with a shock of bright red locks falling to her waist. Her eyes were a deep emerald, reminding her of Aithne's piercing gaze. As she came closer, Abigail realized she was clothed in the moss from the forest. She tilted her head, waiting for a response.

"I was told you could heal Joseph," Abigail said, lowering her bow. She watched as Lady Arianna came closer. "That you could touch the curse in his mind."

Arianna arched a narrow brow. "And why would I have any need to help the Wolf King?" she asked, her soft voice offended.

Abigail felt her heart sink. "He is my friend," she said. "I need you to help me."

Arianna's lips suddenly pulled into a thin smile. "I do not sense friendship in your heart toward the Wolf King, little Guardian," she said. "Do not lie to me about your true intentions."

Abigail straightened her shoulders, her ice blue eyes narrowing as she gazed at Arianna. "Then what do you sense?" she asked, confusion in her voice.

Lady Arianna held her gaze for a long moment, the silence heavy between them. She tilted her head lightly, smiling thinly. "Come," she said, turning. "It is of no consequence to me what is in your heart for the Wolf King. I will give you the answers you seek."

Abigail felt relief surge over her, and she followed Arianna, her eyes widening as a cabin came into view. She knew that it was hidden by magic, and she gasped as, when Arianna passed through the grove, the mist suddenly cleared, flowers opening to bloom around them. Animals suddenly began to appear around them.

"Enter," Arianna said, stepping through the door to the cabin.

Abigail followed her, her nose wrinkling as the scent of moss and mold hit her nose. She glanced around, seeing books and potions lining the walls. The cabin was extremely neat, not a single vial out of place.

"Tea?" Lady Arianna motioned toward a kettle, which was sitting on a table.

Abigail shook her head. "Not to be rude," she said, "but I am only here for the cure. I do not have time for idle pleasantries."

Arianna smiled her thin smile, nodding her head. "Do not think that the Wolf King's cruelties have escaped me, Guardian," she said, stepping toward a shelf.

"So then you do know what is wrong with him?" Abigail asked. Her ice blue eyes followed Arianna as she pulled a book from the shelf.

"He is still bound by his curse," she said, opening the book. "Bozal's body may have gone, but his spirit still lingers."

Abigail felt a sick feeling curling in the pit of her stomach. She watched as Arianna handed her the book. "How can this be?" she asked anxiously. She could see the sun setting through the window, and she knew that she wouldn't have much time. Joseph would be here soon.

"There is a place," Arianna said, moving toward a sitting chair. She poured herself a cup of tea, lowering herself gracefully into a chair. "A place to where the shadows flee."

Abigail looked down at the book in her hands, her eyes widening. "The Land of Shadows?" Her eyes skimmed over images of spirits trapped there. It was only the cruelest and darkest of spirits that could garner the strength to cling there.

"Bozal is trapped there," Arianna said, lifting the tea cup to her lips. "You must go there. In order to destroy his spirit and to cure Joseph, you must trap it wholly inside a vessel."

Abigail frowned. "A vessel?" she whispered. "What kind of vessel?"

Arianna's lips quirked in a thin smile once more. "Once you command the spirit of the evil one, it will enter any vessel of your choosing," she said, setting her tea cup down. Her emerald eyes shifted toward the window suddenly. "You and I are out of time, little Guardian."

Abigail rose to her feet, hearing the fading sound of howling through the mist. "How do I find this Land of Shadows?"

"You must travel to the place where the sun sets in the sky," Arianna said. "And you must take the Wolf King with you. Only together can you remove Bozal's control."

Abigail pulled Shalamar from her back, turning toward the door. "Thank you for your help, Lady Arianna," she bowed briefly, before reaching for the handle. She was surprised when Arianna's hand suddenly appeared on hers.

"Take this," she said, holding a silver chain out to her. From the end dangled a wolf pendant. "It may lend you safety in dire need."

Abigail took it, feeling the weight of it as she placed it around her neck. Her ice blue eyes met Arianna's emerald ones. "Thank you."

Arianna smiled suddenly, tenderness in the gesture. "Let your heart guide you, Abigail," she said gently.

Abigail nodded, before pulling the door open and emerging into the night. The air was hot and stale as the mist fell heavily around her. She glanced back after several steps, surprised to see that the cabin was gone. She felt gratitude in her heart suddenly for Arianna's help, and she turned, pushing her way back through the trees. Her senses were suddenly on high alert as another howl echoed across the mist.

Somehow she needed to make Joseph follow her. And somehow she needed to travel to the end of the earth, where the sun set and the evil spirits lived.

King Alabaster was a cruel man.

Harlie could see it in the tautness of his face, in the way that his mouth pressed into a thin, hard line. His blue eyes were pale and cold, much more so than the icy gaze of his sister. His graying hair was pulled back from his face, a gold crown nestled on his head. He was large for a mortal man, tall and broad. He rose from his chair with the air of a soldier and of a hard-handed ruler.

"You dare set foot in my kingdom, Guardian?" he ground out, his voice booming as it filled the hall.

Harlie glanced at the guards on either side of him, feeling uncomfortable. They had taken his weapons at the door, leaving him defenseless. One guard held his sword in his hands.

"I come with a message," Harlie said evenly, knowing he needed courage. What he was doing was difficult, but what he had left his sister to do was dangerous.

The king's eyes narrowed dangerously. "Speak."

"You cannot hope to win a war against the Wolf King," Harlie said. He watched as Alabaster's face hardened, his jaw clenching. "His army vastly outnumbers your own. And his warriors are not of this realm. You will not win."

"You dare lecture me about my people, Guardian?" Alabaster advanced toward him, his eyes filled with rage. "Your Wolf King has murdered my citizens! I will have his head!"

Harlie stood his ground as Alabaster towered over him. "You must listen to me," he said, trying to keep the edge from his voice. "I do not come on Joseph's behalf. You must let me deal with the Wolf King. His army of wolves is borne from a place where life is sustained through violence. They are not made from the soil of the ground as you and I." He could hear the pleading leaking into his own voice. "They will annihilate every last mortal. You cannot stand against him."

Alabaster's icy eyes narrowed at Harlie. "You and your sister are both pathetic." He leaned down to see into Harlie's face. "Idiot is what you are. When this is over, I will bear the hide of that disgusting demon. I will destroy every last one of those wretched creatures, ridding the land of them once and for all. Magic does not belong in the world of humans."

Harlie arched a brow at him. "Humans do not belong in the world of magic," he said quietly. "If you proceed, your time as king will be done."

Rage suddenly filled Alabaster. Without warning, he swung at Harlie.

Sensing his attack, Harlie dodged him, easily dispatching his soldiers and taking his sword back. He drew it, watching Alabaster clench his fists tightly to his sides.

"You are not welcome in my kingdom, Guardian," he said, lifting his chin. "If you or your meddlesome sister set foot here again, it will be your death."

Harlie grunted an amused sound. "You go to your own end, mortal king," he said, sheathing his sword. He turned without another word, leaving the king standing among his guards, who were groaning on the floor. As he came out into the sunlight, he looked up, seeing Aithne swoop down from the sky.

He heard the gasps of the guards around him as the phoenix landed before him. He leveled an emerald eye over Harlie's shoulder, causing him to turn.

King Alabaster stood behind him, his eyes widened in surprise.

'Do not presume to look upon me, mortal,' Aithne suddenly hissed.

Harlie raised his hands as Aithne flapped great, burning wings. Waves of heat fell over them, causing the guards around them to step back. Harlie could tell Aithne was furious. And he knew Alabaster was too disconnected from the magics to hear the enraged phoenix's voice.

"Great phoenix," the king said, falling to his knees. "Please guide my people as we march to war. Lend our hands strength!"

'There will be no blessings from me,' Aithne said, turning away.

Harlie climbed onto Aithne's back, holding tightly as the phoenix launched into the air. Below, he heard the mortal king yell after them. The mortals worshiped the phoenixes as gods. As much as the king despised magic, for some reason the old ways persisted and the people still looked to the phoenixes for guidance and protection. Perhaps there were some things that were too embedded in their culture to be removed.

'Do you think he will go to war?' Harlie asked.

Aithne banked into a turn, spiraling high into the air. *'I have no doubt.'*

Harlie heaved a sigh, leaning into his flaming feathers. *'We must assist Abigail.'*

A screech left Aithne's mouth as the phoenix turned suddenly, rocketing into the direction of the Arianna's forest.

Abigail pulled herself up onto a low-hanging tree branch. She pulled the arrow from between her teeth, notching it into Shalamar. She crouched low, waiting for her target. Her senses were on high alert as she listened for any sounds through the trees. She sighted down the shaft of the arrow as a shadow suddenly began to materialize.

Joseph's breath caused dust to stir from the ground as he paused to sniff for her scent. He raised his head as he caught her scent, his golden eyes fixing on her quiver, which she had left on the ground. He growled softly as he stepped toward it, taking a deep whiff.

Abigail drew a slow breath as he suddenly looked up. Just as he realized it was a trick, she loosed the arrow, watching it strike him in the heart.

A yelp left his lips as he leapt back, before collapsing to the ground with a groan. He was motionless for a long moment before Abigail swung down from the branch. She landed in a crouch on the ground, her eyes trained on Joseph. When he didn't move, she stood, stepping toward him.

A long, slow groan left his lips, and his eyelids fluttered slightly. He was still on the ground.

Abigail smiled to herself as she pulled her quiver over her shoulders. Her potion had worked. It was a simple sleeping spell that she had conjured from plants she had found in the forest. She knew it would work for a time, but it would wear off. She whistled low, listening as the sound of galloping hooves met her ears.

"We don't have much time," she said, looking up as Snow Belle emerged from the trees.

She threw her head, lowering it to press her nose against Abigail's cheek. Sadness flooded through their touch, causing Abigail's icy gaze to shift to her.

"What is it?" she whispered.

'You don't really know what you're doing,' Snow Belle said.

Abigail shook her head. "Yes I do," she said. She turned her eyes back to Joseph when his body suddenly shifted, morphing slowly into his human form. "You must take me to the Vale."

Snow Belle's heart sank. She lowered her head, kneeling to the ground as Abigail wrestled Joseph's sleeping body onto her back.

It had been easy for her to find Abigail once she awoke from the phoenix's slumber. She had been fully healed, and the phoenix had left her in the forest. Once they reunited, Abigail formed a plan to sedate Joseph and to take him to the Land of the Shadows. It didn't make Snow Belle comfortable, because she knew how to get to the Land of Shadows.

She lurched to her feet as Abigail held on. *'You might not come back, Abigail,'* she said as she trotted through the trees.

Abigail held Joseph tightly against her chest. He was awkward and heavy, but the scent of his hair under her nose made the rest of the troubles fade. He groaned softly as Snow Belle moved into a gallop.

'Everything will be fine,' Abigail said.

As the trees began to give way to the plains, Abigail could feel restlessness coming over her. She knew that Joseph would awaken before they reached the Vale. Her potion would be wearing off soon. And if she didn't bring him into the Vale, he wouldn't follow. He was blood-thirsty, but he was smart enough to know that following her into the unicorns' sacred home was not a battle he could win.

"You must go faster, Snow Belle," she said, leaning forward. "My potion won't make it."

Snow Belle snorted, charging hard across the land. *'You forget that the Vale isn't a where,'* she said. She suddenly lunged forward, a burst of magic casting a tunnel before them.

Abigail gasped, her ice blue eyes widening as Snow Belle lunged into the tunnel. "It's a when," she whispered. She raised her hand to shield her eyes as bright light suddenly besieged them.

When it faded, Abigail realized they were standing on a field of blue grass. The sky was a distressing orange color, and she glanced around, her world feeling tipped as she saw that the trees were zigzagging into the sky.

Snow Belle suddenly reared, sending both Abigail and Joseph to the ground.

Abigail felt her heart lurch into her throat. She remembered this part from the last time they had come here, many years ago. She had been frightened then, but now she just felt out of sorts.

Snow Belle turned on her heel, magic swirling around her like a veil. She was hidden in a cloud of magic as light engulfed her, before the magic shattered, falling away like pieces of glass. A fair maiden stood in the falling pieces, her eyes white and piercing like Abigail's.

"Snow Belle?"

Her eyes softened with humor, and she inclined her head. "Words feel foreign in this place," she said. She turned, her body lithe in the tight-fitting clothing that barely covered her.

Abigail moved to her feet, feeling dwarfed by Snow Belle's human form. She rose barely to her shoulder, and she had to look up to see into her face. She felt captivated by her beauty, strange as it was. She took in how Snow Belle's hair stood in white strands from the top of her head, and the way she regarded her with silence, as if she were still in her earthly form.

"Do you remember this place, Abigail?" she asked, her eyes glancing around the Vale.

Abigail nodded, standing beside her. "I was too small to appreciate it for what it is," she whispered. She looked up at the tall woman beside her.

Snow Belle smiled, looking down at her and taking her hand. She didn't say anything as she turned back to Joseph's sleeping form. "We must take him to Irene."

Abigail nodded. She watched as he began to awaken, his eyes fluttering. "He's going to shift soon," she said, her heart skipping a beat. "We can't let him change here."

Snow Belle raised her hand, catching Abigail's shoulder as she stepped toward him. "Let him," she said. She waved her hand, a cloth forming in her fingers. "He will still be out of sorts when he changes." She handed the cloth to Abigail. "Tie this around his mouth."

Abigail nodded, taking it. Snow Belle's hands were very warm as their fingers brushed.

Joseph suddenly lurched, hair covering his body.

Abigail kneeled beside him, watching his golden eyes flutter as teeth began to form. She swallowed thickly, knowing her timing had to be right. His muzzle formed solidly before her, and she lunged forward, wrapping the cloth tightly around his mouth. She jumped back when he suddenly thrashed, a snarl tearing from his throat.

Abigail leapt to her feet, running toward Snow Belle as Joseph struggled to his feet. She grabbed her arm, pulling her behind her as they ran down the hill. She hated that Snow Belle's legs were so much longer than hers. She was like a gazelle as she ran ahead of her.

Barking and snarling made Abigail run faster after Snow Belle. "Irene!"

Abigail looked ahead as Snow Belle splashed through a stream, golden water soaking her. Trees were like a wall on the other side.

An image suddenly appeared inside the tree line. Fierce, crimson eyes stared out at them, and Abigail felt a chill run down her spine. She knew Irene.

Irene's aura was dark and hard as she stepped from the trees. Her ebony skin was bare and in sharp contrast to her flaming eyes and hair. She was tall, like Snow Belle, but with an air about her that made Abigail want to run away.

Her eyes passed over Snow Belle to Abigail, causing her to freeze knee-deep in the water.

Abigail felt fear chill her down to the bone, stilling her. She couldn't tear her eyes from Irene's gaze. Even when Irene's eyes shifted to the hill, which Joseph was stumbling down, Abigail still couldn't move. She could feel her heart beat slowing, her body losing strength. She fell to her knees in the water, feeling warm hands catch her.

"You must go to the light."

Her ice blue eyes focused on Snow Belle's face. She felt cold as she realized that she was dying.

"Find Joseph and go to the light."

She clasped Snow Belle's hand to her face, shivering. She could barely draw a breath as her vision faded. "S-s-snow Belle," she managed. "The a-a-amulet."

She felt Snow Belle press something cold into the palms of her hands.

"Find the light."

Chapter Five

Abigail looked around, the familiar sense of floating engulfing her. She knew where she was as her eyes adjusted. She was in the dream world.

She had been here before.

She righted herself, looking down at the black boots, black pants and black jacket she wore. A bow was heavy at her back, and a clip of arrows were at her side. She realized she was fisting her hands tightly, and she opened them, seeing the wolf amulet that Arianna had given her.

She knew Irene had sent her here. She was the only one powerful enough to send her and Joseph here.

Irene was the queen of the Vale, and the leader of the unicorns. She had once been a pure unicorn, a bearer of white magic, but the corruption of Phoenix had turned her into a shadow unicorn. Snow Belle assured her that Irene still held the best interest of the magics at heart, but Abigail couldn't be sure. When she was around Irene, all she felt was fear and death.

Abigail turned her head, wisps of her blonde hair falling around her. She needed to find Joseph. The white around her began to form into hazy shapes, and she blinked, watching a door materialize in front of her. She stepped toward it, grasping the handle and pulling it open.

Her breath caught in her throat as she stepped forward through it.

She was in a forest. It was dark as a cloudy night, and it was cold. Fear pulsed through the air around her, making her shiver. She didn't let the feeling catch hold of her, though. She knew it was an illusion of whatever other beings were surrounding her. Her heart had to be strong.

She stepped forward, the door shutting and vanishing behind her. As the forest became solid in front of her, she could see that the trees were twisting in ugly shapes into a tall canopy. She could feel the presence of demons around her, and she could hear the sounds of them moving about. Faint whispers were following her as she walked down a path that was forming beneath her feet. She had to keep reminding herself that she needed to find Joseph.

She turned her head slightly as she walked, hearing the demons whispering her name. She knew it was dangerous to respond, but they knew she was listening. She gritted her teeth as their words began to become clearer.

"You will fail, Guardian."

"His soul belongs with us, little girl."

"You will fail, Abigail."

"You cannot hope to save him from our fires."

She pressed her hand to her arrows at her hips. "Take me to Joseph." Her voice was strong and loud over the sounds of their whispering. "I command you to take me to him now."

Her ice blue eyes widened as the trees suddenly began to twist beside her, winding to clear a new path. Just beyond the trees, Abigail could see the mouth of a cavern. She walked toward it, her pace hurrying. The voices faded away as her attention focused solely on the cavern. It was pitch black as she leaned into it, trying to force her eyes to see in the darkness.

"Hello?" she called. She heard her voice echo back. "Joseph?"

A soft scuffle made her heart jump, and she stepped back.

"Joseph, if that's you, come out," she called. She notched an arrow in her bow, the magical steel cold in her hands. She stepped back as soft growling filled the cavern, and suddenly a shape began to move.

A black wolf stepped into the mouth of the cavern. He was snarling, but not in the vicious way Abigail remembered.

"Joseph?"

The wolf tilted its head, the snarling cut short. It stepped closer to her, stretching its nose toward her.

Uncertain, Abigail lowered her bow, reaching out her hand. She gasped when the wolf pressed its nose into her palm, the sudden connection shooting through her like electricity. A trail of thoughts and images crossed between them, and the wolf lowered his head, his eyes holding hers.

"So you are Joseph's demon?" Abigail asked, trying to process what it had shown her.

The wolf held her gaze calmly. Images flooded her mind, making her gasp.

She could see the forest flashing by, the sensation of cold air in her lungs. Soon the trees came to a stop, a castle materializing in front of her. She realized it was her castle, and she realized that she was seeing herself through Joseph's eyes. She was standing in the snow in her nightgown, the breath frosting as it left her lips. Her ice blue eyes were trained on the trees, but never saw her watcher.

The scene suddenly jumped, changing to the throne room in Castle Quasar. The sound of fierce, angry growling filled her ears, and she saw a guard and a servant girl flee from the room as another guard was attacked. Pained cries filled the air, before the killing blow was landed. She could feel bitter anger burning inside, as well as confusion and fear.

She drew a sharp breath as the images stopped, understanding filling her. Her eyes focused on the wolf.

"You knew," she whispered.

The wolf whined softly.

"But how could you stop it?" Pity filled her. Despite being a somewhat sentient being, the wolf could only do what Joseph wished. He had complete control over it. It was what set men and wolves apart; men fought for control and took it over their demons, while wolves took control of their men's souls and became animals.

"Where is Joseph's soul?" Abigail whispered.

The wolf raised its head, looking into the cavern. Abigail took it to mean that the cavern was the doorway. To reach where Joseph was trapped, they had to descend into hell. She drew a steeling breath, before stepping forward.

"Let's go then," she whispered.

The cavern was extremely dark. Abigail tripped and stumbled, falling to her knees. She couldn't see her hands in front of her face, and she felt the wolf press against her side. She caught her hands in its fur, allowing it to lead her forward. She wasn't sure that it could see any better than she could, but it seemed more certain as it led the way.

Soon the floor of the cavern began to slope, and Abigail gasped, her boots slipping on the floor. The wolf growled softly, a cautionary sound, catching her sleeve in its teeth. The air started to become hot and stale, and Abigail paused as she regained her footing, wiping the back of her hand across her brow. She didn't know how much deeper they had to go, and her heart was racing in anticipation of what lie ahead for them.

She grabbed a fistful of the wolf's hair again, taking a cautious step forward. She felt her feet slide slightly, and she squealed when the floor seemed to turn to ice. She was suddenly catapulted through the darkness, sliding deeper and deeper into the unknown. It seemed like an eternity before she finally slammed into the rock floor again. She heard the wolf land near her, and she gasped, pain shooting up her side.

She looked around, struggling to her feet as she realized that there was red light around a bend ahead. She looked to her friend, seeing that it was growling softly. The scent of burning cinders and flesh suddenly struck her mind, and she knew the wolf could smell it. Her heart suddenly began to race in her chest as she held her bow.

They walked slowly around the curve of the cavern, the light becoming brighter and brighter. She could hear the sound of crackling flames, and suddenly the path opened up into a fierce, fiery pit. The sounds of screaming suddenly met her ears, and she winced, looking at the wolf. It was snarling fiercely, its hackles raised.

"What is this place?" she whispered.

The wolf looked at her, passing thoughts. Images of bound and chained souls filled her mind's eye, the flames licking eternally at their skin. Their jailers were dark entities, which Abigail understood to be evil souls. She realized that if she found Joseph, she would find Bozal.

"We must hurry," she said, looking around the pit for a path. She found one easily, but it was treacherous, and the pit spiraled down and down into an infinite pool of fire and pain. If they fell, there was no way to know when they would stop.

The climb down to the closest landing was long and arduous, and by the time Abigail touched down, she was sweating and her arms and legs were screaming. She realized that her pants and jacket were protecting her from the flames, and she looked around. She could see the wolf at the top of the pit, its golden eyes watching her with concern.

She was starting to think it was hopeless, when suddenly the sound of laughter filled the air.

"So here you are!"

Abigail's head snapped up as a shadow figure suddenly formed in front of her. She gritted her teeth as she realized it was Bozal.

His eyes were frightening as he stared at her, black pools of nothing, and his grin was fanged, teeth like a shark's bared. The only thing she recognized of him was his face, although it was becoming grossly disfigured. She knew she should have been afraid, but anger replaced her fear.

"Where is he?" she demanded.

Bozal laughed again, suddenly springing at her. He slammed her into the hot rock, squeezing her throat to the point she thought her neck would break. "He is mine," he said, his voice suddenly morphing.

She could see the demons in his soul swirling in his eyes. "Joseph's soul belongs to me!"

Abigail grabbed his wrist, using the leverage to swing her feet at him. Her boots caught him square in the chest, the blow hard enough to force him back. She fell hard to the ground, coughing and choking as she drew an arrow. She loosed it at him, watching as it struck him clean in the right eye.

He was still for a moment, before him demon grin widened, baring more teeth and contorting his face in an unnatural way. He reached for the arrow, ripping it from his eye. Abigail felt her stomach turn as he threw it away, his socket bleeding.

"Your mortal tools won't work on me, girl," he said. He stepped toward her, grabbing her by the front of her jacket. He lifted her easily from the ground, the mirth returning to his face. "If you want your wolf-boy, then go get him!"

Abigail screamed as he suddenly threw her over the edge. The rock walls were flashing past her in a blur, and she knew she was dead when she landed. She spun out of control through the air, before she forced her mind to slow down. If she was smart, she could be okay. This was the dream world, and she could control it with enough will.

Gritting her teeth, she summoned all her courage and strength, forcing her body to slow down. She could see the ground rushing to meet her, and she fought harder. It still seemed as if it was coming too fast, but she didn't stop trying, gasping just short of the ground. She landed easily on her feet, looking up to where Bozal stood, extremely high above her.

His roar of rage filled the air, making the walls tremble, stones raining down onto her. His body suddenly morphed into a beast, and he leapt from the top, landing hard on the ledge beside her. It growled, baring rows and rows of razor teeth.

"You will be my next victim," he growled.

Abigail fisted her hands. "No I won't," she said. Anger fueled her.

"I will kill you." Her mind suddenly supplied her with the image of a sword, and she moved her hand to draw it, feeling it form solidly in her hands. As her eyes raked across it, she felt her heart fill with courage. It was her father's sword she had seen in her mind.

Bozal's demon eyes widened. "No one has that kind of control here!" he howled.

"Are you afraid?" Abigail quipped. "You forget, Bozal. I've come back from here." With a cry of rage, she swung her sword, cleaving clean through Bozal's body.

He howled as he disintegrated before her, before reforming into the hard, scaly body of a dragon. He snapped at her, trying to dig long fangs into her, but she blocked him with her sword. She could feel the wolf amulet suddenly become heavy around her neck, and she realized that it was now or never. She had to trap him now.

She pulled the amulet from her neck as she rolled out of his path, holding it out. "I command you to submit to me!" she yelled. She watched as Bozal spun on her, and she focused her will. "Your soul belongs to me!"

Bozal screeched with rage, lunging for her, when a bright light suddenly burst from the amulet. It became like a vacuum, the light pulling Bozal's spirit into it. His horrible screaming filled the air, before the light vanished and the air became still.

The sound of Abigail's heavy breathing was all that surrounded her as she realized that she was no longer in the pit. The flames and heat had suddenly been replaced by nothing but familiar white haze. She looked around, seeing the wolf standing next to a limp form behind her.

The amulet was heavy as she put it back around her neck, before walking toward them. She knelt slowly, pressing her hands to Joseph's face. He was pale and weak, and his dark hair hid his golden eyes.

"Joseph," she whispered. She looked up at the wolf, seeing it watching him intently. "Joseph, wake up." She pulled him into her arms, brushing his hair from his face. "Please, wake up."

He drew a slow, hard breath, soft sounds leaving his throat. His eyes fluttered slightly, before he turned to look at her. "A-Abigail?"

Relief suddenly flooded her, and she couldn't stop the tears that filled her eyes. "I'm here," she whispered. She leaned into his touch when he pressed his hand against her cheek.

"What happened?" he whispered.

Abigail shook her head. "You are safe," she said. She helped him sit forward. "We have to leave this place now."

Joseph looked around, before his eyes suddenly landed on the wolf. He drew a sharp, surprised breath as they stared at each other, golden eyes to golden eyes, before the wolf suddenly snarled. It lunged at Joseph, and Abigail gasped.

She was surprised when the wolf suddenly melded into Joseph, vanishing. He doubled over, grasping his chest.

"Joseph!" She caught his shoulders. "Are you okay?"

He nodded, a pained expression on his face. "Are we in the dream world?" he whispered.

Abigail nodded. "Your wolf led me to you," she said. She watched as he drew his hand away, black clothing like hers suddenly forming on his body.

He seemed steadier and stronger, and he moved to his feet, flexing his fingers. Abigail realized that being separated from the other half of his soul like that must have been what made him so weak. He wasn't two beings; he was one part wolf and one part man, and together they made him whole.

"We have to go," she said, moving to stand beside him. She watched as his eyes shifted to her, suddenly brighter and more wolfish. An air of mischievousness came over him, and he smiled.

He took her hand. "Lead the way."

Abigail smiled up at him, before turning her ice blue eyes ahead. A bright light suddenly appeared, and she led Joseph toward it, Snow Belle's words echoing in her mind.

Go to the light.

Abigail knew she was dreaming.

She wasn't sure how she knew, but that was the first thing she thought as she looked around the castle hall.

She was back in Corona, standing in the grand entry way. She wore a blue, floor length gown embroidered with snowflakes, and she felt the weight of a tiara in her hair. She knew she was dressed for some grand occasion, and she looked around. Her ice blue eyes suddenly landed on a familiar figure.

"My sister." A tall man was walking toward her, smiling gently.

Unlike the rest of her brothers, he had dark blond hair and green eyes. He was very broad, and his hug was crushing as he pulled her to him.

"We have been waiting for you," he said.

Abigail grinned lightly. "What is this place, Michael?"

"You know this place," he said dismissively. He turned, an arm around her to lead her forward. "The others are waiting for you."

Abigail felt hopeful as she let him lead her into the hall, where there was a long table set as if for a party. Her brothers and her father sat at the table. When she entered, they all rose, a chorus of happy voices and faces greeting her. Her eyes turned from Michael to her father.

"Hello Father," she said softly as he walked to her.

He smiled lovingly down at her. "Daughter," he said. He didn't move to hug her as they held each other's gaze. "We will continue to wait for you."

Abigail frowned, before looking over his shoulder. She wasn't sure what he meant by that. She looked back at him, her eyes widening in surprise when she saw that he was holding a sword in his hands.

It was the sword she had summoned during her battle.

Her father held it out to her, watching as she took it in her hands. The crest made the hilt heavy in her hands and a phoenix was etched across the blade.

"This is your sword," she breathed. She hadn't seen the blade since they buried her father with it. She looked up at him. "What is this for?"

"Listen well, daughter," he said gently. "You and Harlie are rulers. You are a prince and a princess. We were crowned by the kings of old to protect the peace between the mortals and the magic world. Under old laws, you command every magical creature. As a Guardian, if you summon, they must obey." His eyes searched hers. "Do you understand?"

Abigail frowned, shaking her head. "What does this have to do with me?"

Her father grinned suddenly, pressing his hand to her cheek. "You will understand," he said. He turned to look over her shoulder at Michael. "We will wait for you."

Abigail didn't know what to say or do, but before she could ask more questions, she suddenly felt the sensation of falling and her world became black.

The sound of Abigail choking made Snow Belle's heart stop. She was by her friend's side in an instant, brushing her cheek soothingly.

"Abigail, come back to me," she whispered. "Follow the sound of my voice. Come to me."

Abigail's ice blue eyes suddenly flew open, and she gasped, surprise and confusion on her face. She realized that she was lying inside a tent, Snow Belle's hands warm on her cheeks. She blinked as her eyes focused on Snow Belle's face.

"Snow Belle?" Her chest was heavy and her mind was cloudy. She remembered this feeling from the first time she had come back; when she had woken in Harlie's arms.

Snow Belle suddenly threw her arms around Abigail. "Oh, thank the gods," she breathed. Her pale eyes were filled with worry. "I didn't know if you would ever find your way back."

Abigail held on to her, something about Snow Belle's touch comforting. "How long has it been?" she whispered. She let Snow Belle help her to sit.

"Three days," Snow Belle said.

"And Joseph?"

The sound of rustling caught her ears, and she looked up, surprised when he suddenly materialized. Relief flooded his face, and he was on her in an instant, scooping her into his arms. "Abigail," he breathed, pressing his hands into her hair.

Abigail drew a sharp, surprised breath, inhaling his scent. It sent a tingle through her body, down to her toes, and she knew this was where she belonged from now on. She held tightly to him, feeling his breath hot on the top of her head.

"She doesn't know," Snow Belle's voice was soft, and mildly irritated.

Joseph released Abigail slowly, looking from Snow Belle to her.

"Know what?" Abigail asked, looking between them.

"We've been waiting for you," Joseph said, concern on his face. "We were starting to think that you couldn't come back this time."

Abigail frowned, stepping away from him. "How long have you been awake?" she asked.

"For three days," he said. He looked at Snow Belle. "Snow Belle said that it was as if I had been asleep for an hour, and then I woke again. But you didn't."

Abigail looked at Snow Belle.

There was sadness on her face. "I've never heard of someone dying twice and making it back again," she said softly.

Abigail swallowed thickly as she tried to digest what they were saying. She remembered moving toward the light with Joseph, and then nothing. Why had it taken so long for her to wake? Where had her soul gone if it hadn't come back to her body?

"The most important thing is that you're okay," Joseph said quickly, drawing her gaze.

"But we don't know the repercussions of this," Snow Belle whispered, crossing her arms. Abigail could see her shooting daggers at Joseph.

"Irene said she would just need time," Joseph said gently to her. "She said that everything would be fine."

Abigail looked at him. "You talked to Irene?"

Joseph turned his eyes on her. "I had to," he said. "She doesn't scare me as much as I thought she would." He grinned lightly.

Abigail felt her heart melt at his smile, and she wondered if it showed on her face, because Snow Belle suddenly stepped toward them.

"She needs to rest," she said, an edge to her voice. She towered over Joseph, and she was menacing with the scowl she wore.

Joseph was still for a moment, before he nodded. He turned to Abigail. "I'll be right outside if you need anything," he said softly. He leaned in to kiss her cheek gently.

Abigail felt her cheeks flush as he left. She looked at Snow Belle as she sighed in disgust.

"I'm sorry if I sound jealous, but you were mine first," she said, turning to look at Abigail. "And he has a lot to atone for."

Abigail felt her eyes soften as she looked at Snow Belle. She knew that feelings were difficult things for unicorns to understand; they only truly had them when they were bonded to a rider, and it was something that was unlike any other relationship. She let Snow Belle wrap her arms around her and pull her against her chest, holding her as she lay on the cot beside her.

Her embrace was comforting as Abigail relaxed beside her. She knew Snow Belle liked to be able to touch her when she was in her human form. It was something she didn't normally have the chance to do, and, at first, it had been weird, but Abigail understood now. When you loved someone so much, no matter what that love was, it just couldn't be helped. She realized that she was still very tired as her body began to relax.

"Thank you," she whispered suddenly. She felt Snow Belle shift beside her.

"You don't have to thank me," she whispered, combing her fingers through Abigail's hair. "I swore to protect you and to take care of you." She kissed the side of Abigail's head. "I will never stop doing that, and it will never become a burden."

Abigail felt sleep close in on her, and she let it take her.

Joseph was uneasy as he stood outside the tent. He didn't want to be away from Abigail for one more minute. He had spent too much time hiding from her, and now that she was here, so close, he couldn't just walk away again. He must have stared at the tent until well into the night, when Snow Belle finally emerged. He took a step back as he realized that her pale eyes were angry.

"You have a lot of explaining to do, wolf-boy," she growled low.

He took several steps back as she advanced on him. He didn't know why, but he was afraid of her suddenly.

"You don't know how long I have waited for this moment," Snow Belle said, her eyes flashing. "You don't know how many times I've thought about what I would say or do." She paused, crossing her arms. "And now that we're here, the only thing that I can offer is that you hurt her. You left her to cry alone every night, wondering what she had done wrong and why she wasn't good enough for you. It's because of you that she fled her home and her duty." Snow Belle's eyes were filled with bitterness and sadness. "You broke her."

Joseph felt her words cutting into him like a knife. He never intended any of those things. He never wanted that. Maybe a beating would have been more tolerable.

Anger suddenly flashed across Snow Belle's face again. "And you're lucky that I don't break you," she said. "She saved you out of the kindness of her heart, and if you care about her, you'll *never* do that to her again."

Joseph looked down, knowing he deserved this. "I never wanted to be without her," he said softly. "I didn't want to hurt her like that."

"Then when she is rested, you will apologize," Snow Belle said. Her face suddenly became a mixture of conflicted emotions. Her voice softened. "And you will promise to love her and cherish her for the rest of her days."

Surprise flashed across Joseph's face as he held her gaze. He knew how Snow Belle felt about Abigail. He couldn't ever really understand it, but he knew that they were almost in competition with each other. But was she conceding? Was this her way of saying that she knew she couldn't be everything Abigail needed?

"And you should know," Snow Belle said, turning away slightly. "I love her, too. And I have loved her more and longer than you ever have or will. If you hurt her, I will kill you." Her eyes left no room for argument as she turned and walked away, leaving him standing there.

Unicorns were complicated beings.

As she vanished into the village of tents around them, Joseph turned his eyes back to the one in front of him. He didn't know if it was her intent, but he was alone now. He stepped toward the entrance, pushing it open.

Abigail was sleeping soundly on the cot, her golden hair fanning around her.

He stepped toward her, kneeling to sit beside her. She didn't wake, and he took a moment to really look at her.

How long had he wanted this?

He tried to slow his breathing as his heart began to race.

This was it. This was the moment that he had been waiting for. He only wanted to be beside her. He only wanted to tell her how much he cared for her, and to never leave her side. He felt his chest constrict with the onslaught of feelings he suddenly felt.

He knew he loved her. He loved her more than his life, but he had wronged her in so many ways. How could he ever hope to make it up to her? She had risked everything to come back and to help him, despite the fact that she felt abandoned.

He couldn't make his body move as he stared at her. He was caught between wanting to pull her into his arms and wanting to leave the room. Did he even have any ground to stand upon anymore with her? Would it even be right to try to keep her?

He drew a slow breath, trying to calm himself. Snow Belle's words came back to him as he watched Abigail sleep.

You will promise to love and cherish her...

Joseph knew that wasn't an issue. He just didn't know how to make peace with her.

He pressed his lips together tightly as his chest tightened. Now wasn't the time. He rose to his feet, casting his golden eyes over her one more time. For now, he needed to keep his distance.

Chapter Six

Harlie knelt down to press his fingers against the scorched earth. He could see a trail, and he knew where it led to.

'They have gone to the Vale,' Aithne said.

Harlie nodded. He felt his heart sink. If they had gone to the Vale, then it meant that Abigail had gone into the dream world. He thought she was foolish.

It was silly and risky for her to go into the dream world to chase after Joseph. He couldn't understand what her desire to save him was, but there was nothing he could do to stop her. He could only hope that she succeeded. Then they could put this whole mess behind them.

Aithne suddenly shifted beside him, and Harlie looked to him, seeing Aithne staring into the distance.

Harlie's eyes widened in surprise as he realized that a white wolf was trotting slowly toward them. Harlie rose slowly to stand as she came closer. He frowned in confusion when Melanie's body suddenly shifted. She staggered forward toward him, swaying dangerously.

"Melanie." Harlie stepped forward quickly, catching her in his arms. "What happened?"

Melanie's grip was weak as she held to the front of his tunic. "My body hasn't healed fully," she whispered.

"Healed from what?" Harlie asked, looking down at her.

Her amethyst eyes were distant and dim. "I had to protect your sister from Joseph," she whispered. Pain suddenly furrowed her brow. "He would have killed me if the phoenix hadn't stopped him."

Harlie felt his heart twist in his chest. His arms tightened around her. "It wasn't really him," he said softly, understanding her hurt.

Harlie knew, from their conversations, that Melanie had known

Joseph since they were very young. They had been raised together and trained together. He knew that some of Melanie's jealousy toward Abigail stemmed from the fact that she and Joseph were intended to be mates.

Mating was a very formal union between wolves, but Harlie knew that Melanie cared about Joseph. And it pained her when she realized that Joseph was willing to throw away old traditions for the sake of a mortal girl. But something must have changed her mind if she was willing to sacrifice her life for Abigail.

"I hope your sister can help him," Melanie whispered, her voice suddenly thick with emotion. She knew that she and Abigail were very different, and she had seen the strength that Joseph had spoken of in Abigail. She knew that Abigail could do things to help Joseph that she would never have been able to do.

Harlie wasn't sure what to say as he held her, hearing the angst in her voice. He decided that all he could offer her was comfort, and that had to be enough. There were no magic words that could heal her broken heart.

His eyes shifted to Aithne when the phoenix suddenly shifted, his eyes trained on the sky.

Above them, a red star was twinkling into sight, forming into the shape of a phoenix. It circled above them for a moment, before landing silently beside them. Flowers sparked to life under its feet.

Harlie felt Melanie pull away from him as they watched the phoenixes' silent exchange. They gazed at each other for a long moment, before the phoenix fluttered into the air, vanishing as it had come. Harlie looked to Aithne, feeling confused.

"What was that about?" he asked slowly.

Sadness and uncertainty began to radiate from Aithne, and Harlie felt his jaw clench. *'The mortal king has declared war on the Guardians,'* Aithne said.

Harlie felt his heart drop into his stomach. "What?" he breathed.

He glanced at Melanie beside him, seeing her face tense. He had expected war on Joseph, but not on his home. They did not have any
way to raise an army in defense, and Harlie knew they would be an-
nihilated. What had Joseph started?

Guilt suddenly flitted across Melanie's face as she looked at Harlie.
"It is because of us," she whispered.

"That doesn't matter now," Harlie said gently. He looked at
Aithne. "We need a plan." He looked back at the scorched ground. He
needed Abigail. She always had a plan.

'We must defend our home,' Aithne said.

Harlie shook his head. "That's impossible," he said softly. "We
don't have access to an army."

There was no one to fight for them or with them. And he knew
that the phoenixes would not stand against an army of men. Even
though it would be simple for them to fight them, the phoenixes were
too passive to agree to it, even with Aithne's encouragement.

"I would stand with you," Melanie said softly, drawing Harlie's
gaze. "I will fight with you. I can't promise you an army, but I can find
others who will fight with me."

Harlie felt his heart ache suddenly as he held her gaze. "I'm not
sure that's the right answer to this," he said slowly. "I don't want a
war." He turned his eyes across the plains, brushing his hair from his
face. "Abigail would know what to do."

Sudden irritation began to roll off Aithne. 'You are just as keen as
she is,' Aithne quipped. 'You should learn to trust your own instincts instead
of relying on others.'

Harlie felt the weight of Aithne's words sit in his chest. He knew
he was right, and he knew that he could find a solution, but it was
hard. Being a Guardian was more difficult than he could have ever
imagined, especially after Abigail left him on his own. He hadn't been
ready to step into her shoes, and he found out the hard way that they
were large shoes to be filled. She carried the weight of the world on

her shoulders, and she did it with a smile. He didn't think he could ever be the way she was.

'*You must find your own strength,*' Aithne said. He lowered his head to look into Harlie's face. '*Make your own path.*'

Harlie sighed, glancing at Melanie, who was watching him attentively. He knew Aithne was right, and he nodded. He couldn't wait for Abigail forever. They would run out of time.

Abigail knew what she had to do when she woke a few hours later. The dawn was closing in over the Vale, and she rose from her cot. There was much work to be done. She sat on the edge of the cot, reaching down to pull her boots on. As she did so, her thoughts began to drift back to her strange dream.

Is that what her father had meant about waiting? That they were sending her back to her body?

Anticipation was racing through her as she left the tent, surprised to see Joseph curled in the doorway. As she came out, he woke, seeming initially startled. He wagged his tail and stretched as he realized it was her, rising to his feet. She said nothing to him as she held his golden-eyed gaze, before she inclined her head.

"I must go to Irene."

She could feel cold fingers of fear creeping over her. The closer she came to Irene's tent, the worse the feeling became. But she had to talk to Irene about what she knew.

Since she had woken, all she could think about was what Snow Belle had said and her dream about her father and brothers. It was true, they didn't know the consequences of her returning from death's door a second time. Did it mean that she could lose her soul at any moment? Could she leave her body in her sleep and never find her way home? Had her father sent her back again?

The only one who could know the answers was Irene.

She paused as she came to the entrance to her tent. She didn't know what to do or say. She could feel Joseph hovering a step behind her, and the sudden soft wind let her knew he had shifted.

"Are you sure you want to go alone?" he asked softly.

Abigail nodded.

She flexed her shoulders slowly, trying to ease the tension from her body. Her ice blue eyes ghosted over the entrance to the tent. "I must do this alone," she said, hearing how callous her voice sounded, even to herself. She knew she was putting up a good front, but she didn't feel it.

"Enter."

Irene's voice was sharp and crisp, and it made Abigail jump. She glanced over her shoulder at Joseph, who nodded encouragingly, before she pushed open the tent. Her eyes widened as she struggled to adjust to the bleak darkness. It felt as if Irene's space was a vortex, sucking the life and energy from the room.

Abigail cast her eyes around, feeling her heart skip a beat as she saw Irene stand suddenly. Her crimson eyes glittered in the dark.

"Tell me why you have come here," Irene commanded. Her voice was dark and commanding.

Abigail swallowed thickly, steeling herself. The weight of the amulet around her neck was suddenly a stark reminder. She had commanded a demon into it. Irene should be nothing. "I need to know why I didn't come back," she said. "And what will happen to me."

Irene made a sound that Abigail assumed was supposed to be a laugh. She stepped closer to Abigail. Her nearness made Abigail cringe, but she held her ground, looking steadily into Irene's face.

"You are strong, little Guardian," Irene said, a hint of admiration in her voice. "That is the only thing that brought you back to our realm a second time."

"What do you mean?" Abigail asked, a sinking feeling in her chest.

"Most mortals do not come back a first time," Irene said. "A second is unheard of." She tilted her head curiously. "But your will to fight is strong. It is the only thing that kept you from the darkness. There are forces that would seek to keep your soul from this world."

"But why?" Abigail asked. She could feel the fear she had previously felt easing away.

"Your light is pure, little one," Irene said, her voice suddenly softening. "You are destined to do great things. There are those that would see your destiny undone." She suddenly narrowed her eyes, waving a hand. "But you have been shielded from their eyes."

Abigail pressed her lips together. "My father?"

Irene nodded. "My soul may be blackened from the terrors I was faced with, but I see the things that need to be seen," she whispered. "And I also see that you must return to your home. You must protect what belongs to you." She suddenly reached out a hand, pressing her finger over Abigail's heart. "Including what is in here."

Abigail looked from her hand to her face, feeling uncertain. Was she speaking about Joseph? She opened her mouth to question Irene, when suddenly Irene's eyes snapped away.

She turned and moved back toward her corner and Abigail could see her reaching for a bundle. As she straightened, Abigail felt her heart lurch in her chest.

Irene's eyes were trained on her face as she held the wrapped bundle out to Abigail.

Abigail realized her hands were shaking as she reached for it, unwrapping it. She knew what it was just from the familiar weight in her hands, and she felt tears crowd her eyes as silver light began to emanate from her father's sword.

"How do you have this?" she whispered as a tear fell down her cheek.

Irene couldn't hide a smirk. "It was given to me," she said. "To be given to you."

Abigail shook her head. "This isn't possible," she whispered. "My father was buried with this sword."

Irene did laugh then, a dark, foreboding sound. "All is not what it seems, little Guardian," she whispered darkly. "Magic works in ways that even I do not understand."

Abigail looked up at her. She watched as Irene turned away from her.

"You must go," she snapped suddenly. "I can tell you nothing else."

Abigail swallowed thickly, before turning to the door.

"Abigail."

Abigail paused, surprised by Irene's use of her name. The other magical beings rarely used it. She looked over her shoulder.

"You must take control of your kingdom," Irene said. Her eyes seemed to be looking through Abigail.

Abigail nodded mutely, remembering her father's words. She exited Irene's tent without a word, the sun light disorienting as she stepped into it.

She felt as if she was in a dream as she saw Snow Belle talking to Joseph.

"Abigail, we must go," Snow Belle said. Her pale eyes were wide. "Aithne has summoned us back." Her eyes suddenly widened further as she saw the silver sword in Abigail's hands.

Abigail wiped at her face as she raised the blade.

"Your father's sword," Snow Belle whispered. "But...how?"

Abigail shook her head. Her ice blue eyes looked over the phoenix on the blade. "I have been instructed to take control of my kingdom," she said softly. She looked at Joseph, who was watching her carefully, his face guarded.

"We must return to Harlie," Snow Belle said, trying to recover from her surprise.

Abigail nodded. "Let's go."

Harlie leaned over Aithne's shoulder as they swooped down. He could see figures on the horizon, and he felt his heart skip a beat in his chest. As they came closer, he could see Snow Belle's pure white coat glittering in the sun. The joy that overcame him to see his sister standing in the sunlight was something he couldn't explain; she had spent so much time gone recently, and he wouldn't let her go again.

As Aithne's feet touched the ground, Harlie swung from his back, catching Abigail in his arms. "I'm so glad you're okay," he said, hugging her tightly. He felt her return his hug. "You're so stupid, Abigail."

Abigail felt her heart ache at his words. Maybe she was. She had made a lot of mistakes recently. But it wasn't because she didn't care. If anything, she cared too much.

She looked up at him. She could see the worry on his face. "I did what I had to do," she said. She stepped back from him, seeing Melanie slide from Aithne's back as well. She nodded a silent greeting as Melanie approached. "I'm glad to see you are healed."

Melanie offered a small smile. "I'm glad you were able to return to the land of the living," she said softly. Her eyes widened suddenly as she caught sight of her leader standing behind Abigail.

Harlie followed her gaze, his sea-green eyes widening when they landed on the black wolf as well. He felt his jaw clench. He didn't know if he should be happy or if he should beat the pulp out of Joseph. He watched as Joseph materialized into a man before him.

"You have some nerve," he said suddenly, his voice bitter. He watched as Joseph lowered his golden eyes briefly.

"I owe you an apology," Joseph said. He glanced at Melanie, who was watching the exchange. "And more."

Quickly, Harlie advanced on him, swinging his fist. The blow landed, knocking Joseph to the ground. Abigail gasped, but didn't move as she looked at her brother. His eyes were blazing with rage. Joseph wiped the blood from his chin, holding his hand up to still Melanie, who had moved toward him, something akin to a soft growl on her lips.

"That's for putting my sister's life in danger," Harlie said darkly.

Joseph's golden eyes were shaded as he watched Harlie. Abigail couldn't tell if he would duck another blow or let Harlie strike him a second time. After a moment of tense silence, Harlie looked at Abigail.

"I'm sorry, Abby," he said softly.

Abigail looked from him to Joseph. She watched as Melanie offered him a hand, pulling him to his feet. Bitterness filled her at the way Melanie's eyes softened as unspoken sentiments passed between her and Joseph before he pulled her into his arms, hugging her tightly. Regret was clearly etched across his face.

"We have more pressing matters to attend to," Abigail said softly, averting her eyes and refocusing her thoughts. "Our father gave me instructions to take back our kingdom." She pulled the silver sword from her side.

Harlie's eyes widened in surprise. "You are foolish, Abigail," he whispered. "If you saw our father, then you were close to death." His eyes didn't leave the blade. "How did you get that?"

"It was given to Irene, who gave it to me," she said softly. She put it back into the sheath at her hip. She watched as Harlie scowled lightly.

"And how will we take control of a kingdom?" he asked. "There is no army to fight for us."

Joseph shifted, drawing their eyes. "I have an army." Abigail's eyes shifted from him to Melanie, who was staring up at him silently.

Harlie's gaze was bitter as he looked at Joseph. "Your army is the reason we're in this mess," he said bitterly. "I daresay you've done more than enough."

Abigail watched Joseph's eyes shift from Harlie to her, waiting for her word. It was true that Joseph could lend them strength, but Harlie's words struck her as she remembered fleeing from Carmen. More bloodshed did nothing to help them.

"We can't," she said softly, shaking her head. "There will be no more killing." She caught Melanie's gaze as her amethyst eyes shifted to her.

Harlie scoffed. "And how will you ensure that?" he demanded. Desperation filled his eyes suddenly. "Alabaster sits with a force of thousands and we have nothing." He glanced at Aithne, who was watching the exchange silently. "Even the phoenixes refuse to stand against him."

Abigail felt her heart ache at their plight. She stepped toward her brother. "Father told me that we have been appointed, under the old laws, to protect Gandora and Phoenix," she said softly. She pressed her hand over the sword. "If I summon them, the creatures that are sworn to us will follow."

Harlie didn't seem convinced as he looked away.

"You have to trust me," Abigail whispered. "Alabaster will know he must concede to us. There is no victory for him."

Harlie shook his head, a dark scowl on his face. "We are sentenced to death," he said bitterly. His eyes shifted to Joseph. "All because of *him*."

Joseph's golden wolf-eyes narrowed. He remained silent, although Abigail could read the accusation in his face. Melanie had shifted at his side, her eyes suddenly angry at Harlie's words.

"Placing blame doesn't change our hand, does it Brother?" Abigail suddenly demanded. She watched as Harlie's eyes snapped to her, surprise and resentment forming on his face.

"Would you choose his side over mine?" His voice was low and careful.

Abigail shook her head, feeling mentally exhausted suddenly. "There are no sides," she said softly. "There is only life and death." She looked to Snow Belle, who was standing silently. "We must go back to Corona. We will assemble what little we have, and we will meet Alabaster." She looked back to Harlie. "You must trust me, Harlie. I have never steered you wrong."

Harlie sighed deeply. It was true. Abigail always had a solution for everything. He just wasn't sure that she was making unbiased choices. He looked to Aithne, seeing him lower his magnificent head.

"We will meet you there," he said finally. "We will begin preparations."

Abigail nodded, watching as he climbed onto the phoenix's back. Once they were gone, she blew a soft sigh between her lips. She took a moment to gather her thoughts before stepping toward Snow Belle.

"What will you have me do?"

Joseph's soft question gave her pause, and she turned to look at him over her shoulder. She felt pity for him suddenly. It must be difficult for him, knowing the turmoil he had caused.

"Go home," she said softly, her eyes shifting from him to Melanie as she pulled herself onto Snow Belle's back. "Set your kingdom right." She looked down at him, seeing the displeased look on his face. "When the time is right, we may need you."

"And how will I be of any assistance if I am not with you?" he demanded suddenly. His golden eyes were bitter. "I realize that I have a lot to atone for, but shouldn't I start by standing by you and your brother in battle?"

Abigail shook her head. "There will be no battle," she said.

"You can't guarantee that," Joseph snapped.

Snow Belle shifted uncomfortably beneath her, and Abigail narrowed her icy gaze at him. As much as she wanted him to stand with her, she just couldn't allow it. There was too much at stake for her to let her feelings cloud her judgment. Despite it not being his fault, he was still the cause of their plight, and she felt bitterness fill her.

She knew she had to choose her words carefully.

"Your presence will do nothing to pacify Alabaster," she said slowly. "Your people need you to return to them and to show them that you are a fit king." She watched as he crossed his arms. "This has become something that only we, as Guardians, can right."

His brow furrowed. "You know it wasn't my fault."

Abigail felt her heart twist in her chest. Of course she knew. That was the only reason she did what she had to save him. She couldn't muster words as she gazed at him.

"And you know I'm sorry," he said softly. His eyes shifted away.

Abigail felt her chest constrict. She knew what he meant. He was sorry for all the nights that she waited for him, and he was sorry for everything that he had done. He was sorry for putting her life in danger.

'We can't waste any more time.' Snow Belle's words cut through her thoughts.

Abigail looked down at her, nodding mutely. "Just go home, Joseph," she whispered. She couldn't look at him. "When things are settled, I will contact you."

She could feel her heart breaking as she let Snow Belle step into a smart trot.

Both missed the way Melanie ducked her head, fighting down her own feelings. It was so plain to her how they felt about each other, and it was plain to her that Abigail had no intention of seeing Joseph again.

Chapter Seven

The castle was bustling as Abigail and Snow Belle finally reached the gates. Anyone able to fight was assembled and being outfitted in armor. Abigail could feel the lengthy ride weighing on her, but she knew that there was no time to rest. They couldn't be at peace until the darkness looming over them was ended.

She swung slowly from Snow Belle's back, trying to fill her mind with other things as servants rushed to her. There was much still to do and to be seen to, even with Harlie's guidance. There was no time for her to let her thoughts linger on Joseph's sad, golden gaze.

There wasn't time for her to think about how he must have felt as she rode away.

As she helped pull swords and other weapons from the armory, she tried to keep from thinking about how crushed he must feel. He had a duty to his kingdom, and he had to know that she was right. He had to know that she had his best interest at heart when she told him to go home. He had to know that she knew he was sorry for what happened, but that it didn't change anything. Despite what she wanted, her place was here, and it could only ever be here, protecting her kingdom.

The evening came swiftly, leaving them still feeling very unprepared.

Aithne was a beacon of light as he swooped down into the courtyard. Abigail paused in her tasks to watch her brother step toward the phoenix. She could tell from the look on his face that the news Aithne was delivering was not good. She let the things in her hands slide to the ground as Harlie walked toward her.

"Aithne has seen them making camp on the plains," he said slowly. "They will be here in days if we don't meet them." His sea-green eyes were filled with worry. "If they lay siege to us, we won't win."

Abigail drew a ragged breath, letting his words sink in. "Then we must go," she said softly. She met his gaze. "We are out of time."

Harlie nodded, turning away from her. "I'll gather the men."

Abigail watched him go, shouting orders for their soldiers to prepare to leave. She turned and walked quickly to the barn, where Snow Belle and the Dream Catcher were standing peacefully.

'It is time,' she said, pressing her hand to Snow Belle's shoulder.

Snow Belle lowered her head. *'Are you certain your plan will work?'*

Abigail shook her head. "I'm not certain about anything," she whispered. She pulled herself onto Snow Belle's back. The weight of her father's sword was comforting against her back where it was sheathed.

Joseph paused as he and Melanie crested a hill.

In the distance was Castle Quasar. The Lake of Fire burned brightly against it, illuminating the castle with an eerie glow. The feeling of home was both comforting and foreign, as was the silence that accompanied them as they stood there.

He tried to force the feelings in his chest away, but they wouldn't subside.

He knew Abigail wasn't mad at him, but somehow that made him feel worse. Part of him wished that she could be mad. Her anger would be justified, but her forgiveness wasn't something he was sure he could deal with. Especially after everything was said and done.

Regret sat heavily in the pit of his stomach.

Had he come to her sooner, would she have been able to help him and to stop this horrible chain of events that was unfolding?

Joseph shook his head, brushing his dark hair from his face.

It was the regret and resentment that had kept him from her in the first place, wasn't it?

He blew a sigh through his lips. It was time to let all of that go. If she could forgive him, then he could forgive himself. And that would have to be enough.

He was surprised when he felt Melanie place her hand on his arm in a comforting gesture. "We'll make things right again," she said softly. Her amethyst eyes were wide and concerned.

Joseph felt gratitude fill him. "I know," he said. He turned to face her. "You have always been beside me, even at my worst. You don't know how much that means to me."

Melanie felt her heart twist in her chest. "You are my King," she said, bowing. "I will follow where you lead." She gasped in surprise when he suddenly pulled her against his chest.

"You are my friend and sister," he whispered softly, pressing his nose into her hair. "I will always do my best to take care of you."

Melanie hated the way her eyes filled with tears. She knew where his heart was. And she knew that she would follow him to the ends of the earth if that was what he asked of her. She blinked back her feelings as he released her.

He focused his eyes on the castle in the distance, his shift seamless. The Phoenixian grass was cool against his legs as he loped toward his home. Once he was close, he paused, throwing his head back, sending a howl floating into the night.

His tail wagged as Melanie joined him and resounding howls echoed his, welcoming them into the fold once again. As he neared the castle gate, he transformed mid-step, his boots settling in the dust as he stepped into the courtyard. He glanced around as servants ran to him.

"Highness!" one of his commanders bowed low before him. "We have received word that the Guardians are marching against the mortal king."

Joseph pressed his lips together tightly.

His commander glanced up at his silence. "Shall we assemble our forces?"

"No," Joseph said slowly. His thoughts were racing. If they were marching, then Alabaster's threat was more urgent than they had originally thought.

His commander rose to his feet as Joseph stepped around him. "Highness," he said softly, his voice meek. He looked to Melanie, who was watching Joseph carefully.

Joseph paused, looking over his shoulder at the man. He could see the fear on his face, and his golden eyes softened. Is this what he had done to his own people? The same ones he had fought so hard to free?

"I was instructed to stay out of their way," Joseph said softly, answering his commander's unspoken question. "Besides, there are things that need tending to here."

His commander's eyes widened briefly in surprise before he bowed once more. "Yes, Your Highness."

Joseph was silent as he walked into the castle, feeling his commander hovering on his heels. He wanted to send Abigail his help, but he knew what she said was the truth.

Alabaster would see their alliance against him and he would stop at nothing to annihilate them. The best way to help her would be to stay out of her way.

Abigail's heart was racing in her chest as she stared across the plains. She could see Alabaster's vast army, stretching out before her like ants. There were too many to count.

Her icy gaze shifted to the horse that was nearing, and she felt Snow Belle tense beneath her. Behind her, Aithne and Harlie were waiting silently.

Alabaster's cold eyes were trained on hers. He drew his horse short several feet from her.

Abigail instantly felt pity for the animal as its eyes met hers. Its head hung low and it looked weary. She could only imagine the things it had seen.

"I didn't think you had the gall to stand against me, Guardian," Alabaster called, tauntingly.

Abigail gritted her teeth. "You are making a mistake," she said.

Snow Belle tossed her head, her horn glinting in the morning sun.

Alabaster's eyes followed her movements. For a moment, Abigail thought seeing her astride her unicorn would be enough, but his face hardened suddenly. "No, you made the mistake, Guardian," he ground out. "And now, I will rid this world of your filth forever."

Abigail drew a ragged breath. "You are outnumbered, mortal king."

Alabaster suddenly barked a laugh. "By whom?" he demanded. "Your handful of men are but palace servants." He motioned behind him. "I have an army of thousands of the finest soldiers."

"Your ignorance has made you forget the old laws, mortal king," Abigail said, feeling anger fill her. She drew the sword from her back. "You forget that Guardians are the rulers of the magic realm. I have insurmountable power at my disposal."

Alabaster's horse suddenly pranced in place, sensing her power. He, however, sensed nothing, and he laughed again. "Your race ends here," he said angrily. "I will destroy you."

Abigail raised her sword, channeling her magic into it. "Behold my army, Alabaster!"

The phoenix on the blade suddenly shifted, glowing with the infusion of her energy. Her father's sword began to glow, magic building inside it, before the light suddenly exploded. Shockwaves pulsed across the land, pushing against her.

Snow Belle reared suddenly as the light vanished and a battle cry filled the air behind her. The startled flapping of Aithne's wings sent hot air coursing over her.

Abigail twisted, looking over her shoulder to see an army standing behind her. Creatures of all shapes and sizes were materializing at her beckoning, with a line of unicorns standing on either side of her.

A chill suddenly ran down her spine as she realized that everything she had been told was true. Her army vastly outnumbered Alabaster's.

Abigail turned her ice blue eyes on him, seeing fear plain on his face. "I have no desire to wage war with you, mortal king," she said easily. "But I am prepared if this is your wish."

An angry scowl suddenly came across Alabaster's face. He was silent for a long moment as he took in the beasts that were backing her. He couldn't seem to find words, fury twisting his features.

"This is not the end of us," he managed finally, reining in his frightened mount as it pranced and turned. "Your day will come, Guardian."

Abigail said nothing as she watched him retreat. She lowered her sword, turning to look at her brother. They had done it.

A black unicorn suddenly stepped forward from the line behind her, lowering its head. Abigail slid from Snow Belle's back, recognizing Irene in her earthly form.

'You are strong, little one,' Irene said, pressing her nose to Abigail's hand.

Abigail slid her sword into the sheath at her back. She didn't have words as Irene lifted her head.

Her black mane fell across equally black shoulders, and her eyes blazed as brightly as Aithne's feathers. Her horn was a dangerous point as she turned her head toward her band. With a silent signal, she bid Abigail farewell, before vanishing into nothing.

Abigail watched as the rest of her army faded away just as they had come, and she felt a sense of relief finally touch her.

Harlie slid from Aithne's back, stepping to fold her into his arms. "You did it," he breathed.

Abigail returned his embrace, nodding. "I wasn't sure it would work," she said.

Harlie grinned. "We never doubted you," he said, releasing her and looking to Aithne. "What will we do now?"

Abigail looked to Snow Belle as she stepped toward her. "Let's go home."

After returning to Corona, Abigail allowed herself some much needed rest. The only problem was that downtime left her mind to wander, and it went places she wasn't willing to go herself. The longer that she sat still, the worse the ache in her heart became. The guilt that plagued her had a death-grip on her heart.

She could never rid herself of the way Joseph had looked at her as she told him to go home. It was almost as if he knew that she was lying, too, but he didn't want to admit it to himself, either. She tried to convince herself that he would be fine without her. If the stories that Harlie had told her about Melanie were true, then he would realize that she was not right for him, and he would take Melanie as his queen.

But that thought was painful and bittersweet. It seemed like the right thing to do, but it would only be another lie. Abigail knew that his heart could never belong to anyone else, even though she hoped it could. It seemed so backwards to her now.

For months, all she had wanted was his attention. She had driven herself mad over what could have been, but once she had come home, she had realized that there was no other option for herself. Her only duty was to her people and her kingdom. She had to protect them and put them first. There couldn't be room for anything else in her life, and she didn't think she deserved more. When she had turned away from her duty, her life had fallen apart.

The nights had been still and silent, and part of her was grateful for that. But another, deeper part of her wished desperately it wasn't so. Sometimes, out of habit, she would find herself standing at the window, staring down into the forests surrounding the castle.

She tried to tell herself that time was all she needed; that the aching hole in her chest would heal on its own. Finally, after a month of feeding herself this lie, she knew that she couldn't fool herself this way anymore. It didn't help that there were daily reminders of Joseph's presence in the form of Melanie's visits. Since they had parted, she made it a point to personally deliver reports on the wellbeing of the kingdom.

From her messages, it seemed that everything was well in Phoenix once more. Joseph was the king that the southern kingdom needed. But there always seemed to be something more that Melanie wished to say.

Abigail could tell from the way her eyes lingered on hers, uncertainty in them. She never went into detail about how Joseph was, and she always made it a point to speak about politics. It was becoming tiresome, but Abigail knew it was for the best. She could only hope that her messages to Joseph about her were equally as vague.

The night was dark as she sat in the library, staring at the wolf pendant. The weight of it was still unnaturally heavy as she lifted it between her fingers. It had posed as a distraction to her from her daily feelings. She had spent much of her free time reading about the best way to destroy it, and she knew her options were limited.

The books had been very specific that the amulet couldn't be smashed without the risk of releasing the entity bound in it. Abigail didn't dare risk setting Bozal's spirit free again. But she knew that the amulet had to be destroyed. It was an accident waiting to happen that Abigail had no desire to try to fix.

After wrestling with what to do with it, she had finally posed her question to Aithne. With his infinite wisdom, surely he would have some advice.

'It must be destroyed by the fires of Olympia,' he said as he lowered his head, his large eye watching her carefully.

Abigail grimaced at his answer, looking up at where he was perched on the balcony. The night wind was cool, blowing away his smothering heat. The last thing she wanted to do was go back to Phoenix.

"Can you take it there?"

Aithne rumbled low in his chest. *'It must be done by the one who put him there.'*

Abigail sighed shortly. She was afraid of that. She closed her fingers tightly around the amulet.

'But I can take you there.'

Abigail's gaze shifted to the phoenix, mild surprise on her face. "This must be done in secret," she said softly. "I don't want anyone to know."

Aithne blinked, understanding her reasons. It was dangerous for anyone to know of the beast trapped inside, just as it was a dangerous trip to destroy the amulet. Without a word, Aithne stepped down from the railing, bowing low for Abigail to climb onto his shoulders.

The night air felt warm as Joseph listened to the sounds of his pack mates. They were moving through the trees, hunting a herd of prey animals. He tried to keep his mind focused on the task at hand, but his human thoughts were so prevalent that they were bleeding into his wolf-mind, threatening to force him to shift.

Finally, as he broke through the brambles and into the open grass, his body began to morph of its own accord. He grimaced as he collapsed to his knees.

It had been nearly a month since Alabaster had retreated back to his kingdom. It hadn't taken him long to realize that Abigail had lied to him when she said she would contact him. He had seen Harlie and Aithne on occasion as they patrolled, but their exchanges were always brief. Harlie didn't have much interest in spending much time around Joseph, and Joseph never had the courage to ask after Harlie's sister.

His only solace had come in the form of Melanie's interactions with the Guardians, but it was hardly enough to pacify the aching in his chest.

He knew it was her wish to remain distant, and so he tried to move on himself. He tried to keep himself busy with his duties and with frequent hunts, but lately it hadn't been enough. This was the first time he had been forced into a transformation because of it.

The sound of howling suddenly echoed in the distance, and Joseph knew his hunters had closed in on their kill. He lost interest as their howling faded into chattering before disappearing completely, and he rose to his feet.

His thoughts turned to Melanie as he pushed his way through the trees. She had done her best to stay beside him and make sure that he wanted for nothing. Most days, she went out of her way to ensure that there was little for him to attend to, and it was frustrating.

He needed something to do to keep his mind busy.

The meadow grass was soft as it wisped against his legs, cushioning his footsteps. His boots didn't make a sound as he walked into the night, seeing Quasar illuminated in the distance. A spark on the horizon suddenly caught his eye, and he paused, realizing it was a phoenix. He was further surprised when he realized the phoenix was flying toward Olympia.

Curiosity suddenly got the better of him as he shifted into his wolf form.

Why would a phoenix be flying to Olympia? It wasn't the time for their reincarnation, which took place at Olympia. Worry filled him as he ran toward the mountains. Powerful magic could disrupt a phoenix's lifespan; magic much like Bozal's had been.

The trek to Olympia hadn't taken much time, but Joseph was panting as he stepped into the shadows of the mountains. He could see that the phoenix had landed near the summit, and he shifted into his human form, climbing quickly.

He was closing in on the phoenix, pulling himself onto the ledge it had landed on, when suddenly the creature turned to face him. He recognized Aithne immediately, and his heart dropped.

"Aithne, what's going on?" he asked.

The phoenix flapped his monstrous wings. *'I cannot say,'* he said.

Joseph could see a tunnel that led into the mountain. "Where is Harlie?"

'Harlie is safe in Gandora,' Aithne said, turning his head toward the tunnel. *'Abigail has come here.'*

Joseph felt his heart skip a beat. "Abigail?"

He stepped toward the tunnel, surprised when Aithne snapped his massive beak at him. He jumped away, narrowly avoiding a painful, crushing bite.

'She does not wish to be disturbed.'

Joseph narrowed his eyes at the phoenix. "Then she came to the wrong kingdom," he quipped, irritation in his voice. He stepped toward the tunnel, watching Aithne warily.

When Aithne made no move to stop him, Joseph squeezed into the gap. He instantly felt claustrophobic as the walls nearly sandwiched him together. He vaguely wondered how Abigail had traversed this narrow space.

He blinked in surprise when the tunnel opened suddenly into the belly of the volcano. His eyes found Abigail as he struggled free of the tunnel. He was silent as he watched her.

She was whispering an enchantment, a silver amulet dangling from her fingers. A single, golden spark of magic jumped around the amulet as she finished her spell, seemingly binding the amulet. Joseph was surprised when she held the amulet, drawing a slow breath. She was lost in thought for a brief moment before she tossed the amulet over the edge, watching it fall into the heart of the volcano.

As it melted into the heat of the fire, a wind suddenly whipped through the cavern. Joseph watched as she lifted a hand to block her face from the warm blast. As the wind passed, a dark shadow curled in the lava, a soft cry echoing around them, before it faded away to nothing. A chill shook Joseph as he watched Abigail's lip curl in disgust as she turned away from the fire.

When her ice-blue eyes landed on him, she froze.

"Joseph," she breathed. Surprise was etched on her face. "How long have you been there?"

"Long enough," he said. His golden eyes shifted toward the lava below. "What the hell was that?" The unsettled feeling was still heavy in his chest.

Abigail followed his gaze. "In order to release you from Bozal's control, I bound his spirit into that pendant," she said softly. "This was the only way to destroy him."

Joseph's eyes widened briefly. He wasn't sure what to say as he watched her eyes shift back to him. He was suddenly filled with millions of questions to ask her, but none of them came out. He felt silly when she stepped toward him, awkward silence dispersing the eerie chill.

"Harlie doesn't know I came here to do this," she said. "I need to return to him." Uncertainty flashed across her face when he moved to block her.

"I can't let you leave," he said quickly.

Indignation crossed her face and her hand slipped to the hilt of her sword.

Joseph realized how that sounded as soon as the words left his lips, and he raised his hands. "If I let you go, I know you won't come back," he said softly. His golden eyes searched her face. "I can't just let you go again."

Abigail frowned at him. Guilt suddenly consumed her. "Joseph, you know that I have things to do," she whispered. "And you and I, we're just so different..." She looked away.

Joseph surprised her when he stepped toward her, catching her chin in his hand. "We aren't different at all," he said, his eyes searching hers quickly. "I know I hurt you. And I can't tell you how sorry I am. I would spend the rest of my days making it up to you, if you would let me."

Abigail's icy gaze widened. Was it really that easy? Somehow things didn't seem so simple, especially when she looked back over the last months she had spent wishing things would be different.

"I never blamed you," she whispered suddenly. "I was never mad at you." She felt tears fill her eyes as her mind reminded her of how close he had always been, but how far away. "I just couldn't understand why..." Her voice stuck in her throat. "I waited for you."

Joseph felt his heart twist in his chest as a tear streaked down her face. He didn't know what he could say to tell her how sorry he was. From the moment that he met her, he knew there had been something inside her that he would never find again. He had known, so long ago, when they were fighting for their lives, that there was a fire inside her that blazed brighter than the fires of Olympia. She had an insatiable desire to do what was right and to fix a wrong that wasn't even hers to mend.

He had spent a long time trying to understand his feelings about her. It was easy to love her, and he had fallen for her quickly. She was so different from anyone he had ever met. Her allure to him was like a beacon in the dark. He could never turn his thoughts from her, and he had tried. He'd buried himself in tasks and business to the point of exhaustion, but he was never able to outrun her memory.

But it had never seemed right, even when she had stood right in front of him. There was always a wall of guilt in his heart over the fact that he hadn't been there when she needed him. He should have been able to save her. To him, she was like a stone; firm and unmoving. She never wavered, even when everything seemed stacked against her. The least he could have done for her was stop Bozal from hurting her.

Unthinkingly, he sighed deeply. "I never felt like I was strong enough for you," he said suddenly. "You could stand up to anyone, and I always felt so weak. And then the voices..." He shook his head. "I made mistakes, but I should have been there for you."

Abigail felt her cheeks flush darkly. She had never considered how he must have felt when she was nearly destroyed by Bozal. She had been so consumed by her own feelings that it never crossed her mind why he couldn't step from the darkness and reveal himself to her. Was it even right for her to try to mend things with him now? How selfish had she been?

"I need to go home," she softly. She needed to get away from him for a moment and clear her head. She couldn't think with all of the feelings bubbling inside her.

Joseph's lips pressed into a thin line, but he nodded. "Wouldn't want Harlie to worry," he said vaguely. He watched as she stepped past him, slipping through the tunnel. He followed closely behind her, the scent of rain suddenly hitting his nose as they reached the exit.

Lightning split the sky, illuminating dark rain clouds. Abigail looked around, realizing that Aithne was gone. Fat rain drops began to fall slowly from the sky, hitting the ground around them.

"Aithne is gone," she said, looking over her shoulder at Joseph.

He glanced around as lightning lit the forest around them, followed closely by booming thunder. "It's dangerous here," he said. He tilted his head. "We need to climb down."

Abigail frowned, following his lead. She hated climbing. She stayed close behind him as he found a trail down. Her mind supplied her with images of the last time she had followed him through these mountains and she felt her heart twist. Even then she would have followed Joseph to hell and back. She just hadn't known at the time that's what it would take.

No sooner had they reached the bottom when the sky suddenly split, letting loose pounding rain. They were soaked in seconds.

"Come on!" Joseph yelled, catching her hand. He led her into the trees, which barely offered any cover from the downpour.

Abigail used her free hand to brush the water from her eyes. She wasn't sure where he was leading her, but it didn't matter as she followed him. She was surprised when a small outcropping appeared and Joseph ushered her into a niche that would shield them from the rain.

As she slipped underneath the jutting rock, she brushed at the water on her face, feeling a chill shake her as the wind began to pick up. She sank down to sit, wringing the water from her hair. She looked up at Joseph as he joined her, a small grin on his face.

"Looks like you'll have to wait until the rain stops," he said.

Abigail rolled her eyes. She watched as he sat close to her, so that their shoulders were touching. Exhaustion suddenly swept her as the warmth from his body flooded her, and she unthinkingly let her head rest against his shoulder. Memories flooded her mind. There had been a time when all she had wanted was this closeness.

She hadn't had a peaceful moment in longer than she could remember. She hadn't realized how weary her mind and body were. She blew out a soft sigh as she closed her eyes, the sound of the pounding rain lulling her to sleep.

"Abigail?"

Joseph's voice was soft as it broke through her mind, and she blinked, looking up at him. His golden wolf eyes were glowing softly in the darkness.

"I don't want you to leave," he whispered.

Abigail felt her heart twist in her chest. She sat up slowly, feeling the weariness ebb away. "I have things to do at home," she said softly. More than anything, she just needed to be in a place that she could think. She didn't know what to do with him, and his confessions had only thrown her into more confusion.

Joseph's eyes were searching hers. "You could do those things here," he said softly.

Abigail frowned at him. "Here?"

"In Phoenix," he said. "With me."

Abigail felt her heart catch in her throat. What was he saying?

"You could stay here with me," he said slowly. "You could be my wife."

Abigail frowned at him, her heart suddenly racing in her chest. She sat back. "Are you asking me to marry you, Joseph, son of Jarlath, Wolf King of Phoenix?" She heard the incredulousness in her voice. What in the world had spurred this? They hadn't even really resolved anything.

Joseph turned to face her, shaking his head. "No," he said. "I, Joseph, am asking you, Abigail, to marry me." His wolf eyes shifted down. "No titles, no complications." When he looked back to her, his golden eyes were smoldering. "Will you?"

Abigail couldn't find her voice as she stared at him. She was completely unprepared for this. Did she even have an answer for him? She could tell that her silence was not what he expected, and she looked away, shaking her head.

"I don't even have an answer," she whispered. Was it wise to jump into this with him? When she had forgotten her place last time, it had taken all of her strength to bring everyone back from the brink.

"Yes would be an appropriate answer," he quipped.

Abigail felt her heart catch in her chest, and fear seized her. This was a dangerous line they were toeing, wasn't it? She wasn't sure how she could even think about an answer. There seemed to be so many uncomfortable feelings in the way.

She rose quickly to her feet, surprising Joseph.

"Where are you going?" he asked, standing quickly.

Abigail ignored him as she started into the rain. She couldn't be here with him, having this conversation. The rain was cold and stinging as it pelted her skin. It brought a sense of clarity to her thoughts that seemed to evaporate when she was close to Joseph.

THE HEART OF THE GUARDIAN

"Abigail!"

She paused at the sound of desperation in his voice. She hated the way that he made her feel, and she gritted her teeth, preparing herself for what she knew she had to do. She had to protect her heart.

She turned slowly, seeing him watching her helplessly, the rain plastering his dark hair to his face. "I can't do this with you," she said. Thunder was deafening as it shook the ground around them.

"Do what?" Joseph demanded, stepping toward her. His golden eyes were glittering with irritation. "I'm not asking you to do anything other than be you."

Abigail brushed her wet hair from her face, blinking raindrops from her eyes. "I can't be that with you," she said accusingly. Her heart ached in her chest. She didn't like the person she was with Joseph. She turned into someone she didn't recognize; someone with feelings and fears.

"You can," Joseph said firmly. "I'm sorry that I hurt you. I know how you feel, and it doesn't feel good." He watched as her brow furrowed lightly. "But I want to move past that. And I want you to be beside me."

Abigail swallowed thickly. As much as she wished he wasn't, he was right. She looked up at him when he stepped closer to her.

"I know you, Abigail," he said gently. "This is the easy way out for you, and you aren't that person. You aren't a quitter." He could remember her words spoken to him about fighting for things she believed in. They never left him. "You taught me to fight for what I believe in and for what is right, and I believe in us." His golden eyes softened. "*We* are right together. I'll never stop fighting for you."

Words failed Abigail as she stared at him. She felt her face flush as his words sank in and she realized that he was right. Her eyes widened when he stepped closer, reaching for her hands.

"I love you, Abigail," he said softly.

Abigail felt her heart twist in her chest. Tears flooded her eyes suddenly, mixing with the rain drops on her face. She had waited so long to hear someone utter those words to her. She never imagined that they would be from him.

"I love you," she whispered.

She closed her eyes when Joseph suddenly caught her face in his hands, pulling her toward him. Her legs turned to mush as he pressed his lips against hers. She could feel the desperation in his kiss as he held her tightly to him. Months of questions and doubts suddenly melted away with his touch.

He pressed his forehead against hers as he broke the kiss. For a moment, neither one of them could move.

"So what is your answer?" Joseph asked finally, brushing his fingers across her cheek. "Will you stay?"

Abigail shifted her ice-blue gaze to him, feeling her uncertainties ebb away as she realized that, maybe, this was her place, here with the man she loved. "Are you sure this is what you want?" she whispered. "A lifetime of only me?"

Joseph leaned toward her, catching her face in his hands. "Forever could never be enough of only you," he breathed, pressing his lips to hers again. "You're the love of my life. I've kept you waiting too long."

Abigail felt more tears spring to her eyes as he pressed his lips against her skin. Somewhere deep inside her heart, she knew that he was right. They had kept each other waiting for too long. She pressed her hands against his chest, breaking the kiss. There was confusion on his face as he looked at her.

"I will marry you," she whispered. "I will."

Chapter Eight

The night was silent as Abigail stood in the palace garden. It was heavily wooded, made to look like the forests of Phoenix. Her white wedding gown was spread around her, diamonds sparkling in her yellow hair. Her thoughts were far away as she stared up through the trees into the night sky.

She wondered what her father would think of her. Would he be proud of her?

She liked to think that he was. She had done everything he had told her to do. She had protected her kingdom and those she loved, never forgetting his words to her. But this was a new chapter of her life, one she had no instruction on. She didn't know if she was ready.

But that was how she had felt when the task of being a Guardian had been forced upon her. She had carried that burden with pride and ease. Being a wife and a queen should be easier, right?

Abigail blew a soft sigh. She wasn't so sure.

A soft sound caught her ears, and she turned slowly. She was surprised to see Melanie materialize from the darkness. Her amethyst eyes were glowing softly as she approached.

"You are a beautiful bride," Melanie said, her eyes taking Abigail in for a moment. "I daresay that I am jealous of you." She offered a small smile.

Abigail felt her heart ache suddenly for Melanie. "Thank you, Melanie," she whispered softly. She watched as Melanie stepped closer to her.

Her eyes were downcast as she came to stand in front of Abigail. "I must be honest with you, Abigail," she whispered. "This is hard for me."

Abigail didn't know what to say as she gazed at Melanie. She had been surprised that Melanie had been in attendance at the ceremony earlier. She knew that it was a difficult reality for Melanie to accept, and there were many days when Abigail did not see Melanie around the palace. Joseph explained it as her being busy, but Abigail knew better. How would she feel if the man she loved was marrying another?

"Joseph and I grew up together," Melanie continued. "I helped him shoulder the burden of being the king's son." She paused, drawing a ragged breath. "But there was nothing I could do for him when Bozal took control." She shook her head, and Abigail could see tears rolling down her cheeks. "I could only stand by and watch him suffer." Bitterness had filled her voice. "As much as I loved him, I couldn't do anything."

Abigail felt her heart breaking for Melanie. She knew what it felt like to suffer in silence. She stepped toward her, placing her hand on her arm. "You did the best you could," she whispered, watching as Melanie's eyes shifted to her.

She shook her head, wiping at her face. "It wasn't enough," she said. "But I realized it was because it wasn't my job." Her tears were drying. "Joseph and I had grown distant in the time that he was away. And it wasn't until the moment that you saved him that I understood why."

Abigail felt her face flush when Melanie suddenly sank to her knees before her. "Please, this isn't necessary..."

Melanie shook her head. "It is," she said firmly. "You are my queen now. I will serve you in the same way that I have served Joseph." She kept her eyes downcast. "I pledge my loyalty, and my life, to you."

Abigail had no words as she stared at Melanie. In so many ways, she knew how Melanie felt. She knew the feeling of being helpless. But she also knew that there was a point that she and Melanie separated. Finally, she drew a ragged breath.

"You may rise, Melanie," she said softly. She knew that wolves were bound by strict laws. As queen, she was due a certain amount of respect, but she also had to return the same respect to her subordinates.

Melanie moved slowly to her feet. She didn't say anything as she looked at Abigail one last time before turning and vanishing into the trees. Soon, a chorus of howls began to echo from outside the castle walls. Abigail couldn't be sure, but she guessed it was a song of celebration. Save for a single, mournful note that floated beneath their song.

Abigail turned her eyes back to the sky. She couldn't fathom what Melanie must be feeling, but she knew she would do her best to be sensitive to her. All she knew was that the past few weeks had been crazy for her.

Getting married wasn't something she had spared much thought to. She never thought she would find anyone worthy of marrying, or anyone who would want to take her as a wife. The feeling was surreal as she stood alone now, thinking on the words she had exchanged with Joseph. Somehow the future seemed more certain, and just that much brighter.

"Here you are."

Abigail jumped, looking over her shoulder. "Here I am," she whispered. She watched as Joseph crossed the grass toward her, his soft gaze making her heart flutter.

"And what are you doing out here by yourself?" he asked, pulling her into his arms.

Abigail leaned into his kiss, closing her eyes, wanting to remember this moment. "Reflecting," she said softly as he released her.

Concern filled his golden eyes. "On what?" he asked.

Abigail drew a slow breath, looking away. "My father," she whispered. "Everything that has brought us to this point." She leaned into Joseph's embrace as he wrapped his arms around her.

"You know he is proud of you," Joseph whispered, pressing his nose into her hair. He drew a slow breath, memorizing her soft scent.

He held her tightly when she didn't respond. After a moment of silence, he looked down at her. "We shouldn't dwell on sad things."

Abigail nodded. He was right. This was her wedding night. She had much to celebrate. There was time for contemplation later.

She let him take her hand, leading her back through the trees, toward the palace. The brightly lit ballroom was like a beacon, casting light into the trees of the garden. Inside, she could see the smiling faces of their guests, and she looked up at Joseph as he led her up the stairs.

"Joseph?"

He paused at the top step, turning to her. His golden eyes were watching her patiently.

A moment of doubt suddenly caught at Abigail's heart, and she looked away, grimacing. "Will you always love me?" she whispered. Her heart was torn by Melanie's words. Was it so easy to fall out of love with someone and leave them behind?

Joseph frowned deeply, stepping down onto her level. "Loving you isn't something I just woke up and decided to do one day," he said slowly, catching both her hands. "Every part of me needs every part of you." He pressed her hands against his chest, searching her gaze. "I will need you forever."

Abigail felt her cheeks flush suddenly, and she looked away. She knew what he meant. Their type of love wasn't fleeting or weak. It was strong and lasting and potentially destructive. She could never love another, and she never wanted to try.

"It was just a silly thought." She turned to go up the steps, but Joseph held her still.

"Abigail," he said gently. His eyes were searching her face in a resigned way. "I saw you with Melanie."

She paused, feeling her heart catch in her throat. Had he heard what Melanie had said to her?

Joseph sighed shortly as he thought about the best way to put her at ease. "You have to understand," he said softly. "I *do* care about

Melanie. She has always been my friend and she was a constant companion. I knew, no matter what I did, Melanie would always be there for me." He frowned lightly as he held her gaze. "I loved Melanie because I had to. But I choose to love you. And I need you more deeply than I have ever needed anyone. You complete me in a way that I never realized I needed."

Abigail could feel a flustered blush heating her cheeks. What could she say to that? "So you did love her then?" she whispered finally.

Joseph pressed his lips together. "We were children, Abigail," he said gently. "There isn't anything more to it than that. And she clings to that when she knows she shouldn't."

Abigail nodded, searching his gaze as his words sank in. She knew what he meant.

"Do you believe everything that I've said to you is the truth?" he asked.

Abigail felt a blush heat her cheeks. She could never choose to believe he was lying to her, even if he really was. "Of course," she whispered, holding his gaze.

Joseph offered a soft smile, leaning forward to catch her in a tender kiss. "That's enough of that, then," he said softly.

Abigail frowned at him. Part of her was still amazed at how easy it was for him to turn her thoughts. He didn't let her dwell on it long as he took her hand and led her into the bright warmth of their party.

The sun was bright as it streamed into the windows. Outside, Abigail could hear the sounds of laughter, and she rose from where she sat to cross to the window. Below, in the courtyard, a small gray pony was prancing, tossing his head, a small girl bouncing on his back.

Abigail watched as Joseph reached for the girl, laughing as he lifted her from the pony's back. Her dark curls bounced around her face as she laughed.

"Again, Daddy!" she squealed. "Again!"

A soft smile creased Abigail's face as she watched Joseph pull their daughter against his chest. His words were lost as he spoke softly to her, carrying her inside the castle. It was lunch time, and Abigail left the window to make her way down to her family. As she reached the bottom of the stairs, she was greeted by little giggles and a kiss.

"What are you laughing about?" Abigail asked, holding out her arms as her daughter reached for her.

Her eyes were wide and bright as she caught her mother around the neck, specks of blue catching the light in her golden gaze. "Daddy silly!" she yelled, grinning broadly.

Abigail slid Joseph a glance, seeing him watching their little girl. "Daddy will get you!" he said teasingly.

Abigail let their daughter down as she screamed, running into the dining hall playfully. She turned to look at Joseph as he caught her around the waist.

"I'm afraid we have a problem," he said, smiling softly as he kissed her.

"And what's that?" Abigail asked, leaning into his embrace.

"It would seem that Bellaliza has quite a penchant for horses and swords," he said slowly.

Abigail's steps slowed, and she looked up at him. She could see the mirth in his eyes. "Smart girl," she said blandly. She was surprised when Joseph laughed.

"Just like her mother," he said.

Abigail shook her head. "You realize this is Harlie's fault," she said.

Joseph frowned playfully at her. "Oh, absolutely," he said. "Your brother is a terrible influence."

Abigail grinned at him. Harlie came to visit often, bringing his niece toys and weapons. Abigail didn't see any harm in it. She wanted her daughter to learn to be courageous and self-sufficient. She was the next heir to the Guardian title, as well as a princess of Phoenix.

Abigail prayed that her life would never be as hard as theirs had been, but she knew the value of being prepared.

"We'll have another discussion about this in a few years when she learns how to shift, okay?" Abigail said, walking toward the dining hall. She was surprised when Joseph paused, letting go of her.

A surprised look had come across his face. "Do you think she will?" he asked softly.

There had been much debate about whether she would learn in time. Most shifters were born with access to their ability, but they hadn't seen it in Bellaliza. She was nearly five years old now, and elders had told them that she would never learn. She was too old. Abigail knew Joseph had been disappointed, but he never said anything.

A wry grin came across her face suddenly. "Didn't I tell you?" she asked coyly. "The other day she was running around here with a little wagging tail."

Joseph's golden eyes widened. He was silent for a long moment as he seemed to process what she had said. After a moment, a pleased look crossed his face.

"She's just a late bloomer," Abigail said, stepping toward him, reaching for his hand.

Joseph remained silent at he took her hand. Abigail could tell that her news meant the world to him.

If you enjoyed this book, please leave me a review on your outlet of choice! Reviews are crucial to little authors like me and to help other book lover find great books!

Thank you for your support!

Check out my other titles:

Return to Royalty

Available on all major retailers!

Return to Gexalatia

Coming in March 2018!

Jewels for Gemma

Available on Amazon in ebook format!

www.ingramcontent.com/pod-product-compliance
Lightning Source LLC
Chambersburg PA
CBHW031237120726
47905CB00002B/632